# WITCH WAY AFTER FORTY

## SILVER SISTERS BOOK 1

### JENNIFER L. HART

ELEMENTS UNLEASHED

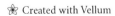 Created with Vellum

# WITCH WAY AFTER FORTY

## SILVER SISTERS BOOK 1

Witch Way After Forty
Hart/ Jennifer L.

1.Women's—Fiction 2. North Carolina—Fiction 3.
Paranormal—Fiction 4. Witches—Fiction 5. Werewolf—
Fiction 6. Humor—Fiction 7. Small Towns—Fiction 8. Home
Renovation—Fiction 9. American Humorous—Fiction
10.Mountain Living —Fiction 11. Divorce— Fiction 12.
Alpha Male—Fiction I. Title

ISBN: 978-1-951215-66-8

*For:*
*Mamacitia, Jeannette, Billie Jackson,*
*Amy Duncan, and Katherine Meachen.*
*Thank you for helping keep the dream alive.*

# WITCH WAY AFTER FORTY

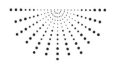

# CHAPTER ONE

## ALYS

My first thought when seeing the naked blonde riding my husband in our bed was, *Of course, the selfish ass insisted she is on top.* Never mind that those clearly artificial double Ds were bound to cause her slight frame serious back pain in a few years. He wasn't much for manual labor. Not old Kyle. His idea of getting a workout involved mowing the lawn or shoveling the driveway. Which he never did well and I was usually forced to go back over it to clean up the sloppy job.

In some shadowy corner of my mind, I recognized that it probably wasn't normal to feel sympathy for the woman boinking your spouse.

Then again, I'd known it was coming.

Just like Kyle was about to. I could tell by the way his face turned red and he bucked beneath her spastically.

The hell with that. He hadn't respected me enough to keep his side dish on the side, well, then he could just deal with blue balls.

The bedroom door was open so I strode in, doing my best to keep from snagging a heel in the filmy bits of lace that obviously didn't belong to me. Perhaps when I was three, I could have fit that size. Then again, I might have had a Barbie once that could wear those skivvies.

What was this woman even doing with Kyle? It seemed like a pertinent question so I tapped her on the shoulder. "You know, honey, you can do better."

She screamed and scrambled off of him, about two seconds before Kyle was about to nut. I reached down and grabbed him by the balls and twisted. I'd boil my hand later. Or maybe chew it off.

For his part, Kyle's groan turned to one of sheer agony. "Alys," he gasped.

"Oh, you remember me?" My tone was even, almost bored.

"Who's this?" Blondie asked.

"His wife. I'd offer a handshake but mine are busy at the moment."

The woman's big green eyes went from me to Kyle, whose skin had flushed purple. His whole body shook. "You know it costs more for another girl, don't you?"

Her accent was clear New Jersey. That combined with the fact that I had never seen her before topped with her mention of cost had me turning back to the worm in my bed. "A prostitute, Kyle? Seriously?"

He made a gargling noise and I sank my nails in, just a little.

My sister had told me Kyle was a bastard-coated bastard with bastard filling. I should have listened.

"You ought to leave," I nodded to the dental floss that passed for her undergarments.

"Nu-uh," Blondie folded her arms over her implants. "Not 'til I get my scratch."

I sighed. "How much?"

"Four hundred."

I raised a brow. "Seriously? For what, twenty minutes of work? Considering how he performs you would have time for a shower after."

She reached for her bra and I had a moment of envy when her breasts didn't alter an iota as she snapped it on. "I charge double for the uggos. Plus, there's the drive."

The gurgling sound Kyle made when Blondie called him an uggo was worth four hundred bucks. My purse was downstairs in the hallway, but Kyle's Rolex was on the nightstand. With my left hand, I retrieved it and lobbed it to her. "Keep it."

"Do I look like a pawn shop to you?"

Her words didn't fool me. I could see her assessing the watch and the gleam in her eye. The watch was worth a lot more than four hundred.

"It's the best you're gonna get. He's in no position to finish, so unless you want to wait around until he recovers…." I smiled sweetly at the puce color of my husband's face.

She pulled her micromini up and then threw on a jacket. "I'm good."

I released Kyle the moment the front door shut behind her. He curled onto his side in the fetal position. Fitting, since he was such a big baby.

I didn't say a word. Instead, I kicked off my heels and turned to the bathroom. I let the water run as hot as it could go, then used half a bottle of antibacterial soap. For the record, that was the last time I was touching that man's privates. The thought filled me with a giddy sort of relief.

The signs had been there for months. Internet porn had been constant throughout the marriage and easy enough to ignore. But then the credit card charges had popped up. Sites that were clearly shell companies with BS names to protect privacy. Phone calls to numbers I didn't know. Him never going to bed at the same time as me. I thought it had been a run-of-the-mill affair, something middle-aged men did to prove they were just as young and virile as they had once been.

In Kyle's case, the bar wasn't set too high. It was probably even lower now, between Blondie's dismount and my claws. I hadn't drawn blood, but the thought of leaving him emasculated was far too tempting.

If he had been discreet, I could have gone on feigning ignorance. But he'd forced me into this position, into being the victim, the foolish wife.

The thing that hurt most was my pride. And in my book, that was unforgivable.

I stared at my reflection, at the crow's feet lining my eyes, the silver that had overtaken the black in my short bob, and winter pale skin which was even paler than usual. I pinched a little color into my cheeks, then turned to the medicine cabinet. After sorting through its contents, I scooped what I needed into one hand and then carried it out to the bedroom.

Kyle had extracted himself from the bed and pulled on a pair of sweats. "You can't honestly be surprised, Alys."

I didn't bother to look at him as I snagged my overnight bag from the top of the closet. My toiletry bag was inside and I took the time to separate the liquids from the pills, from the make-up brushes. *Everything in its place. Don't let him see the wound.*

"When was the last time we even had sex?" Kyle sounded triumphant, as though he had just scored a point.

I tapped my chin as though contemplating the question and then shrugged. "I really couldn't say, Kyle. Seeing as it wasn't all that memorable."

His brown eyes narrowed. "You're a frigid old bitch."

I went back to my packing, trying to figure out what exactly

4

I would need for my new Kyle-free life. Clothes for work, both demo and client meetings. Jeans, sweatshirts, and work boots as well as twinsets, slacks, and heels. And it was fall now, heading toward winter. What about a coat and snow boots? Maybe I'd have to get another bag out of the attic. The thought made me tired. I just wanted to leave the house that I had lived in for twenty years and never really liked, and not look back.

"I should have kicked you to the curb years ago." Clearly irritated that even his blatant act of defiance didn't get my undivided attention, Kyle began to rant in classic dipshit monologue.

No to the slog to the attic, I decided. I'd come back with Maeve at some point and get the rest of it. When I was in a better place to deal with this crap. Keep it simple. *Think capsule wardrobe. Black pairs with anything. Neutrals are good too.* I added two pairs of slacks, a twinset, and three different blouses along with the set of black heels I had been wearing and then crammed as many jeans and sweats on top as I could fit. Making swift decisions always helped fuel me so I zipped the bag, snagged my e-reader off my nightstand, my jewelry box from the top of the dresser, and headed for the door.

"Where are you going?" Kyle called as I descended the grand staircase to the bottom floor. He chased me down, looking none too healthy. I hoped he wouldn't have a heart attack. I didn't want to stick around long enough to let the EMTs in.

At that, I rounded on him. "If I'm so awful, why not just go file for divorce like a decent human being?"

His lips parted but he didn't say anything. We both knew why. He liked having money. Liked the lavish lifestyle my business had afforded us. He'd retired early and that was when the trouble began.

"You're not getting a dime." Thankfully Aunt Jess had taught me to keep my finances separate from my spouse's.

"It's half mine," he snarled.

"Like hell it is. You spent every dollar you made on this mausoleum." Done with him, I turned to the door.

He folded his arms over his chest. "Do you really want the entire town to know that I paid a prostitute for sex?"

I froze with my hand on the door and a sliver of fear ran down my spine.

He pushed on. "Think of the gossip. Alys Stevens can't hold her man."

My heart pounded and for a moment I was afraid I would be the one to pass out. "You can have the house. And your damn Corvette. But no money."

"We'll see." He looked smug.

I should have gelded him when I'd had the chance.

MY BRAIN HADN'T SWITCHED on and I drove on autopilot back to town. Maeve and I had lived in Eckhart most of our lives and the small Southern town felt like home. I stared at the sleek two-story white brick storefront with the name *Silver Demo and Design* on the plate-glass window. Maeve had taken a course to learn calligraphy just so she could design our logo. When my sister did something, she did it with her whole heart.

I should have gone to Maeve's. But so early in the afternoon, she'd be busy with the twins. Getting them snacks and set up with homework, or maybe afterschool activities. The last thing she needed was me dumping my purse out all over her life.

Better if I did something useful.

I stepped out of the Suburban and slid my sunglasses

onto my face. Took a breath of fresh mountain air, squared my shoulders, and headed inside. My hand shook a little as I reached for the door and I clenched it into a fist.

*This isn't the time or the place.* Aunt Jess's voice popped into my head. I let out a slow breath, tamping my feelings back down as far as they would go. *Control it. Don't let it control you.*

I reached again and my hand was steady.

No one would guess the sordid scene I'd left in my wake. Or that my insides were raw and bleeding. I would not give Kyle the satisfaction of a public breakdown. He wasn't worth it.

Though it was late afternoon, the office stood empty. Lora, our executive assistant, had asked for the afternoon off. Her desk was pristine with only a picture of her, her mother, and her son stationed in a place of honor next to her computer. Her milk chocolate skin tone was much darker than her son's and lighter than her mother's but they all had matching happy smiles. I hoped the three of them were out hiking or kayaking, enjoying the last of the warm weather for the year.

Most of our clients were by appointment only since we only worked on one renovation project at a time. The bungalow we had just finished was under contract and I'd just signed the closing papers on the Mid-century Modern home that was our next project.

I headed to my desk, across from Maeve's, and booted up my computer. I hadn't had a chance to go over the new floor-plan with our contractor yet. We'd have to set up a walk-through ASAP as the demo was scheduled to begin next week.

I studied the design I'd come up with. Having never had the chance to work on a Mid-century Modern before it was an interesting challenge. The house lent itself to an open floorplan but there were all of these hideous plaster columns interspersed throughout the space. Totally killed the flow as well as the sightlines between the kitchen and the living area. My fear was that they'd be structural and we'd have to leave the eyesores in place. Or sell a kidney to pay for the steel beam we'd need to support the roof.

I was so lost in thought that I didn't hear the door open so I jumped when a deep voice tinged by an Australian accent rumbled my name. "Lys?"

My hand flew to my chest. "Brock! You scared the hell out of me."

My GC scowled down at me, which would have been more intimidating if he was a day over thirty and wasn't cute as a button. I clenched my fist as that familiar urge to brush his shaggy blond locks away from his face arose. Probably some stupid latent maternal instinct, since I was old enough to be Brock's mother. Well, if I had started really *really* young. Kyle and I never had kids, had never wanted them.

He crouched down beside me until we were at eye level. "I didn't mean to. What are you doing here?"

I raised a brow at him. "Is that a trick question?"

The corner of his mouth twitched but he stifled it before it became a full-blown smile. "No, smartass. You told me you were taking some time for yourself."

I'd always liked Brock. He was a straight shooter and didn't play word games or make phony promises the way some contractors did. If he said he would do something, it got done. Of course, it was my name—albeit my maiden name—on the sign, so I always double-checked.

"Change of plan. Are you busy? We need to do a walk-through on the new house."

"I was just packing it in for the day." He gestured toward the front window where his shiny red pickup reflected the sinking sun-kissed, distant blue hills.

"Crap, I didn't realize it was so late. You probably have a

date or something." Because that's what virile young men that could pose for a fireman's calendar did on a Friday night. Head down the mountain to a club with too loud music, overpriced drinks, and too many sweaty bodies crammed in together. Not go home, fill a tub full of bubbles and pour a glass of wine, and get lost in a good book.

Suddenly, I felt a million years old.

"I'm not seeing anyone." Brock's chocolate brown eyes had the most intense golden ring around the iris. It seemed to flash for a moment when he looked directly at me. "We can go over now if you'd like."

I would, but it seemed selfish to shanghai him after hours. "I don't mean to impose on your free time. Just because I have no life doesn't mean you have to jump to my beck and call."

He shrugged and the motion caused a hypnotic ripple of muscle beneath his long-sleeved black t-shirt. He really was too damn pretty for my own good. "Spending time with a beautiful woman on a Friday evening is my idea of living it up."

My badly battered pride preened at the compliment even as I scolded myself not to let it go to my head. Brock couldn't call me a frigid old bitch the way Kyle had because he worked for me.

"Okay, sure. Let me just check the rear door and make sure we're all locked up."

He leaned back and it wasn't until then that I realized he'd been invading my space. "I'll wait out front."

I used the bathroom and checked my appearance to make sure the professional businesswoman façade was in place, then secured the building and set the code.

Brock stood by my Suburban. He scowled at the suitcases in the back seat. "Going somewhere?"

Damn. I hadn't wanted to get into it tonight, not with my

GC. Not with anyone but my sister. I didn't want to lie to him and he could be remarkably stubborn so evading him would take more energy than I had in my reserves. Brock would hear about it eventually. Might as well cut out the middle-man. "Kyle and I are separating."

Brock's head whipped around and he stared at me. The intensity there burrowed beneath my skin like a chigger.

"I caught him in bed with a prostitute." *Why* had I said that? I certainly hadn't meant to voice my humiliation.

"What an idiot." Brock's eyebrows pulled together. "Want me to take care of him for you?"

The deadpan way he said it made my lips twitch. "What, do you know a guy or something?" I didn't think Australia had a mob, but you never knew.

"Or something." There was a feral light in his eyes that I didn't know how to interpret. "I'd let you watch."

And didn't that sound dirty as sin? Wait, were we still talking about murdering Kyle?

I cleared my throat. "Yeah, I hate to break it to you but the cops always look at the ex-wife first. Motive and all that. So, while I appreciate the offer, I'm going to have to pass."

Thoughts of all that would happen surfaced like creatures from the deep. The lawyers. The court cases where we fought over petty shit. The gossip. I was so tired. Maybe I needed to change my diet. More iron or something. It couldn't be normal to be so damn exhausted all the time.

"Are you staying at Maeve and Kal's?" Brock asked.

When I nodded, he plucked the keys from my hand. "You're in no condition to drive. I'll take you."

I blinked up at him. "What about the Mid-Century Modern?"

"It can wait until Monday."

My lips parted, a protest on its way up but Brock covered

my mouth with his palm. His skin was warm and a little jolt of electricity went through me at the contact.

"You deserve better than Kyle," he murmured.

I wanted to thank him, but his hand still covered my mouth. A chill breeze blew against the back of my neck and an involuntary shiver raced down my spine.

The moment dragged out between us and I felt as though something shifted. As if I was seeing Brock in focus for the first time.

Then he dropped his hand and stepped back. "Come on, possum. Let's get you home."

I was in the passenger's seat of my own vehicle and well on the way to my sister's house when I realized something. "What about your truck? It's back at the office."

"One of my pack will get it."

"And pick you up?" Maeve and Kal lived twelve miles from the town center.

He made a noncommittal sound.

I reached for the radio but he gripped my hand. "Please, don't. I can't take the noise."

"What?" I blinked up at him. "From the radio?"

"I have an audio sensitivity," he explained. "Loud music can be physically debilitating."

There went my mental image of him at a club. Or riding a fire engine. "So, what do you do for fun?"

He slid me a sideways look. "I run."

"Run for fun?" The skepticism dripped from my voice. "I only run so I can have a second glass of wine." Or cheesecake. But I kept that last part to myself.

His teeth flashed.

"Different strokes for different folks." I shrugged it off as he turned onto Maeve's street. The white Southern-style home was a two-story structure and had been Maeve and my first project together. Maeve and Kal landscaped it beautifully and the wraparound porch was whitewashed every spring, to make the tulips and crocuses pop. Seeing it always brought a smile to my face.

It disappeared when I spotted the motorcycle in the driveway. "Crap."

"What?" Brock asked.

"My sister is here."

His brows drew together. "She lives here, doesn't she?"

I let out a heavy, put-upon sigh. "Not that sister. The bad one."

# CHAPTER TWO

"I didn't mean it that way." *Why* couldn't I seem to hold my tongue around Brock all of a sudden? We'd worked together for almost two years and I'd never felt compelled to burp up private knowledge to him before.

His lips twitched. "It's okay. You don't owe me an explanation."

I didn't, but I was already in it hip deep so I might as well trudge on through. "Siobhan and I are like oil and water. Have been since we were kids. I love her more than anyone—except Maeve of course—but everything about her makes me nuts."

She shaved her head and carved geometric patterns into the stubble and then dyed what was left of it bright colors. She'd dropped out of college and taken various low-paying jobs for most of her life. She'd never been married, a fact she liked to open with when meeting strangers. She called herself "terminally single". Just putting it all out there, like spilling your private business was no biggie. Her whole personality was pure impulse, designed to get the strongest reaction out of those around her. "Sibby is the absolute last person I want to deal with right now."

"Do you have somewhere else to go?" Brock asked. "Someplace else you can stay?"

I hesitated. There was a place I could go, probably should go so that Sibby and I didn't get into a knock-down-drag-out in front of Maeve's kids. But I had to tell my sisters about Kyle first. "Are you sure you don't need a ride back to your truck? Kal would be happy to…."

"I'm fine, possum." Brock moved closer, so close that I could feel the heat radiating off him. He didn't touch me but his gaze left a trail along my neck and down over my cheek that felt like a gentle caress. "You have my number. Don't be afraid to use it if you need anything."

My lips parted. What exactly was he offering? But before I could ask, he dropped my keys into my hand, exited the car, and jogged down the street. I popped the door and watched him disappear into the twilight. The man could really run.

"Alys?"

I whirled around and faced my two younger sisters. They stood in the doorway, side by side, looking like mismatched bookends. At forty-five, Maeve embodied everything a mother ought to be. Her dark curly hair, so like our mother's, was sprinkled with silver. She'd never lost the pregnancy weight that came from bearing her twins six years earlier, but even though she griped about it constantly, I thought it suited her.

Siobhan looked more like my reflection in a funhouse mirror. Her hair was shaved on the left side, with lightning bolts zig-zagging through the stubble and the right was flipped over the top of it and streaked with blue that matched her eyes. She had the family hips, which she accentuated in leather pants or short skirts. There was a new piercing above her left eyebrow and a tattoo of what looked like a snake winding up her right forearm. No one would have pegged her for being in her forties. She looked and behaved as though she were barely old enough to drink legally.

"Who was that?" Sibby craned her neck as though she could still see Brock jogging up the street. "And where can I get one?"

"That was Brock, our GC." Maeve's eyes were full of questions, which she didn't voice.

"We were going to check out the Mid-Century Modern, but he thought I'd better come here instead. Where are Kal and the kids?" The house behind her, usually filled with the scents of cooking and the sounds of laughter, stood quiet.

"He took them camping for the weekend." Maeve shifted her weight, clearly uncomfortable. "I was gonna have you over tomorrow so we could talk. I would have done it today but you said you wanted some personal time so…."

It clicked then. She'd asked Kal and the kids to find somewhere else to be. That way if Siobhan and I mixed it up, there would be no witnesses for the ensuing bloodbath. Not that Sibby and I ever did more than shout.

So what if neither of them had bothered to let me know she was coming to town? It didn't matter that I'd had the same thought myself a few minutes ago. The fact that Maeve had cast herself as the peacemaker, as though *I* were part of the problem, chafed like a sandpaper thong.

"Yeah, well I don't want to interrupt. I just wanted you to know I'll be staying at Aunt Jess's cottage."

"What? Why?" Maeve's dark brows pulled together.

"Because I caught Kyle in bed with a prostitute this afternoon." My gaze strayed to Sibby, waiting for her reaction.

She folded her arms over her chest. She'd never liked Kyle. Had told me not to marry him the night before our wedding. Had insisted he was a bastard coated bastard with

15

bastard filling. Anger still swirled in my stomach when I thought about that night.

The night that had broken us in more ways than one.

Maeve swore. "Are you all right?"

"I'll live."

Sibby snorted.

"But Aunt Jess's place is a mess," Maeve fretted. "It's probably infested with vermin. The roof is in terrible shape. And what about mold? No one has been in there in ages. Hell, there isn't even electricity running to the place anymore."

"Then it will give me something to do in my free time."

Sibby snorted again, as though the idea of me having free time was absurd.

Enough. I'd had enough of this day, of reliving the humiliation to my nearest and dearest. Time to retreat. I stepped back toward the car. "So that's where I'll be. If you need to reach me."

"Alys," Maeve tried again, but I wasn't having any of it. Not pity or condolences or any more of the fraught tension that stretched out between the three of us. I turned and got back in the car. It smelled woodsy and fresh, like Brock, and gave me enough control to turn the engine over and drive off without looking like I was running away from my sisters.

Aunt Jess's cottage sat on the far side of the lake from the public beach. Nestled in the trees, it was private and if I were honest, just a little bit creepy. The three of us had grown up there and it hadn't felt odd when Aunt Jess and our mother had been in residence. Then it had been a bright, happy place, a place where the five of us had belonged.

I drove slowly around the lake, past the battered blue and white sign that read *Eckhart Town Limit* until I spotted the dirt trail that led to the cottage. My headlights illuminated the mailbox as well as the hand-painted sign that proclaimed

"Witch Way." The memory of my mother affixing that sign to the post made me smile.

If I closed my eyes, I could still hear her say, "If everyone already thinks we're witches, we might as well have fun with it." Something in my chest throbbed and I put my hand over the dull ache as though I could physically ease the heart wound.

My car bumped along the rutted dirt for another half a mile. Maple, birch, and oaks flanked the winding drive on either side. In a few weeks when all the leaves came down, the trees would act as guideposts because the dirt would be covered in a colorful blanket handwoven by mother nature.

And then the trees parted, revealing the cottage. The moon hung directly above it, turning the moss growing on the roof almost silver.

Leaving my bags in the car, I snagged a flashlight from the glove compartment. Sure, the place was a little run down, but so what? I just needed space right now and the cottage provided that.

Across the lake, a wolf howled. My heart pounded at the eerie, haunting cry and I hastened up the rotting steps and into the cottage.

The door creaked open. I fumbled for the switch, flicked it a few times. Nothing. No problem. I didn't need electricity. Not for one night. There was a propane-fueled heater in the downstairs bedroom if it got cold. I took a deep breath, scenting dried herbs and old dust and the sickly-sweet tang of memory.

Boards creaked under my weight with every step. I headed for the hutch at the foot of the stairs that led up to the other two bedrooms. I paused, listening for the sound of scurrying—or worse, slithering—but there was only the moaning wind.

The hutch held hurricane lamps as well as several candles

and baggies of dry matches. Even when she had access to electricity, Aunt Jess was always prepared for the worst. I lifted the glass, struck a match, and lit the wick of one, adjusting the flame down to a cozy glow. Setting the lamp on a nearby table, I lit a second, smaller one that I could carry with me as I surveyed the space.

The term cottage was a bit of a misnomer, as it implied that the place was small. It had been tight for the five of us, but as children we'd spent a good deal of time outside, exploring the woods around the lake and just being kids. No television, certainly no internet. Only books and conversation in the evenings. Our news came from the Sunday morning paper which Aunt Jess would pick up along with a dozen doughnuts. Otherwise, it was town gossip, which mostly focused on us.

A simpler way of life to what I had been living.

There were three bedrooms as well as a loft overlooking the great room. The wood-burning stove stood on the north wall of the main space. I didn't bother to light it. It wasn't so cold yet and the exhaust vents needed to be inspected for nests and other debris first. The kitchen stood to the south side of the great room. The long, battle-scarred knotty pine table where my sisters and I had done our homework and we all gathered for meals needed to be stripped, sanded, and refinished, but it was still a good piece. The ancient round fridge was unplugged and the door sat open. I doubted it worked. The gas stove was fueled from a propane tank out back that looked like a tampon only a dinosaur could use. I made a mental note to check the levels tomorrow.

Mom had been a lousy cook, but Aunt Jess was the best. Sibby had learned all of her kitchen witchery, as she'd playfully called it, but Maeve and I hadn't been interested. Maeve's herb boxes still hung below the kitchen window, the wood of them probably as rotted as the steps. The only things that grew there now were weeds.

The thought made me sad. I turned my back and walked to the greenhouse.

Greenhouse implied a structure apart, but Aunt Jess had thriftily utilized the back of the house as one wall. On a standard house, a place like this might be termed a conservatory or later, a Florida room. A place to sit and bask in the sunlight. But this space was not meant for leisure. Three walls and a ceiling of windows were the only things that separated the greenhouse from the true outdoors. It was both part of the house and sacred space. A place where Maeve, Sibby, and I were never permitted. Aunt Jess had been a botanist with a specialty in horticulture and this space had been her livelihood. She'd brought our mother on as an assistant. Being allowed within had been a rite of passage for me and my sisters, one we had never managed to achieve.

Though left untended for the last decade, the plants in the greenhouse still grew. Thrived. It was a living memorial to the women who'd poured so much of their own life and time into the space. I felt a little guilty, not about the plants, but about trespassing into the space without permission. But there was no one left to give it to me. And Aunt Jess had left the place to the three of us, so I guess that was a sort of permission.

My earlier lethargy was forgotten as I set out to explore the forbidden.

HEADLIGHTS BOUNCED along the rutted road, blinding me from the book I had been trying to decipher. After shielding my eyes, I made out the distinct shape of a minivan. Maeve, of course.

Setting the book aside, I moved to the front door and opened it to spy both of my sisters, who each hauled a humongous Rubbermaid bin toward the porch.

"What's this?" I set the hurricane lamp aside and reached out to take the bin from Maeve.

"Stuff for your stubborn carcass," my sister grumped. "Sleeping bags, cleaning supplies, and some food so you don't starve to death."

I rolled my eyes. "You didn't have to."

"Have you met her?" Sibby huffed as she set down her own bin with a thud. "Wow, I can't believe this place is still standing."

"It's got good bones."

"And crap finishes." Maeve huffed. "Is that old fridge still here? And the stove from hell?"

"Did you think it would walk off on its own?"

She shrugged. "A girl can hope."

Sibby turned to me with sudden excitement. "Have you been in the greenhouse yet?"

"I was just in there."

She made a quick circular motion with her hands as though prompting me to get to the good stuff. "And?"

"And nothing." I shrugged. "I found a few books but the light is hell and I barely got through a page."

"But what was on the page?" Sibby bounced on her toes. "Was it a spell book?"

I shook my head. "Nothing that interesting. More like some musty geology project."

"That doesn't sound like Aunt Jess. Or Mom." Maeve shook her head. "Okay, so let's get to cleaning the kitchen, and then we can eat."

"Why do you always make us work first?" Sibby grumbled as she took the rag Maeve thrust at her. "I'm hungry now."

"You're worse than my kids." Maeve handed me a broom and then snapped on a pair of rubber gloves.

"Kinky," Sibby muttered, earning a sharp look from Maeve. "I didn't know you and Kal were into all that dominance stuff. Do I want to know what the gloves are for?"

I choked back a laugh. I'd forgotten what a genuine smartass my youngest sister could be. And how much I enjoyed her sass.

Maeve bristled. "Shut up, both of you, or I won't share Kal's double dark chocolate torte."

Maeve's husband was a pastry chef for one of the local resorts and his double dark chocolate torte was the stuff of legends.

"Yes, Mistress Maeve," Sibby muttered but then set to wiping down the dining room table.

"Are you really okay?" Maeve asked me, too low for Sibby to hear when I swept close to where she was scrubbing.

"Yes and no." I paused, glancing over my shoulder. "I knew something was going on with Kyle. And I ignored it because I didn't want to deal with it, you know?"

"I do." Maeve's eyes glittered in the low light from the hurricane lamp.

She must have been talking about the twins. Maeve and Kal had tried for years to have children. Rounds of expensive in-vitro chased by constant disappointment. It had been a horrible stumbling block in their marriage. Family was very important to Kal. He had been shunned by his own family and his tribe for marrying a woman who wasn't Inuit. They only had each other and Maeve had been eaten up with guilt because she couldn't give him a family. Having never wanted children myself, I didn't know what to say to her, how to comfort her when each attempt failed and seemed to carve another chunk out of her soul.

And then a miracle had happened. Two little miracles.

Arabella and Philip. Life between the two of them was better than ever, not the brittle image Kyle and I had projected outward. True joy. It was as elusive to me as the desire to spawn. Though I doted on my niece and nephew, there had never been that pang that other women mentioned, that yearning that must be critical to motherhood.

Some people did get happy endings. And there wasn't a better recipient than my sister. But I couldn't help but envy her such absolute contentment. Maeve was a born nurturer, a mother, a wife.

I was a hard worker.

"Hey, you guys, check this out," Sibby called from…

Maeve gasped. "Did she go in the greenhouse?"

"You know she's always been too damn curious for our own good. It amazed me Aunt Jess kept her out of there as long as she did. Sibby has never respected boundaries." I omitted the fact that I'd done the same thing not even an hour earlier.

"I heard that." Bright blue hair poked around the corner to the door. "You two always treated this place like it was a shrine. But I for one want to know what kind of crazy shit went on in here."

"What makes you think crazy shit *did* go on in there?" Maeve moved to the doorway but didn't cross the threshold.

"Um, you know Aunt Jess was a hippy. Locked green-house? Edible plants? Yeah, she was growing some super shrooms or maybe a little strain of pot that doesn't look or smell like pot but toasts you ever so nicely."

"You're nuts," I muttered. "What are you going to do? Smoke every plant in the place to see if you get a buzz?"

"Maybe?" Sibby's grin turned wicked. "Want to try it with me, Alys?"

I opened my mouth to respond, but Maeve clapped her hands. "There will be no ingesting of plants from this room in any manner. No eating, smoking, huffing, or cooking down to shoot up. Is that clear?"

"Has she always been so bossy?" Sibby whisper-mocked.

"Motherhood made her worse," I grumbled.

"Now, get cleaned up. I have a lasagna as well as a good stout red and if I am going to spend the rest of the night with you two, I need wine." With that Maeve spun on her heel and stalked off toward the powder room.

I moved to follow, but Sibby pulled me to a stop. "Look at this a minute."

Turning, I spotted the yellowed scrap of paper she held out. It was handwritten, and my crap eyesight in dim lighting struggled to read the title. "Empowerment Brew?"

"All the makings of it are right here." Sibby waved around the room.

My gaze narrowed on her face. "How do you know that?"

"Because, unlike you, I paid attention when Aunt Jess and Mom took us on nature walks. See that one right there? That's Belladonna. Nightshade. It is supposed to help people relax. And can also be used as a poison."

A cold chill gripped my spine. "You don't think Aunt Jess was making poisons?"

Even for Sibby's wild imagination, that was a bit of a stretch.

"No. I think she was making natural cocktails. Because that's what this looks like." She took the paper back. "Empowerment was kinda Aunt Jess's thing. Mom's too. And there was no doubt they knew how to cut loose and have a good time. I checked the list here. It seems straightforward enough. I think we should try it out. Couldn't we all use a little empowerment in our lives?"

I rolled my eyes. "If you want to ingest strange plants and risk Maeve's wrath, I won't stop you. But I'm not paying for your funeral, either."

23

At the word funeral, a little light went out of Sibby's eyes. "What?" I asked.

"You know you're almost the same age Mom was when…"

My throat constricted. "I do."

"I had this dream." Sibby admitted "About you. Alone in the darkness. You were trapped and…."

"And what?" My voice was tight, betraying nothing.

She didn't finish. Waved it away. "Nothing. It was just a stupid dream. Don't pay any attention to me. It's probably nothing."

"Probably," I muttered, not mentioning the fact that I'd had the exact same dream.

Except in mine, I was dead.

# CHAPTER THREE

"**G**od, Maeve, this is good." I moaned around my first bite of the double dark chocolate torte. "Like criminally good."

"No wonder Kal is getting so fat," Sibby quipped.

"He is not," Maeve protested.

"Is too. You can't tell me you haven't noticed when he's on top of you. Then again, he's a big old ox of a guy, so maybe not."

Maeve shook her head, the picture of denial. "He's not the fat one. I am."

I hated when she said things like that and decided to keep chipping away at Kal. He wouldn't mind a few good-humored knocks if it made his wife feel better. "You have to admit, he's kinda rocking the Dad bod lately."

"Maybe he has put on a few pounds." Maeve's lips twitched. "We let our gym membership lapse when I was pregnant with the twins."

Sibby leaned forward and lowered her voice to a conspiratorial whisper. "Does he have bitch tits?"

*"What?"* Maeve and I chorused.

"You know, man boobs. Moobs." She gestured to her own chest as if to illustrate. "Does he get all jiggly up top when he's going to town on you?"

"You are way too interested in their sex life." I reached for my glass. "Kyle definitely has bitch tits. The prostitute called him an uggo."

Maeve's jaw dropped.

Sibby barked out a laugh. "Perfect. Couldn't happen to a nicer guy."

Maeve sobered. "You should probably go get tested. Since he was…you know."

"Screwing around with professionals?" I let out a sigh and admitted a painful truth. "Not necessary. Grabbing him by the balls today was as close as I've been to him in two years."

For once neither of my sisters had anything to say. I finished my piece of torte before I added, "It's not Kyle. Well, it's not *just* Kyle. I just haven't felt the urge."

"Not even flying solo?" Sibby gaped.

I shook my head. "It took a while before I realized what was going on. That and my cycle stopped. Full-blown menopause sort of sucked it right out of me."

"Forty-nine. Just like mom." Sibby shook her head.

I shivered and reached for my wine.

"There are hormones," Maeve protested. "Things you can do."

"What's the point?" I pushed back from the table, collecting my plate and heading over to the sink. Maeve had lit some candles and the space glowed with cozy light. "That part of my life is over."

"It doesn't have to be," Sibby urged. "That hottie who ran off earlier was totally into you. Would like to get deeper into you, if you get my drift."

I rounded on her. "Brock? You can't be serious. He's a child."

"He's twenty-nine, actually. Hardly a child." Maeve looked thoughtful. "And Sibby's right. He does have a thing for you. He calls her Lys. And one time I caught him giving her *the look*." She directed the last part to Sibby.

"What look?" I asked even as Sibby nodded.

"You know. That one that's full of heat. Like he can strip you with his eyes and would do you on the nearest available surface?"

I wrapped my arms around myself. "Brock did not give me the look. Or any look. You must be wrong."

Maeve's chin jutted up. "Stubborn. You can't tell me what I did or didn't see."

"He should be your rebound shag," Sibby drained her wine and rose. "And I know just what will help you."

"What?" I asked.

She tossed me a wink and then headed out into the greenhouse.

Maeve got up and started collecting plates. "You know, it's not a bad idea. You and Brock. He's a good guy."

"I work with him," I sputtered. "And he's too young. He doesn't want a woman on the far side of menopause."

"Maybe you should let him be the judge of that." Maeve hip-checked me out of the way so she could set the plates in the sink. She turned the faucet on and waited for the water to heat. "Listen, I'm not trying to tell you what to do. I know you're ridiculously concerned with how other people perceive you. If you don't want Brock, fine. But don't give up on your sexuality. It's about more than the physical sensations."

"Maybe for a happily married woman whose husband worships the ground she walks on," I muttered. "The rest of us get our jollies where we can."

"You don't know what you're talking about." Maeve turned back to the dishes but before I could question her on what she meant, Sibby reappeared with a clear decanter full of...something sparkly.

"No," I groaned. "Why can't you let this go?"

She ignored me, pouring the pale contents into each of our empty wine glasses. The liquid effervesced in the candle-light like champaign.

"Let what go?" Maeve set the last plate in the drainboard and then turned. "What is that?"

"Empowerment brew." Sibby set the empty decanter on the table with a dull thump and then collected the three wine glasses between her two hands and moved toward us. "It's an old family cocktail recipe."

I rolled my eyes as Maeve frowned. "Where did you get it?"

"I made it."

"From things in the greenhouse," I added with a pointed look.

"It's some sort of Wicca-earthy cocktail." She thrust the glasses forward and I took mine only to prevent her from dropping the glass and making a mess.

"This is a horrible idea," I muttered. "We have no idea what these plants will do."

Sibby flashed me a grin. "Sure we do. They'll empower us. It's right there in the name."

It amazed me that she could have so much faith in some-thing that she knew so little about. Times like these, I was sure one of us had been a hospital mix-up.

"Maeve?" Sibby arched her pierced eyebrow and focused on our middle sister. The tiebreaker.

Something seemed to pass between the two of them, a current of communication that I didn't understand and wasn't privy to.

"What the hell." Maeve knocked back the contents of her glass in one gulp.

My jaw dropped. "I can't believe you did that. We have no idea what that will do to you."

"That's the fun part." Sibby let out a delighted squeal and polished off her own glass. I scanned the room for Maeve's keys. Her van was blocking me in and I didn't want to take the time to haul my bags out of the car so there would be enough seats for the three of us. Great, I had to take both of my foolish sisters to the hospital to have their stomachs pumped.

"Come on, Alys," my youngest sister cajoled. "Don't be such a spoilsport."

"You are old enough to know better," I told her.

"But young enough to do it anyway," she winked. "Live a little."

I turned my pleading gaze to Maeve. "How do you feel?"

She considered a minute. "Fine. Better than fine, actually."

"Empowered?" Sibby suggested.

I gave her a sharp look even as I pleaded with Maeve. "Please, let me take you to the hospital. If anything happens to you, Kal and the kids will be devastated."

Maeve blinked once, her pupils huge from more than just the dim lighting. "I want to go outside. Anyone else want to go outside?" Her words were slightly slurred.

"Hell yes," Sibby set down her glass and then grabbed Maeve by the hand. "You coming Alys?"

I followed, terror coursing through me. The drink was still in my hand. I ought to bring it to the ER so the doctors would know what my foolhardy sisters had ingested and be able to treat them. "Guys, I really think we ought to go to the hospital."

Sibby had her arms out and her head thrown back. She spun in circles. Around and around, her face lit with joy and moonlight.

Maeve had flopped onto her back, waving her arms up

and down like she was making a snow angel. Except there was no snow, so all she was doing was running her arms and legs over the grass.

"This tickles," she started to giggle.

The two of them were wasted. Trashed out of their minds.

"Come on, Alys. Pull that stick out of your butt and have some fun," Sibby shouted.

"Weee! Maeve ripped up fistfuls of grass and let them shower down on her.

They really did seem to be happy. Having fun in childlike ways. Was I being unreasonable to want to have them checked out for that?

Maeve rolled from side to side, her long hair picking up dead leaves and sticks. Sibby skipped up to me.

"Trust me, Alys." At that moment she appeared stone-cold sober. "For once in your tightly controlled life, trust me."

I swallowed. I should have trusted her all those years ago, about Kyle. She was my sister and I hadn't believed enough in her then. And we had lost years because of it. Maybe she wasn't the bad sister. Maybe I was.

Suddenly the drink in my hand was more than just a potentially deadly concoction. It was a peace offering. A fresh start.

An empowerment brew.

I brought the glass to my lips and took a cautious sip. It was fizzy on my tongue, bursting with a flavorless sort of effervescence. I tipped the glass higher and swallowed more. It cracked and sizzled like an energy storm as it went down my throat.

Sibby danced back and clapped her hands. "You did it."

I had. I waited for something to happen. Something unusual or different. It wasn't like overindulging at the bar. I felt…better. Less exhausted and more energetic.

I set the glass on the porch and then looked up at the moon. It seemed to be singing. I closed my eyes and swayed from side to side, basking in the glow. The melody. It filled up all the cold, dark places inside me and I let it.

She no longer held sway over me. My tides had stilled. I was my own woman, her equal.

Those were not my normal thoughts. They were hazy and not fully formed.

"I'm stoned," I said in awe.

"No, this is very important," Sibby said, sounding like a stern toddler. She gripped my hand and dragged me to where Maeve lay prone.

"Maeve. Get up." Sibby nudged her in the ribs with her motorcycle boot. "This is serious business."

Maeve rolled over and giggled. Her face was flushed. Her eyes sparkling. "What is?"

"We're not done yet. We have to ask the universe for it."

"It?" I swayed from side to side, again lost in the dulcet tones of the moon.

"Whatever it wants to give us. We need to tell it that we're ready." Sibby dropped my hand only long enough to haul Maeve to her feet. "Are you ready?"

Maeve blew long strands of reddish-brown hair out of her eyes. "Aye aye."

"Then take Alys's hand." Sibby grabbed my other hand with her free one and then closed her eyes. "Al, are you ready?"

"I hate when you call me Al."

"I know. Answer the question."

My eyelids drifted shut and I breathed in and out. Listened to the moon's song. Equals. Powerful equals. "I'm ready."

"We're ready!" Sibby shouted to the night sky. "Bring it!"

"Yeah, bring it, beeyotch!" Maeve shouted, then clapped her hands over her mouth and snort laughed.

"We're ready!" I hollered and then hooted like an owl for no reason other than it felt good to do so. I felt wild, alive, and free.

We screeched like banshees that we were ready for whatever the universe had in store until we ran out of oomph and sprawled on the grass, quietly staring up at the moon.

"This is probably why Aunt Jess wanted to live in the middle of nowhere," Maeve said. "Otherwise, the neighbors would have called the cops if they cooked this stuff up and got wild with it all the time."

"Neighbors can eat a dick," Sibby grunted and rolled over. A few moments later she began to snore.

Somewhere in the back of my mind, it occurred to me that we should go inside. Instead of suggesting it, I basked in the moon's glow and a feeling I hadn't experienced in a long time. Contentment. I shut my eyes and listened to sister moon's song.

I WOKE up feeling every minute of my age. The moon had set, leaving us at the mercy of the morning sun that threatened to crest beyond the distant hills. The dew had soaked through my clothes. My hair was damp, my skin clammy. As I rolled over my back twinged.

"That," I muttered as I sat up. "Was a monumentally stupid plan."

A groan sounded beside me. I turned just as Maeve sat up, wincing. She looked just as bedraggled as I felt, with her hair full of leaves and sticks. And her clothes sticking to her body.

"I don't think I'm hung over?" Maeve said it as a question. "You?"

The birds were singing in the trees but the sweet chirp didn't make me wince. I shook my head. Stiff and sore yeah, but my head felt surprisingly clear. "Nope, no hangover. What about you, Sibby?"

I turned to my other side where she'd passed out. There was an indent in the grass to show she'd been there, but no sign of Sibby.

"Maybe she went in the house?" Maeve suggested. "Started the coffee?"

"There's no coffee pot."

"I brought a French press and grounds. Plus powdered milk." Maeve groaned and climbed to her feet. "All you need to do is boil water on the stove."

"You really do think of everything."

Maeve shrugged. "Just because you decided you would rather be a hermit out here doesn't mean you can't enjoy the modern conveniences."

"Speaking of which, I could use a shower. I have to meet Brock at the Mid-Century Modern at nine." Then find a divorce lawyer and deal with the whole Kyle mess.

"Are we not going to talk about it?" Maeve asked as we headed for the house.

"Talk about what? The fact that we got drunk and howled at the moon then slept outside even though we know better." Seemed pretty self-explanatory to me.

She pulled me to a stop. "You felt it too. I know you did."

"Felt what?" I knew what she was talking about. The moon. The kinship I had felt with what amounted to be a lump of dead rock in the sky.

She hesitated, as though she were trying to put whatever had happened after we screamed at the universe to bring it into words that made sense.

Like we weren't tempting fate with that dumbass maneuver.

"The connection," she said at last.

"Maeve, I don't have time for this." I detoured toward my car and snagged a suitcase out of the back seat. I lugged it up the dicey steps—was really going to have to fix those—and then past where Maeve stood and into the main bedroom.

Praying the pilot light on the hot water tank was lit, I turned on the shower and let the water run. My fingertips grazed the water and I smiled when after a moment it heated up to a decent shower temperature.

After retrieving a towel, washcloth, body wash, shampoo, and conditioner from my bag, I laid out the items I needed and then shucked my damp clothes. I stepped into the avocado green tub and pulled the discolored shower curtain. The warm water helped to loosen the knotted muscles in my back and neck and I had just started lathering shampoo into my hair when the shower curtain was ripped aside by my wild-eyed sister.

"Sibby's gone," Maeve said.

## CHAPTER FOUR

"What do you mean she's gone?" I glared at my sister from behind a sudsy tangle of wet hair. "Did you check upstairs?" It would be just like Sibby to wake up cold and drag herself inside to a comfy bed and leave us to sleep on the cold ground.

"I checked everywhere," Maeve insisted as I rinsed the shampoo from my hair.

"Try her cell." I reached for the conditioner, but Maeve snatched it out of my hand.

"Alys, It's on the table where she left it. She is not here."

A prickle of unease went through me. Sibby was one of those people who was forever texting or screwing around on social media. For her not to have her phone on her...I reached down and shut off the water.

Maeve handed my towel over and proceeded to pace the confines of the bathroom. "Both of our cars are here. Her motorcycle is back at my place. She couldn't have gone far."

"What are you most worried about?" Maeve had a bad habit of catastrophic thinking. Some horrible thought must have lodged itself in her gray matter to get her so worked up.

Maeve stopped and turned to face me. "I'm worried she was all out of her head on that brew and wandered into the lake."

I froze. Outside the bathroom window, the morning went utterly still. No wind, no birds. As if the entire world was on pause. That thought hadn't even occurred to me. But we had all been senseless the night before. Dancing and hearing songs that weren't there. What if, still under the influence, Sibby had woken with some urge to swim, panicked, and drowned.

"Should I call Kal?" Maeve wrung her hands.

My hair dripped water as I stalked out of the bathroom. "We don't want to upset the kids yet. Let me try someone else."

Brock's number was programmed into my phone, as were all my business contacts. I was supposed to meet with him this morning anyway, so I knew he'd be up.

"Lys?" He sounded sleepy as he breathed my name into the phone.

"My sister's missing. Can you help Maeve and I look for her?"

"Where are you?" The grogginess vanished. In the background, I could hear a rustling sound, as though he were pulling on his clothes.

If I hadn't been on the verge of panic, I might have felt embarrassed to be naked while I was on the phone with a man who was also in the buff. But thoughts of Sibby and the lake pushed everything else aside.

"My Aunt Jess's place. It's on the far side of the—"

"I know where it is. I'll be there in twenty minutes." He disconnected and I dropped the phone.

"Brock is on his way," I told Maeve as I reached for my underwear. "Check the house again while I get dressed. Make sure you look for notes or clues."

Maeve nodded and dashed out the door.

I dressed as quickly as I could, wresting to yank jeans up over my still wet flesh. Finally dressed, I ran out into the main room where I bumped into Maeve who was coming down the stairs. "Nothing."

"Did you check the greenhouse?" Not waiting for her to reply, I headed through the kitchen, past the dining table, and out into the greenhouse.

All the plants turned to face me. Away from the sun, they stretched toward me.

I jolted to a stop. Maeve slammed into my back. "What? Is she in there?"

My pulse throbbed in my ears. I could feel them. All of them. Feel their roots sunk into the soil. Feel their need for light, their hunger for my attention.

"Alys?"

Sibby. We were looking for Sibby. I scanned the room, the plants.

"No." Slowly, ever so carefully, I backed out of the room and shut the door. "No, she's not. Let's go look outside."

We burst through the door as though the cottage had ejected us. "Sibby!" We shouted. Waited.

Maeve circled the house and I headed toward the lake.

Sunlight playfully dappled the surface of the lake as we approached it. I scowled at it. The water had no right to look so cheerful when my sister was missing, possibly drowned in its depths.

Clouds gathered before the sun, blocking its rays from the water. There was no wind, no rise in humidity. Nothing that explained where the clouds had come from or why they had formed.

The sound of gravel crunching beneath tires. I turned and spied Brock's pick-up truck barreling down the road. He pulled to a stop alongside Maeve's minivan. I ran to greet him.

"How long?" he asked. "How long has she been missing?"

"We're not sure," I said as Maeve jogged up to meet us. "We were all…drinking last night and fell asleep outside. When Maeve and I woke up, Sibby was gone."

Maeve wrung her hands. "Should we call the Sheriff?"

Brock shook his head. "They'll just tell you to wait twenty-four hours to report her."

In twenty-four hours, Sibby might be dead. Could already be dead. I pivoted to face the lake once more.

Brock surveyed the tree line on the far side of the house. "I'll check the woods around the house. See if we can find her."

"What should we do?" My throat closed up and I had to choke out the question.

"Stay here. Call me if she turns up." He put a reassuring hand on my shoulder. "Don't worry. We'll find her."

He squeezed once and then jogged toward the evergreens.

Maeve came to stand beside me. "You didn't mention the lake."

"There's nothing he could do about that." If Sibby was in the lake, we would need the Sheriff's office to help dredge it to find her body.

The thought of Sibby, cold, lifeless, waiting to be found at the bottom of the lake….

Before the intent was fully formed, I stormed toward the water. Anger was building up in my gut and the sky above me grew darker, more menacing. Behind me, I could hear Maeve calling my name but I didn't pause, didn't alter my stride one bit as I pushed onward.

At the point where my feet should have hit the water, my sneakers sank into the mud. I took another step. Squish. Another. And another.

Maeve gasped. "What are you doing?"

I looked down and saw that the water was retreating from me. The lake retracted like a beaten animal fearful of its abusive owner. I took another step. The water withdrew further.

Was I doing this? Was I somehow responsible for pushing back the lake? Or was the water responding to my rage somehow?

Debris littered the loamy bottom. It lay before me, its secrets unguarded by its familiar liquid blanket. Bass flopped at my feet. A broken fishing pole stuck out of the mud at a sharp angle. Some rotting orange fabric had snagged on a rock. Plants bent low and snails crawled along. No sign of Sibby.

I was thirty feet out into what should have been very deep water. I turned back to the shoreline. Maeve stood there, her hands covering her mouth as she gaped at me, and the wall of water which towered behind me hovered in a way that defied gravity, defied nature.

Sibby was a decent swimmer, but she wouldn't have made it past this point. Not in the state she had been in the night before.

I returned to the shore, could feel the water groveling around my heels, as though begging for forgiveness. A glance back over my shoulder told me all was as it had been before I'd moved into the water.

The plants, the clouds, and the lake.

"What the hell did you do?" Maeve breathed.

I shook my head, unable to tell her what I didn't understand.

"Help!" A voice cried from behind us.

Maeve and I whirled around, saw Sibby standing on the roof of the cottage. Relief filled me at the sight of her. We ran to a spot just below her.

"You scared the hell out of us!" I bitched as we reached the ground. "How did you get up there?"

My youngest sister glared down at me. "I have no idea."

"How is that even possible?" Maeve asked.

I shook my head and scanned the area. There were no ladders or trellises along the structure, no large trees close enough to climb up. The windows had been painted shut to prevent drafts years ago.

"I swear, Sibby. If this is some sort of elaborate prank—"

"It's not," she snapped. "Believe me, Alys. I have no clue how I got up here."

I let out a breath. I believed her. "Why didn't you answer when we called for you?"

"Can you get me down before you start interrogating me?" She crossed her arms over her chest and waited.

My phone rang and I extracted it from my back pocket to see Brock's name on the display. "Hey."

"Any sign of her?"

"Yeah," I cleared my throat. "She's here. On the roof."

And she better have a good explanation as to how she got up there because I was ready to throttle her.

BROCK HAD an extendable ladder in the back of his truck. Maeve and I held it as he climbed up to help guide Sibby down. Something about seeing him touch her bothered me. I turned my back on them and stared toward the lake.

The one I had relocated by sheer force of will.

*Don't think about that. Or the plants.* I didn't want to lose it in front of Brock. Sibby and Maeve had seen me come unhinged more than once but Brock worked for me. I didn't want him to see me like that because when I lost my cool, I *lost* it. No man could withstand Alys Stevens's temper unleashed.

No man would ever want to.

"There you go."

Glancing over my shoulder, I saw that Brock had reached out a hand and laid it on Sibby's back to guide her down.

My fingers curled into fists. The wind off the lake picked up, blowing my hair into my eyes.

"Thanks, handsome." Sibby flashed Brock a winning smile as she bounced to the ground.

Overhead dark clouds blotted out the sun. I clenched my molars together but somehow grit out, "Yes, thank you, Brock. We all really appreciate it."

He dipped his head in acknowledgment and set to work packing up his ladder.

When his back was turned, I snagged Sibby by the arm and towed her over to where Maeve stood, arms wrapped protectively about herself.

"Damn, Alys. You guys weren't kidding about his *rrrower* factor. Break me off a piece of that a—"

"*Inside*," I grated. "*Now*."

The wind yanked on the treetops. Leaves spiraled down to the ground, many of them being pulled prematurely from the trees in the harsh gusts.

Maeve's eyes went wide and she clapped a hand over Sibby's open mouth, preventing whatever smartass remark my sister intended to spew next. "We'll meet you inside in a minute." She half dragged Sibby up the stairs and the sound of the screen door slapped shut behind them.

I closed my eyes and counted to ten. Then twenty. By thirty, I was calm enough to turn back to the truck, where Brock was securing his ladder. Without asking, I strode to the passenger's side, popped open the door, and pulled myself up to fasten the other side.

He flashed me a grin. "You never mind getting your hands dirty."

"Force of habit," I said as I pulled the ratchet strap tight. "When I see something needs doing, I do it."

Ladder in place, I hopped down and shut the door, then rounded the front end to move to where Brock stood. He leaned against the driver's side door, arms folded across his chest, not looking like he was in a hurry to escape the coming storm. "Tell me about how you got into it."

Funny, I'd never actually told anyone the story before. Lora had been with us from the beginning and Kyle and I married. Maeve obviously knew it because we'd been there. "I was working in finance, living in an apartment in the city and hating every minute of it."

He nodded. "I can see that. You're a nature girl at heart."

I stared at him. "No one else seems to notice that about me."

He grinned. "Most people believe the ice queen façade."

They did. The wind died down and the clouds thinned a bit.

"So which house was your first?"

"Maeve's. She'd been living here, taking care of Aunt Jess who had ovarian cancer, when this property came up for auction. She told me she thought it would be a good invest-ment, or a weekend home. As you can see, this place is a little too tight for all of us." I waved at the cottage.

"It was the first time in my life I had ever done some-thing so impulsive. When Maeve and I bought that house, it was just the two of us doing everything. Slithering into crawl spaces to inspect foundations and investigating attics. The more we sub-contracted the more money we spent. I started asking questions of local GC's and watching videos, taking tutorials and going to home improvement centers. It took us almost a year since we had so much to learn and so many other obligations. But eventually, we did everything. From demo to pouring concrete, to installing hardwood floors to landscaping. There was just so much of us in it that by the time we were done, I was equally proud and disappointed."

"And you gave it to Maeve and Kal?"

"Not right away. We sold it, used the profit to invest in a new foreclosure. That one had been in a fire and we had to take it down to the foundation. It cost more, but when it was done it sold for more too. A lot more."

"And you officially had the bug." Brock smiled.

I nodded. "We were several years in when the first house came up for sale, for about twenty grand more than we'd sold it for. But by that point, I could afford to be a little frivolous. Bonus that it royally pissed Kyle off when he found out." I winced, realizing just how passive-aggressive that sounded.

Brock ignored the mention of my husband. "You bought it for Maeve?"

"And Kal. As a wedding present." It seemed only right that one of us should live there.

"And now you're living here." Brock looked back at the cottage. "Got big plans?"

Even though I'd told Sibby and Maeve the day before that I intended to renovate the cottage, I shook my head. "I can't afford to divide my time right now."

Brock studied me, the gold in his irises seeming to glow. "So, you'll give everything to your sisters, but take nothing for yourself. Who cares for you, possum?"

My lips parted and I was about to say *I do*. But the breath was stuck in my lungs because Brock bent down and gently feathered a kiss over my lips. Warm, soft gentle pressure, just a taste. It was over before I could consider how I should react.

He stepped back and was in the truck before my body unfroze.

"I'm glad you called me. Do it again any time," was all he said.

I watched as he drove away.

Overhead, the clouds parted and the sun came out.

I stood there, basking in the warmth of the day, trying to understand what had just happened.

Nothing. At least nothing much. Except that in the last twenty-four hours I had been actively ignoring the line I had drawn between work colleague and romantic entanglement.

Worse, Brock didn't even seem to notice the line. Or care that I was so much older and his source of income. And why the hell did he keep calling me possum?

I moved back to the house on wooden legs and then reached for the screen door handle. Maeve and Sibby were seated on opposite sides of the dining room table, each clutching a cup of coffee.

Maeve looked up at me. "Is he gone?"

When I nodded she cut her gaze to Sibby.

"Good, because you're not going to believe this."

# CHAPTER FIVE

## SIOBHAN

"*What do you mean you woke up in a stranger's bed?*" Alys sounded both horrified and at the same time, not at all surprised. No one could pass judgment like my big sis.

I knocked back my coffee and then headed for the French press just so I didn't have to meet her stare. "It's like I said, I woke up in a bed and some guy had his arm around me."

It had been so much more than that though. The feel of a male body cocooning mine. His warm breath on the back of my neck. The heaviness of a limb slung over me. The undeniably male scent. Smooth high-thread-count sheets. I had been chilled to the bone after sleeping on the damp ground and it had been so damn long since I'd been held.

"What guy?" Classic Alys, always pushing and pulling and shoving her way to more info. And at this point, I had nothing else to give her.

"If I knew his name, I would tell you. But I don't." I left out the part about how he had felt familiar somehow. How being in his arms felt right. She would have just rolled her eyes at me.

"What did the room look like?" Maeve asked.

I shook my head. "I don't know. It was dark. Really thick curtains. I could make out shapes, like maybe where there was furniture, but nothing was too clear."

"And then you were on the roof," Alys said in a flat tone.

I knew that tone. Her quintessential *stop trying to blow smoke up my ass, Siobhan, because the stick I keep up there doesn't leave room for anything else* tone.

It always pissed me off, that tone. It reminded me that nothing I ever did was good enough for my oldest sister. Well, too freaking bad. This time I had logic on my side. I rounded on her. "How else would I have gotten up on the roof? If your boy toy hadn't had a ladder I'd still be on the roof."

Her mouth opened and I saw Maeve put a hand on her arm. "Remember the lake."

If possible, my oldest sister's expression closed up even tighter.

"What about the lake?" I asked.

Maeve's gaze slid to me, her eyes full of stress that she didn't need right now. "We thought…well, we were all acting senseless after drinking that stuff last night. And we were worried that maybe you stumbled into the lake and drowned."

I winced. I'd been so freaked out about what had happened to me that I hadn't thought about what my sisters had gone through when they found me missing. No wonder Alys had called her McNibblet.

"Alys," Maeve swallowed and looked at our big sister as though waiting for her to take over. When she showed no sign of budging, Maeve hurried on. "Alys moved the water back. From the shore. For like a football field's length. It was like there was some sort of invisible wall and she just kept on pushing and pushing." Maeve stopped and looked at our oldest sister again as though waiting for her to add something.

"It's not possible," Alys muttered.

"Which part, teleporting or building a wall of water?" I knew as soon as I said the words out loud that I shouldn't have.

Alys shot me a hostile look. "Any of it. We're probably having some sort of aftereffect from that empowerment thing. Hallucinating."

I ignored her grasping at straws and focused on Maeve. "How about you? Anything out of the ordinary happening to you?"

Maeve shook her head and smiled. "Nope, but it's only nine-thirty. I have plenty of time to develop powers."

This time Alys's poisoned glare landed on Maeve.

"Powers. Empowerment." My lips began curling up at the sides. "I think we woke something up last night."

Alys made a frustrated noise. "You're—"

"What, being ridiculous?" The idea was so thrilling that I thought I might levitate. "How else can you explain this?"

Her lips compressed into a thin line and she said nothing. For a moment I felt sorry for her. Of course, I had known that Kyle was a dipshit, had known since he'd come on to me on their wedding day. It had floored me. How could my strong, capable, brilliant sister tether herself to a bottom-feeder who disrespected her that way?

The only explanation was that she didn't know. So I had told her. And she hadn't believed me. I should have done Alys a favor and slept with Kyle that very day.

He wouldn't have lasted a month.

The mystery guy of the amazing thread count sheets ought to count his lucky stars that I'd vanished before he woke up. Because it had been way too long for me to not use the temptation of morning wood to my nefarious advantage.

"I don't have time for this," Alys pushed herself away from the table. "I have to secure a divorce attorney."

"What about that woman who bought the Alpine Chateau we did last year?" Maeve, ever helpful, offered. "I'm pretty sure she was a divorce lawyer. Or at least she could recommend someone good."

"I need better than good. I need this over, yesterday. I still need to do a walk-through of the Mid-Century Modern and—"

"I can't believe you two." I got to my feet so I could tower over the two of them. "Lawyers and walk-throughs. You guys, we have magic now. Can we take five minutes and just contemplate what that means?"

"It doesn't mean anything." Count on Alys to stick her head in the sand and ignore the obvious. The woman could teach the mountains a thing or two about being an immovable object. "Like I said, it was probably some shared delusion brought on by whatever was in that drink. I told you not to fiddle around in there."

"She's probably right," Maeve put in. "After all, I haven't done anything strange."

Alys moved over to the French press and poured what was left into the travel

thermos Maeve had brought for her. "I'm heading to the office."

I crossed my arms over my chest and lifted my chin. "You haven't even said thank you yet."

"Thank you?" Alys shook her head. "What, for you getting yourself stuck on the roof or for drugging us?"

"Not to me, to her." I nodded my chin at Maeve.

"Sibby," Maeve began. "Don't."

"Don't what? Don't tell her that you leapt into action to make sure she would have everything she needed to be comfortable here? That you dropped whatever your plans were for the night to provide support to your emotionally stunted big sister? How long are you going to let her take you for granted?"

Alys's lips parted and, for a moment, I hoped she would say something profound. But all she said was, "I appreciate you both taking the time to check up on me. But I really need to go."

I watched her walk away and then turned to face Maeve who sat slumped and looking defeated. We listened as gravel crunched beneath her tires as she did a broken K turn and left us behind.

"Alys doesn't ask for help. We have to bludgeon her with it or she goes without. You know that." Maeve spoke up.

"That doesn't mean she gets a pass on gratitude." I sat across from her at the table and took her cold, pale hand in mine. "You need to tell her."

"I will."

"When?"

"Soon." Maeve could be just as stubborn as Alys, though she went about it in a totally different way. "She has to get this business with Kyle settled. Besides, you know Alys. She wants to fix everything. This can't be fixed."

We sat in silence, absorbing the truth of that.

"You should rest," I said to Maeve. "Let me drive you back to your place so you can have a nap before Kal and the kids get back."

"What about here?" Maeve waved her hand around the cottage. "Someone needs to clean this place up."

"I'll come back on my bike after I drop you off." My gaze darted to the greenhouse. I would come back all right. Only I wouldn't spend my time cleaning.

# CHAPTER SIX

## ALYS

"I don't take Maeve for granted," I muttered as I drove back around the lake and through town. "I don't take anyone for granted."

Damn Sibby. She always pulled crap like this, getting inside my head, telling me black was white and down was up. But the pang of guilt worming its way through my stomach told me that she had a point. I hadn't actually thanked my sisters for coming over. Because I hadn't wanted to be alone after what happened with Kyle. And as ridiculous as Sibby's empowerment potion had been, at least it had kept the nightmares away.

I needed something to do. I should have just gone for a run or something until my sisters left. But I hadn't been thinking straight. Work always gave me purpose.

The Mid-Century Modern house sat on a hillside at the outskirts of town. With no better destination in mind, I headed for it and was surprised to find Brock's truck already parked in the circular drive.

"I thought I would find you here." Brock exited the truck. He was freshly showered and his hair was combed back from

WITCH WAY AFTER FORTY

his face. "Still want to do that walk-through?"

At least he didn't want to talk about the kiss.

"You don't have to—" I began and then cut myself off. That was the same sort of thing I'd said to Maeve the night before. Telling someone they didn't have to do something did not equal a thank you. He was already here and willing. "If you wouldn't mind, I'd appreciate it."

Brock nodded and then took the keys from my hand and led me to the front door. "So, what's the damage?"

Brock knew me well enough. I didn't flip houses the way some designers did. I fixed the ones no one wanted. Sometimes taking the structures down to the studs.

The door opened into the great room with a massive stone hearth and wall of windows that looked out over the evergreen trees. The smell answered his question but I tacked on, "There was a fire in the kitchen."

"Drugs?" He asked with a raised eyebrow.

I shook my head. I had once gutted a house that had been inhabited by meth addicts. There was very little left to work with on that job. Drugs destroyed lives and so much more.

I shoved the thought of that stupid empowerment brew away. "My understanding was the house belonged to an elderly woman. She forgot she had something in the oven and went to bed."

We passed through the living room, over the dated octagonal tiles, through the dining room, and toward what remained of the kitchen.

Brock whistled low. "Not much left. The bedrooms are right behind here, too. Did the owner get out?"

I laid a hand on one blackened wall. "No. The batteries in her smoke alarm were dead. The smoke got her before anyone knew what was happening."

"A perfect storm." Brock shook his head. "Damn. We're

really going to have to go to town on this place. What have you got planned?"

For the next hour, we walked through the house, discussing possibilities. Brock tried—and failed—to talk me out of moving the kitchen to the dining room's current location. I knew it would be expensive but I had a vision of some man cooking dinner while his wife sat on the couch and drank wine and I refused to let it go. Mid-Century Moderns were all about clean lines and despite some of the bizarre style choices, like the tile and that seafoam green pedestal sink in the master bath, others could be celebrated.

Brock went into the crawlspace, climbed onto the roof, and checked the attic. He did tell me that the ugly columns were decorative—why bother, for the love of grief—and that they could be removed sans the expensive steel beam. We talked about adding a mudroom and a powder room, two guaranteed strategies that would open the house up to buyers with young children. If the spirit of the former owner was lurking around, I think she would like my plans for her home.

"This is going to be one of your best yet," Brock said as I locked the door. "I'll make some calls and have numbers by Monday."

That was how it worked. Brock gave me an estimate on labor and materials and then Maeve and I would go over how much we had left to spend on finishes and still turn a profit. Some designers tried to skimp on the structural end, to the new owner's detriment. Rotting wood looked good with a fresh coat of paint. Maeve and I never did things that way. Better to have a clean, inexpensive tile shower than a marble one if the plumbing wasn't up to code. High-end finishes didn't equal a quality home.

"Did you hash things out with your sisters?" Brock asked as we walked back to our vehicles.

"As much as we ever do. Sibby thinks—" I cut myself off, unable to believe I'd almost confessed my sister's wild theory to him.

"What?" The golden ring around his irises expanded.

"It's silly. And I'd feel silly repeating it."

"Nothing wrong with being a little silly. Laughter is one of the best things there is, possum."

"Why do you keep calling me possum? Did I suddenly grow an ugly hairless tail that I'm not aware of?" I glanced over my shoulder at my posterior.

He laughed. "It's a term of endearment where I come from."

I sucked in some air. This was it, time to discuss the kiss and redraw the line. There could be no bizarre nicknames, no more kisses. "Listen, Brock. I've been a little off-kilter since yesterday. While I appreciate that you've been helping to steady me, I don't think that this is such a good idea."

"What?" Though his tone was all innocence, it didn't fool me at all.

"You and me. Getting closer."

"So, this is a bad idea, is it?" He took a step forward, deliberately invading my space. He bent down next to me and inhaled.

"What are you doing?" It was a stupid thing to ask. He was clearly smelling me.

"You desire me," he said. It wasn't a question. "And you smell like the moon."

How was a woman supposed to respond to that? "I—"

"And you're no longer mated."

"Mated? You mean married? Well technically I am, we have to work out all the legalities."

"You aren't using him as a buffer anymore. You cut him loose." The golden ring flared brighter. "That means you're fair hunting."

The way he spoke was downright unnerving. Like his words had a totally different meaning than the ones I knew. "I'm not looking to be hunted or chased or whatever game you are playing."

"This isn't a game to me, Lys." He tipped my chin up and held my gaze. "I've never been more serious about anything. I want you. Have wanted you since the moment we met."

My lips parted and I wanted to tell him that what he was saying was wrong, impossible. All the things I constantly told myself. My chest constricted tightly and, for a moment, I thought I was about to have a heart attack. Instead, what came out were words that ripped free from my soul, "I'm not ready for this."

"I know." There was no way to describe what he did, but he somehow dialed his intensity down. The golden rings shrank until it was just the barest highlight ad his brown irises. And he was just Brock again. "I know you're not ready. But when you are, I'll be here for you, Lys. I have been waiting for you. I will keep waiting for you."

And then he turned and walked to his truck, climbed behind the wheel, and drove away.

Leaving me breathless and shaky and wondering how I had lost control of my life so completely.

SIOBHAN'S MOTORCYCLE was parked in front of the cottage when I pulled up. My eye began to twitch at the sight of it. Sibby sans Maeve was way too much. I didn't want to talk about her hallucination from earlier or her accusation that I was some ungrateful shrew. I definitely didn't want to talk about Brock and whatever the hell was going on there.

*I have been waiting for you. I will keep waiting for you.*

He made it sound like I was some soldier gone off to war,

he was my affianced left to wait and worry. Yet at the moment, it hadn't felt melodramatic or ridiculous. His eyes had been sincere. And intense.

I fanned myself a little remembering the look he gave me.

Sibby opened the screen door at my approach. "How goes it sister-witch?"

I cast her a black look. "What are you talking about?"

"Only this." She pointed to a heavy tome that she had left on the dining room table.

"Sibby, I'm not in the mood for…whatever this is. I just met with a divorce lawyer and I have a ton of things to do." Things like check my accounts. Because according to her, disgruntled spouses sometimes did sneaky things like move money around before filing for divorce. Kyle's name wasn't on my accounts, but he might know passwords. And he was a big enough hemorrhoid to try to pull something like that.

"Well, get in the mood. This, Alys, is our family legacy." Her eyes sparkled. "Magic."

"What?" I moved closer to the book and stared down at the slated cursive.

"We are the latest in a very long line of witches. See here? Mom traced her lineage back to a Scottish indentured servant in the early seventeenth century. That woman, Margret Ellen Silver, was traded from her village to the indigenous people."

"Traded?" I gaped. "As in, they exchanged her like last year's unwanted sweater?"

"Apparently, she wasn't all that popular. Or rather, she was *too* popular with some lord of the manor where she served. Unmarried, no kids, and from all accounts, quite a looker. Must be good genes running in the family, huh?" She nudged me in the ribs.

I was getting caught up in the story despite myself. "So, because some land-owning jackass or whatever couldn't keep it in his pants, this whole village drove her out of town?"

"Must have had all her teeth in her forties. Yeah, the women banded together and convinced the men they'd be safer if they gifted her to the local tribe. To keep the natives from raiding the village."

I blew out a breath. "Bastards probably thought they'd kill her for them."

"It gets better." Sibby bent low, her finger skimming along the lines written in the book. "It says here she was adopted by the crone of the tribe, a wise woman and a healer. It was while apprenticing there that Margret Ellen called magic to her family line."

"Called magic how?" I bent low over the book to try to decipher the words.

"I'm not really sure." Sibby shook her head. "It's not super clear. There's something about magic being like energy, free-floating, and all around us. Some people can sense it, some can tap into it, casting spells and whatnot. And only a very few can wield it in line with their own gifts."

Looking at the book was giving me an eye strain headache. "What gifts? What are you even talking about?"

"People who can harness the magic, tap into it and use it in line with their gifts, they're witches."

The word hung between us for an endless moment. Witches.

"Are you saying Mom and Aunt Jess could…?"

Aunt Jess had been an honorary title bestowed on our mother's closest friend. Her lineage was from the Caribbean. "I think Aunt Jess was something else. But Mom…"

Our mother had been a chubby, soft-spoken woman who'd been emotionally and mentally abused all her life, first by her father and then by her husband. She hadn't found peace until the last few years when she'd come to live here.

She wasn't exactly the poster child for female empowerment. Or witchcraft. "If this is true, why wouldn't they tell us?"

"No idea. Maybe they didn't know we would want to be empowered." Sibby licked her lips. "I can teleport."

I folded my arms over my chest and raised a brow.

"Well, I'm not exactly sure how it works." Sibby pushed back from the table and began to pace. "I did it before I woke up. And then again, when I was…er…that is to say…"

"When you were what?"

She put her hands on her hips. "When I was turned on, okay?"

"Oh." Heat crept up my cheeks.

"How about you? Were you all hot and bothered when you did, whatever you did?"

I shook my head. "Not the way you mean."

It was her turn to raise a brow. "Alys, this might be important. We need to figure it out."

"I don't know, I wasn't lolling in bed with some random, I was looking for you! At first, I thought you were playing some sort of trick on us. That's when the thing with the plants happened."

"What thing with the plants?"

It sounded insane. If it had been anyone but Sibby, I never would have brought it up. But she would badger me until I gave her every last detail. "We were looking for you in the house and I went into the greenhouse and all the plants… turned toward me."

She blinked. And then before I realized what she was doing, she grabbed me by the arm and hauled me into the greenhouse. "Wait, I don't think this is a good idea."

"Don't think." She paused in the middle of the room and waited.

I held my breath.

The plants didn't so much as rustle.

Sibby released my arm and I sagged against the workbench. "You see? It's just some silly story."

"Just because you want something to be true doesn't make it true, Alys," Sibby said. "What about the lake?"

"I told you it was some sort of drug-induced hallucination from that empowerment crap."

"You're doing that thing again."

"What thing?" Annoyance coated my tone.

"Stuffing your head up your ass to avoid dealing with reality."

"I avoid dealing with reality?" The laugh that burst from me was a hollow sound. "Look who's talking. What have you got to show for your life other than a string of ex-lovers and bad debt?"

Sibby wasn't even paying attention, her gaze had gone past me. "Alys?"

"What?"

She pointed.

I looked over my shoulder. And screamed.

# CHAPTER SEVEN

## MAEVE

Much to my surprise, I did manage to nap after Sibby dropped me off. My doctor had cautioned me to avoid stressful situations. Ha. Even when Kal took the twins out for the weekend, my sisters filled in the gaps. First, Alys's announcement that she was getting divorced and oh, by the way, going to live in Aunt Jess's musty cottage. Then Sibby's disappearance and subsequent insistence that yes, she had in fact teleported and she and Alys had awakened powerful magic wasn't exactly calming. After all that, my body and mind had shut down hard.

I rolled onto my back and stared at the flat ceiling. Alys and I had scraped the yellowing plaster treatment off the ceiling ourselves before spackling and sanding and spackling and sanding some more before it was finally smooth enough to paint. It was a messy job that took days and had left my arms aching.

Alys derived so much enjoyment from projects like that. The work gave her a sense of purpose. I always enjoyed the end result but was happy to outsource the harder labor. Alys was all about utility, form, and function. I was better with natural things and decorative touches. We had been a good team, had worked hard to build a brand, a life. And now it was all starting to crumble.

A tear trickled out of the corner of my eye. I had to tell her. I couldn't believe I'd revealed all to Sibby first. But even though I was closer to Alys, my younger sister was easier to manage. I snorted. Probably because she couldn't be managed by anyone.

And Sibby was keenly observant, a fact most people missed about her. Her wild hair and smart mouth, tattoos, and piercings hid a sharp mind that didn't miss a trick. She could tell immediately that something wasn't right with me, and had persisted until I told her. Sibby was like that—utterly relentless.

Or maybe I had needed someone to talk to and knew she wouldn't drive me insane with questions I didn't have answers to the way Alys would.

She wouldn't treat me differently. The way I knew Kal would.

*Don't think about that,* I told myself. *Get out of bed and do something.*

I threw back the covers and shifted my weight until my feet hit the floor. I was much more careful than I had been. Had taken something as simple as getting out of bed for granted. But that was before my body had betrayed me.

*Don't think about it. Keep moving.*

It had become my mantra. I braced a hand on my night-stand and pushed up, just in case of muscle spasms. Every-thing seemed steady and I let out a breath I hadn't realized I'd been holding.

The soft autumn breeze drifted in through the open window and I closed my eyes and let it caress my face. When I opened them, I spied Peter Green standing down by the mailbox staring up at me. He held his leaf blower, though he wasn't actively using it.

"Nice day, isn't it?" I called down to him.

He just gaped. The damn leaf blower still going. Maybe he couldn't hear me. The thing made an awful racket. But why was he looking at me that way?

I glanced down to make sure I didn't have a boob hanging out. Kal's gray t-shirt covered me to my knees and I wore panties beneath it, but Pete could only see the top half of me. That stare was so bizarre, unnerving.

Of course, Pete was a bit of an odd duck. But he had never made me feel uncomfortable before. Time to end this one-sided conversation.

"Good talking to you, Pete," I said and shut the window, then pulled the drapes.

Dismissing the odd encounter, I headed into the shower while I mentally made a task list for the day. What was left of the day. Philip had a bake sale coming up for the soccer team on Monday. They were hoping to raise enough to buy new uniforms. Alys had offered to sponsor them, which seemed like the easiest way. My sister was not just a hard worker, but a financial genius. She had the golden touch when it came to making money. And she was generous, especially when it came to Arabella and Philip.

But her offer had been shut down hard. Missy Hargraves, the coach's wife, had said that it would show my son favoritism if his aunt bought the uniforms. And then she proceeded to voluntell me that I was making cupcakes. Five dozen of them. I really hated making cupcakes. And dealing with bossy PTO mom types who never seemed to say thank you.

But it's what a good parent would do.

I dressed in jeans and a blousy white cotton top with puffy sleeves and pulled my hair up into a messy bun. Not one of those stylish Instagram-worthy ones. Just a classic I'm a mom getting hair out of my face because I have crap to do bun. I slid my feet into sandals, probably the last time I would get to this year, and then headed down the stairs.

My cell was plugged into the kitchen island. I unplugged it and checked my texts. One from Kal. *Kids are bored and I miss my wife. Can we come home yet?*

I chuckled a little and I typed back. *You make it sound like I put you in timeout. You're supposed to be bonding with your offspring.*

Three little dots appeared. *Been there, done that, got the t-shirt. Everyone knows you're the fun parent.*

I shook my head. *Liar. You can come home whenever you want.*

*Love you, Evie.*

Tears misted in my eyes. Kal was the only one other than my mom who ever called me Evie instead of Maeve. There was something so personal in the nickname, as though they were the two people in the world who knew me best. Sibby was just Sibby to everyone. Her full name didn't fit her. Most of the time, I didn't mind my old-fashioned name. It was unique, original, and memorable.

But secretly I preferred being Kal's Evie instead of everyone else's Maeve.

It reminded me of the way Brock referred to my big sister as Lys.

I hoped she went for it with him. She may be on the verge of fifty, but so what? After Kyle and his crap, Alys deserved to have some studly fun. If she could get over her own insecurities about their age difference and the BS about him working for her, which he didn't technically do since he was a contractor free to seek work elsewhere, she might actually be able to let go.

The image of that wall of water formed in my mind and I shivered. Maybe Alys shouldn't let go entirely.

"And how the hell come I'm the only one who doesn't get powers? Huh? How is that right? What, am I the classic forgotten middle child or something? Marsha, Marsha, Marsha." Not that I particularly *wanted* magic. But I'd made the call to down that stupid cocktail. Sibby had shown me the recipe and I knew there was nothing toxic in it. Being magical sounded so much better than having a degenerative disease.

I turned to the pantry, saw that it was practically empty, and sighed. I'd have to go to the store. I'd taken almost everything edible over to the cottage last night. And then there were those stinking cupcakes. Well, if the kids were coming home, I could put them and Kal to work. He was the baker in the family.

I shut the pantry door. Movement out of the corner of my eye pulled my attention to the back porch and I yelped.

Pete Green stood on my deck, and he was holding a bouquet of flowers. That same stupid, not all there look on his face.

I clapped a hand over my chest, right above my thundering heart. "What the hell are you doing?"

He shook his head, indicating that he couldn't hear me.

"Go home," I snapped and pointed to his house the way I would a dog that had escaped from its yard.

Pete gave me a woebegone look and then set the bouquet down reverently on my doormat. He backed away slowly, his eyes fixed on me the whole time. I watched him go, waited until I saw him cross into his own yard.

My gaze fell on the flowers. *What the hell is going on?*

# ALYS

*"What the hell is going on?"* I screeched.

Just as they had that morning when Maeve and I had been looking for Sibby, the greenhouse plants were stretching out, leaves splayed wide as though absorbing sunlight. Only they weren't facing the sun.

They were reaching for me.

"Amazing," Sibby stepped past me and held out a hand to the plants.

"Are you insane?" I gripped her wrist, preventing the contact. "Don't touch those."

"You're angry." Sibby's thick brows drew together as though she were trying to puzzle something out.

"No shit, Sherlock," I barked. "What does that have to do with the greenhouse and these crazy plants?"

"Were you angry this morning?" Sibby asked.

"I don't remember." The lie fell easily from my lips.

Sibby gave me a flat stare. "I was missing and since you're emotionally stunted, let's just say that yes, you were angry then too."

"I am *not* emotionally stunted."

There was a tapping sound, and we looked over to see more greenery pressing against the glass on the outside. Dandelions, ferns, blackberry bushes, and even what looked suspiciously like poison ivy all trying to get in and join the party.

"I rest my case," Sibby said.

I wanted to ask what case but the urge to get out of the greenhouse was more immediate. Using my body to shield Sibby, I skirted along the plants making sure none of them touched us as we made our escape. I shut the door and backed away from it.

"That must be your trigger." Sibby still held the book and placed it on the dining room table where she pointed to a section. "See here where it says an emotional trigger will kindle the magic? Mine is desire. Yours has to be anger."

I wanted to refute her words. It wasn't possible. How could I control plants or water just by losing my temper?

But I had seen the proof with my own eyes and my heart was still racing at the prospect of what would have happened if those plants had made contact with my sister.

It was almost as if they had risen up...to protect me.

I let out a slow breath. "How do I get rid of it?"

"Get rid of it?" Sibby shook her head. "Get rid of your newly developed magical powers? Powers that we asked the universe for? You're not serious."

I took a slow breath, trying to calm myself. From behind the closed door to the greenhouse, I could hear rustling as the plants resettled themselves. "I am completely serious. I don't want this, Sibby. I didn't want to drink that empowerment brew, to begin with."

"But you did drink it. We all did and then we summoned magic." Sibby wasn't paying any attention to me, her focus back on the book. "What do you think Maeve can do?"

I put my hand over the page she was perusing. "Sibby,

listen very carefully. You just finished telling me a story about how some ancestor of ours was run out of town. I am in the middle of a messy divorce with a cheating bastard who hired a prostitute and brought her into our bed. What do you think the likelihood of us remaining undiscovered is under those circumstances?"

"This is the modern age," Sibby shrugged it off. "People don't burn witches at the stake anymore."

I took another deep breath, determined to keep my temper on a short leash. "No, but they do expose them on social media. Maeve and I have a business to run. The last thing we need is some sort of crazed witch enthusiasts following us around town and smearing our professional reputation with rumors of black magic and deals with the devil. This is the South, for the love of grief. That sort of thing just won't fly."

Sibby seemed to be listening so I pushed on.

"Maeve's got, kids. What we do affects Bella and Philip. Kyle is looking for ammunition to take as much as he can from me. You were too little to remember that summer with Mama after Daddy left. Before Aunt Jess took us in. Mama had nothing. No one to ask for help, no money, no place to go. We drove from place to place, camped in the woods, bathing ourselves using people's garden hoses and eating packages of crackers for days on end. So please, do me a favor and see if you can find out how to undo that brew. Because I never want my niece and nephew to have to live that way."

Sibby was looking at me oddly. "You're scared."

"You're damn right I'm scared. I don't know what this is but it's just...it has to go back." Before it ruined everything.

My sister licked her lips. "We're not talking about a pair of pants here, Alys. I don't think we can return it."

"Will you at least look?"

JENNIFER L. HART

"I will, but only if you promise that while I do, you consider what this could mean. The good you could do with it." Her eyes sparkled.

My lips parted but before I could say anything my cell rang.

"It's Maeve," I said extracting it from my back pocket. I swiped to pick up the call.

"Help me," my sister begged through the phone, her voice a low hiss. "Alys, I don't know what is going on."

"Where are you?"

"The Farmer's Market bathroom."

Since it was Saturday afternoon I knew she meant the local store, not the outdoor venue.

"Are you sick?" I asked.

All the hairs on my arms rose up at her hysterical laugh.

"Just…hurry," Maeve whispered. "Before they get in."

68

## CHAPTER EIGHT

Tires screeched as I took the turn that would lead us to the heart of town. Sibby's shoulder connected with the door. She cast me a wary look. "I can't believe I'm saying this to you of all people but you need to slow down."

My hands tightened on the steering wheel. In the distance, thunder rumbled. "What did she mean by they? Who are they and why is she so afraid of them? Why not call the police to help?"

We'd lost the cell connection when we'd dashed out of the cottage and Maeve didn't pick up when Sibby tried calling her back. My adrenaline was spiking and my heart racing at the thought of what that might mean.

"I don't know. Unless…." She trailed off.

"Unless what?"

"Unless it has something to do with magic," Sibby suggested.

"Don't." I barked.

She huffed out a breath. "Don't what? Tell the truth? Because, um, in case you have forgotten, Alys, we do have magic. And in every book I've ever read, people who have magic are always threatened by people who want their magic. Supply and demand, baby."

"This isn't some fairy tale, Sibby. Maeve is in real trouble." All sorts of possibilities lurched through my mind like a monster parade.

"Which means you're the heavy hitter here."

I blew through a stop sign on an abandoned logging road. "What do you mean?"

"Only that you are obviously pissed. Which means your powers are ready to rock. Mine aren't, since I'm neither hot nor bothered and am unlikely to get there. At least not without a little pocket rocket action. Which even I am not willing to test out in public."

She'd lost her last freaking marble. "You're telling me that you're expecting me to use…whatever this is, in the middle of downtown Eckhart?"

"I'm just saying we should be prepared. Like the Boy Scouts."

My foot slammed down hard when the light at the edge of town flashed from yellow to red, sending my Suburban fishtailing.

Sibby was tossed against her seatbelt. "I don't want to hear another word from you about my speeding tickets. You drive like a crazy person."

The light changed and I stomped on the gas, but then eased up when the Farmer's Market storefront came into sight.

The place was crowded, not at all unusual on a clear autumn weekend. What was unusual was that the bodies all seemed to be logjammed to the back part of the store. Near the restroom door.

I stopped the Suburban in the middle of the street and threw my door open. My heart pounded as I rushed through the open store door and into the crush of bodies. It was like a concert. Only there was no music and other than the rustling of clothing, there was no sound. The people weren't speaking, didn't interact at all. It was like they were all waiting for something.

Or someone.

I elbowed my way to the front and slapped a flat palm against the door. "Maeve?"

"Alys? Thank God." The door opened a crack. Behind me, the crowd surged forward. I was jostled and would have landed face down if Maeve hadn't grabbed me by the shirt and yanked me into the bathroom with her.

There was a meaty thud, the sound of bodies hitting against the closed door.

"What the hell, Maeve?" I blew the hair out of my eyes. "What did you do?"

My sister's eyes were red-rimmed. "Nothing, I swear! I just came into town to buy a few groceries. Kal and the kids are on their way home. I barely made it through the door when I felt someone touch me."

My shoulders stiffened. "Who?"

"Herb Paxton."

"The bee keeper?" Herb Paxton was eighty-six years old and weighed about twenty pounds less than I did. He only came to the market to sell his wildflower honey. Not exactly someone I would have thought would accost my sister.

"It was just a hand on the shoulder. But he had this odd look on his face. Like he wasn't all there. It spooked me. I tried to back away from him and the next thing I knew, every eye in the store was on me and all these people were coming at me." Her voice quavered.

It didn't make any sense. The whole store was acting like a pack of tweens and Maeve was a hot new boy band.

Unless….

"Has anything else strange happened since this morning?"

Maeve fidgeted. "Well, my neighbor was staring at me. And he brought me flowers."

"Which neighbor?"

"Pete Green. But you know he's a little cracked." Maeve said.

"And...how were you feeling when all this started?"

"What does that have to do with anything?" Maeve glared.

"Were you frightened?"

"How did you know?"

I let out a breath. "Damn it. I really hate it when she's right."

"Who?"

"Sibby." I leaned back against the wall and scrubbed a hand over my face. "I think this, whatever this is, is your power."

Maeve's lips parted. "My power is to make people act like zombies who chase after me?"

"I don't know, Maeve. I don't have any answers."

Maeve wrapped her arms around herself. "How do we get out of here?"

Sibby popped into the little remaining space beside us. Maeve let out a shriek and the pounding on the door increased.

I frowned at our youngest. "Not the pocket rocket thing...?"

She rolled her eyes. "No. Since you basically abandoned me in the middle of the street, I moved your Suburban around the corner. There was this guy there, mmm, shoulders for days. He was wearing a suit too. Perfectly tailored. You ever notice how all guys look good in a suit? It was all the juice I needed."

"Can you get us out of here?" I asked.

Sibby bit her lip. "Maybe if I just take one of you?"

"Go." I pushed Maeve into her arms. "She's the one they want. Go back to the cottage if you can. Away from town."

"But my groceries," Maeve gestured to the basket sitting on the back of the toilet tank.

"I'll take care of it. Go, Sibby. Get her out."

Sibby wrapped her arms around Maeve and the two of them vanished.

I blew out a relieved breath, picked up Maeve's basket, and then turned to the door and slowly opened it.

The crowd had dispersed. People wandered down aisles and chatted with neighbors. Like nothing unusual had happened.

I really hated it when Sibby was right.

"I CHECKED in on your neighbor when I dropped off your groceries," I said to Maeve as I entered the cottage. "He, much like everyone else in town, seems fine."

Maeve lay back on the couch. A wet washcloth covered her eyes. "I guess, whatever it is, it isn't permanent?" Her voice was weak and reedy.

"Enchantment." Sibby breezed in from the kitchen, carrying that damn book again. "You are officially an enchantress."

Maeve plucked the washcloth off and glared at her. "That's not funny."

"It's no joke. I was reading up about the different witch castes. In our line, there are three types. The enchantress, the traveler, and mother nature."

I collapsed into a chair that sat kitty-corner to Maeve. "That doesn't make any sense. Out of the three of us, Maeve is the maternal one."

"We're not talking about actual mothering here, Alys. It's

the maternal instinct, the drive to fix and nurture and protect. And the fury that is unleashed when something you love is threatened."

Maeve was shaking her head. "Whatever that was that happened in town, that was not me enchanting anyone."

"Technically, it was." Sibby put a hand over Maeve's. "Enchantment is about bending people to your will. You were feeling frightened or sad or anxious and all those people stopped what they were doing and responded to you."

"And when she left, they went back about their business, as though nothing had happened." I let out a breath.

"You can command them, too," Sibby added. "You could have told them all to leave you alone and they would have done it."

"So, it's like mind control?" Maeve's eyes were huge. "I don't want that."

"Not mind control. More body control. They are responding to your emotional turmoil, not mentally, but physically."

"How come we weren't affected?" I wondered out loud.

"Don't know. Maybe because we are all magical, we are immune?" Sibby suggested.

"What about Kal? And the kids?" Maeve put her head in her hands. "I can't deal with this."

"You can keep it locked down." Sibby handed her the book. "See here? Enchantment was the same gift our ancestor had. If she'd wanted, she could have manipulated the whole village. Bent them to her will. But she left instead because she valued their freedom to live their lives and be dicks. You can learn how to wield it."

"What about getting rid of it?" I asked.

Sibby shook her head. "There's nothing here."

"Damn it, there has to be." I got up and stalked into the

kitchen. My hand was on the door to the greenhouse before I remembered the plants.

Mother nature. The plants had responded to me as though I radiated the sunlight that they needed. Just because I'd been angry. And more than that, I had a sense for them. Could feel them even now.

"Alys?" Maeve stood behind me, her arms wrapped around herself. "I'm sorry."

"It isn't your fault."

"It is, though," she insisted. "I was the one who drank the brew. And just this morning I felt sorry for myself that I hadn't gotten what you two did." A tear tracked down her cheek.

I went to her and tugged her into an embrace. "It'll be okay."

If only I believed that.

Her phone rang and she pulled away and wiped at her eyes. "That will be Kal wondering where I am."

"Tell him about Kyle. Tell him I need the emotional support so you're staying with me."

Maeve hesitated. "I…I don't think I can lie to him."

"Want me to do it?" Sibby offered. "I have no problem lying to anyone you want."

"You say that like it's a good thing," I grumbled.

She shrugged. "In my world, it kind of is."

The phone stopped and Maeve stared down at the missed call. She swallowed. "Will you give me a ride back into town?"

"Are you sure?" I put a hand on her arm.

She nodded then looked at our youngest sister. "You coming home with me?"

"It might be a good idea," I suggested. "In case she needs another quick escape."

Sibby gave me an indecipherable look. "If you don't want me here just come out and say it."

"That's not what I meant." Though I did need a break from all this witchery. I had work to do, a divorce to strategize and Sibby just seemed to push everything else out of the way to take up residence in my gray matter.

We piled into the Suburban and I drove back to town. No one spoke. Maeve was taking slow, steady breaths. I recognized the Lamaze breathing from when she'd had the twins.

We saw a few people out walking down the main drag. Some waved, most went about their business.

I pulled up beside Maeve's minivan. "You sure about this?"

She nodded. "I'll call you tomorrow."

Sibby popped her door but I caught her arm. "I need space. I get that you are really into all this magic stuff. But I just…I can't…."

Her palm covered my hand. "I know, Alys. Believe me, I know."

She got out of the car and climbed into Maeve's ride.

All the hairs rose along the back of my neck.

Someone was watching us.

I did a quick scan of the area. Nothing seemed out of sorts. I popped my door and slid to the ground, turning in a full circle.

"Alys?" Maeve rolled down her window, her brow furrowed as she watched me. "What is it?"

The last thing I wanted was for her to have another panic attack in public. "It's nothing. See you tomorrow."

I watched as my sisters backed out, shifted into drive, and disappeared around the bend.

The presence lingered for a moment longer before it also vanished.

Thoroughly unsettled, I drove back out to Witch Way.

Maeve had left makings for peanut butter and strawberry jam sandwiches, a staple from our childhood. I fixed myself two and then headed out to the front porch to enjoy the quiet night.

And froze.

# CHAPTER NINE

## SIOBHAN

"Aunt Sibby!" Arabella rushed toward me, a grin showing off the gap in her teeth. She looked exactly as Maeve had as a child. Solid, stocky body and long dark hair flying every which way.

"Hey there, peanut." After Alys's curt dismissal, it was nice to have such a genuine welcome.

"Did you hear the news? We've got dogs!" She practically squealed with enthusiastic delight.

Beside me, Maeve groaned. "Kal, you didn't."

"Didn't what?" The hulking form of my good brother-in-law filled the doorway. Kallik was well over six feet tall and had a bulky build. His long dark hair and deep-set eyes came from the Inuit tribe he'd been born into. The same tribe that had rejected his choice of wife. But Kal maintained many of the traditions he had grown up with and taught them to Bella and...

"Where's Philip?" Maeve eyed her husband dubiously.

Kal winced. "So yeah, I meant to talk to you about this, but you weren't picking up your phone and well, I had to make a choice."

"What choice?" Maeve was interrupted by the sound of running feet pursued by nails scrabbling on hardwood. Multiple sets of nails.

Philip rounded a corner and behind him came what looked like two very furry and enthusiastic sausages.

"Maeve, meet Gimli," Kal scooped up one of the sausages and held it out to his wife. Its nose was black as ink, its dark eyes bright with mischief.

"And this is Grogu!" Philip squealed as the puppy wiped out on the hardwood floor and almost took the boy down with him. Unperturbed, the dog struggled up and lifted a hind leg.

"No!" Maeve shouted.

"Guys, get them out," Kal shepherded the kids and canines to the backyard.

"The G&G wrecking crew." Maeve closed her eyes and I could see her counting to ten so she didn't lose her cool.

I put a hand on her arm. "You need to tell him."

"Back off," she snapped.

I recoiled.

Maeve was immediately contrite. "Sorry. I didn't mean to take it out on you. It's been a day is all."

Understatement of the year. "What kind of dogs are those anyway?"

"Corgis." Maeve moved into the kitchen where she could watch the action as it progressed outside. "Bella's been obsessed with them since she saw a video on YouTube. They're very smart, though you wouldn't know it from those two."

I winced as Gimli dashed between Philip's feet and ran smack into Kal's legs.

She shook her head. "They're ridiculously expensive. And why would he get two of them?"

"Maybe Kal can take them back?" I suggested.

She gave me a droll look. "Would you want to explain that to the kids?"

Hell to the no. "I'll leave you all to talk." I headed for the front door.

"Aren't you hungry?" Maeve asked.

I shook my head. "Nah."

"I'll leave you a plate in the fridge," she called out.

I shook my head. My sister, the mother hen.

The enchantress. Who'd have thought?

I headed down the street and took a turn off the cul-de-sac that led to a small stream. There was a footbridge over the stream that led to a winding nature path that snaked past Maeve's development and back into the heart of town. I figured I would follow it, giving Maeve and Kal and their kids and the G&G wrecking crew time to do whatever families did.

Wandering aimlessly was what I did. Ever searching, never finding. The caste of the traveler fit me well. I never took a job I couldn't walk away from. Never stayed in any one place for too long, never settled down.

In some ways, it had been a great life. I didn't have anyone to answer to and, other than my sisters, no one to worry about. Which I usually didn't bother with since Alys worried enough for all of us.

But somewhere along the way, things had changed. Oh, I still wanted to travel and have adventures, just not flying solo. And I wanted a real home base. Not just my sister's guest suite, or a random apartment but somewhere that was mine alone. I'd been toying with the idea of taking up residence in Aunt Jess's cottage. After all, Maeve and Alys had other homes. But Alys had beaten me to it. And she made it clear that the place was hers.

So I was left to wander again.

I'd come to the footbridge. Instead of crossing it and

continuing on, I sat down with my legs dangling over the edge, ignoring the twinge in my knee, and watched the dark water eddy before it disappeared beneath me.

"You look lost," A lilting male voice said from behind me.

I jumped and my hand went automatically to my heart. "You scared me."

"Sorry," he said. He had a strange accent. One I didn't recognize. It was melodic and rolled gently as he spoke. "That wasn't my intent. I was just wondering if you needed some help."

I looked from him in his black trench coat and wool slacks then down at my ripped jeans and battered sneakers. His tone rankled. "You mean, I'm not good enough for your fancy little subdivision?"

His grin was disarming. "Actually, I meant you're too good for this fancy little subdivision."

"My sister lives here." Why was I trying to pick a fight with a handsome stranger?

*The answer's in the question, Sib.*

Because he was handsome. And well-spoken and had shoulders that went on for days. Plus, that accent was a total panty dropper. And his eyes. There was something…off about his eyes. The color seemed too dark for the rest of him, almost muted as if he wore contacts.

I quickly looked back at the dark stream before the urge to teleport away overcame me. Suddenly Alys's admonitions about being careful not to use our powers in public made a lot more sense.

"No offense to your sister, but I bet she fits right in here. Drives a minivan. Probably baking cookies as we speak and haranguing her husband about some perceived misdeed."

Maeve had enough to deal with without tackling a baking project. But the haranguing line was spot on. "You're very judgmental, aren't you?"

He shrugged. "Most are far too easy to judge. They stay in their lanes and live their lives in malcontented silence as their souls wither."

The way he spoke unsettled me. Mostly because I had the same sorts of thoughts. "But not you?"

"No." There was a flash of something behind those eyes, again muted. "No, I take what it is I want. I throw elbows and fight to attain higher ground. There's too much in the universe that needs to be explored. Too many foods to eat, sweet vintages to be sipped. Too many beautiful women to be kissed."

I got to my feet. "Listen…?"

"Sebastian," he supplied.

"I'd say it was nice to meet you but it really wasn't. So I'll tell you to have a good night."

I was a few steps away when he called out. "You never told me your name."

I shouldn't. He was a power-hungry weirdo lurking in the woods. Yet I had a fondness for the off-beat types. Probably because I marched to the sound of my own drum. "Siobhan. Siobhan Silver."

And then I strode away, wondering why a smile was tugging on my lips.

"Siobhan Silver," Sebastian whispered her full name and smiled as he watched the witch walk away. The stunning woman had no idea of what she'd just done, by giving her full name to one of the fae. Her scent lingered in the air, sweet and hot. Newly empowered, perfect in her ripeness. He could have plucked her like forbidden fruit from the tree of knowledge and he would have savored every last bite.

So, this was where the magic had manifested. He'd felt the

first tingle of it that morning, right as he had awoken. For a moment he could swear that there was someone in bed beside him. But the presence had dissipated as soon as he'd come to full alertness.

The scent of magic remained.

He'd been tracking it all day at random places all over the small mountain community before he finally spotted Siobhan and her sister. Immediately he knew Siobhan had become empowered, had been given something that didn't belong to her and she probably had no idea how to use it.

What was her caste? Did she even know about the magic yet?

Of one thing he was certain. She didn't hold all of it. Mortals rarely could contain the power of the fae. It took scores of bargains to hold enough of the free-floating power to truly be formidable. It was the way of the fae, at least those who still lived in the light.

Sebastian and those like him had found another way to attain power and stay on this side of the veil. Hunting down the magic thieves.

"Did you find the one you seek?" A sibilant voice hissed from behind him. "Did you find the witch?"

Sebastian turned and looked down at his anchor. He tipped his head to the side and studied the thing that had once been a man. "I have. And her last name is Silver."

The creature hissed. Its flat, snakelike eyes glittering malevolently.

Sebastian studied him. "Yes, I thought you would remember that name. Your dealings with that line of witches are what indebted you to me in the first place."

"Are you going to drain her?" His anchor—which Sebastian referred to as Louse having stripped the being's power from his given name at the onset of their bargain— looked hopeful.

"Eventually." Sebastian stared off in the direction that Siobhan had taken. He needed to know more about her and her potential power before he could siphon it. "Like a fine vintage, magic only improves as it ages. And there is time. Come, Louse. We have work to do."

# ALYS

"I have work to do," I said to Kyle, the absolute last person I expected to see on the doorstep to my aunt's cottage. "You need to leave."

"Not until you hear me out," Kyle said.

He looked sickly in the moonlight, really unwell. His complexion was too pale coming off of summer. Was he ill? I was annoyed because I didn't want to feel sorry for the cheating bastard who hadn't had the decency to just end things but had decided to humiliate me instead.

I blew out a breath. "What is it you want?"

"Money."

I laughed. "Get stuffed."

"Come on, Alys." Kyle practically whined. "All the bank accounts are in your name. I have expenses."

"Get a job. Or sell some of your toys. Or cram them up your ass. Whatever you do, leave me out of it."

"You owe me."

"I don't owe you a damn thing. The last time we talked, you called me a frigid old bitch. And let me remind you, that was after I caught you in my bed with a prostitute. So no, I don't need to listen to any more of your crap. I'm done."

"There must be something you want," he insisted.

"All I want is a nice, peaceful divorce so we can move on with our lives."

"That's not how it's going to be." His nostrils flared, signaling a full-blown mantrum in progress. "I've got a damn good lawyer, one of the best in the state. He'll make sure I get everything that you owe me."

"That I owe you?" I shook my head. "Get real, Kyle. You're the one who was screwing around."

"Did you really think I could go on without sex, Alys?" In classic Kyle fashion, he never knew when to shut the hell up. "It's not natural. A man has needs."

A snort escaped. "Well, it's not like you were going without, were you? You were spending my hard-earned money to import paid professionals to take care of your needs."

"Would you rather I have screwed your sister?"

The wind picked up, ruffling the waters of the lake. "Maeve wouldn't have anything to do with you."

"Not the fat one." Thunder rumbled and Kyle glanced uneasily over his shoulder. "The firecracker that you despise. I hear she's back in town."

"Keep your disease-riddled needle-dick away from my sister." Any idiot would have heard the warning in my voice.

Any except the idiot I'd married.

He licked his fleshy lips. "You know she's into me. Has been from the beginning. Didn't she tell you how she came onto me the day of our wedding?"

Lightning flashed down about a foot from where Kyle was standing. He yelped, and the whites of his eyes showed all around.

"You need to leave, Kyle." The wind picked up my hair, blowing it away from my face. "And don't come back."

He opened his mouth but just at that moment gravel crunched under tires. Brock's truck rounded the bend.

Kyle turned. "What's he doing here?"

"I work with him." The reply was automatic and I was sorry I'd said anything because I sounded defensive.

My ex watched as Brock slid down from behind the wheel, then rounded on me. "You have got to be kidding."

I scowled at him, but Kyle's grin unsettled me.

"I'll get what I want from you, Alys. One way or the other." With that, he scuttled back to his car. I waited until he executed a broken K turn, narrowly missing running Brock over as he sped down the drive.

"Are you all right?" Brock asked as he came up the steps.

My hands were balled into fists at my side and the peanut butter and jam sandwiches were completely mangled within. I stared down at the sticky mess cursing Kyle and his timing.

Another deep rumble of thunder echoed around the peaks. The storm had blown up out of nowhere. Was that just treacherous mountain weather? Or was my mother nature witchery to blame?

"Come on. It's starting to rain." Brock's touch was gentle as he took me by the wrist and held open the screen door for me. The interior of the cottage was dark. I hadn't lit any candles when I came home, but he didn't seem to have any trouble navigating around the furniture and leading me to the kitchen sink.

I held still as he worked my fingers open and used a paper towel to remove the worst of the mess. He tested the temperature of the tap water, then held my hands beneath the faucet. It should feel ridiculous, having someone else wash my hands for me. I was a grown woman. But I couldn't have moved if I tried.

"I tried calling you," Brock said. "A few times."

"Why?" My mind immediately went into problem-solving

mode. "Is something wrong?" Shit, my cell was probably dead. I didn't think I had charged it the night before.

Those intense gold eyes fixed on me. "Not about work. About earlier. With us."

Us. The word sent out tendrils that wrapped around me, around him, binding us together somehow. I swallowed and took a step back, needing more space. "It's not a good idea."

"Why?" Brock asked.

"Pick a reason. For starters, I'm too old for you."

He shrugged. Shrugged! As if to say, so what. Like the two decades that separated our ages were no big deal.

My brain scrambled for another reason. "And you work for me."

"I work with you," he corrected. "As a contractor."

"It's the same thing. Your livelihood depends on my business."

"Have you been paying attention, Alys? Contractors are in high demand. I have to turn down jobs all the time, especially when I'm working on restoration with you."

I shook my head. "Why would you do that?"

"Because I like working with you. I like what you do, how you restore houses and turn them into homes. And because I want to be around you. It…eases something in me." His gaze searched my face. "What did that bastard say that has you so upset?"

I shook my head. "I don't want to talk about it."

"Don't do that," Brock gripped my chin. "Don't shut me out."

I wanted to pull away, wanted to protest that my divorce wasn't any of his business. But the intent look in his eyes telegraphed something else entirely.

"Let me in," he breathed. "Trust me, just a little bit. I've earned honesty from you, Alys."

A lump formed in my throat. This was all kinds of wrong.

I mattered to him. What I was thinking, feeling. He wanted to know those things. Wanted me to share something private with him.

But where would that lead? My future consisted of getting rid of my loadstone husband and trying to make it to my next birthday. A fact that was seeming less and less likely every time I lost my temper. I didn't have room in my head or my heart for Brock.

Yet the words tumbled out. "Kyle said…he said Sibby came on to him."

"Do you think she did?"

"Something happened on our wedding day. Sibby came to me and begged me not to marry Kyle. She wouldn't tell me why. I think," and I paused to truly consider what I did think. "It's much more likely that Kyle came on to her."

"Why wouldn't she tell you?" Brock asked.

"I don't know." I closed my eyes and let out a breath. "Sibby and I…we aren't close. Not like I am with Maeve. Maybe she thought I wouldn't believe her."

And that fact shamed me. I loved my sisters. Both of them. And if she had said something, I would have believed Sibby.

Wouldn't I?

Of course, I would have believed Maeve. Because it was Maeve. She didn't lie the way Sibby did. Just to be dramatic or to snag attention. And that's what I'd thought, that Sibby was trying to make my wedding day about her, by insisting she had a feeling that Kyle wasn't right for me.

Well, she was right. Until a few moments ago Kyle had been…all right. Never more than that and sometimes a whole lot less. He'd never made me so angry before. Even when I'd caught him in bed with a hooker, it had been the sting of wounded pride that hurt, but my emotional investment had been nil. Not when he threatened my sisters. The

89

cold fury that had bubbled out of me was like nothing I'd ever known.

"Shit." Horror filled me at the memory of that lightning. I almost killed him.

Kyle was middle-aged and out of shape. That bolt would have stopped his heart. My hands trembled as I raised them to cover my face. I wasn't sure if I was upset because I had almost hit him or because I hadn't.

"It'll be all right, possum." Brock pulled me against him. My lids slid shut and I breathed him in. So steady. So reassuring.

He pulled away before I was ready. "Come on."

"But the storm." A glance out the window showed the clear night sky dotted with stars.

"It's over." He studied my face. "At least for now."

"Where are we going?" I asked as he tugged me along.

He flashed me a wicked grin. "To my house. I have something I'm dying to show you."

# CHAPTER TEN

"Y̶our place?" I asked with a raised brow at the three-story split log home with a wall of windows that overlooked the lake. We'd driven for ten minutes, but as the crow flew, we were only about three miles from Witch Way. The bend to my hidden cove was out of sight of the house, but there was a private dock and even a boathouse. Light spilled from sharply angled windows and solar lanterns lined the white gravel walk that led up to the front door. Carved jack-o'-lanterns sat on rustic end tables, electric candles animating them against the gloom. A howling wolf's head had been etched into the glass of the door. The entire picture was one of cheery autumnal welcome. It was incredible, the kind of lake home that would grace the cover of an architectural magazine.

"Not just mine," Brock murmured. "There are almost a dozen of us in residence at present."

My eyebrows lifted. "Wow, big family."

"That's one way to put it." His tone was dry. "It's more like a job than a family."

"How so?" I asked but he was already out of the truck. I

stared at the house again, trying to put a finger on the pulse of exactly what the situation was that I was about to enter.

"You're not part of some commune, are you?" I swallowed as Brock opened my door. "Or a cult?"

He grinned as though I amused him. "Nothing like that. It's more of a halfway house for those who need it."

"Halfway house?" I frowned up at the estate that had to cost a cool million.

"Privately owned." Brock shut the truck door behind me. "Don't worry, everyone here is stable… at present."

With those ominous words, he escorted me over gleaming pea gravel and up to the door.

"You guys really go all out for Halloween, huh?" I traced the wolf's head etching with my finger.

Brock cleared his throat. "That's more of a year-round thing. Come on."

He depressed the latch and put a hand out, holding the door wide for me. I crossed the threshold, curious despite myself.

The layout was incredible. Three stories above us, long exposed beams came to a summit above an open catwalk. To our left was a palatial great room with a massive stone fireplace in one corner. A slate gray sectional filled the space and I could hear the sound of voices, male ones as well as the blaring sirens from some sort of video game.

Dead ahead was the curved staircase that led to the catwalk above. Music drifted down from a room upstairs. Something low and soothing. Classical, though I didn't recognize the piece.

Brock gestured that I should go right. It led to a hallway. A few closed doors and no signs of life, at least not until we reached….

"Oh," I blinked at the enormous eat-in kitchen. The L-shaped island could easily fit six people along its length. The waterfall edge of marble ran down to gleaming wood floors. Cabinets reached the ceiling. Double ovens had been built into the wall beside an eight-burner gas stove top. A massive deep sink was flanked by two humongous refrigerators and beyond….

My feet carried me to the sliding glass door. Alongside the house, an outdoor kitchen boasted three gas grills, a stone pizza oven, as well as a covered seating area. Beyond that stood a white gazebo, strung with faery lights. It was currently occupied by three women who sat chatting and laughing.

Form and function, design, and décor. It was a space that I wouldn't touch, wouldn't change a thing because everything about it was perfect.

"This is incredible." Had I used that word before? It was the only one that fit.

Brock moved up to stand beside me. "It was my father's design." There was a hint of sadness in his voice. I turned to him, my gaze questioning. "He died a few years ago."

"I'm so sorry." My hand raised again to my heart as the remembered pain of losing my mother when I was eighteen was still fresh.

Brock's golden gaze turned distant. "I found the plans when I was cleaning out his house and I thought…it seemed a fitting tribute. I'm just sorry he never had the chance to see it."

"You did an amazing job." I put a hand on his arm. "I'm sure he would have been pleased. And proud."

"Thank you." He threaded his fingers through mine. "I've wanted to show you this place for a long time."

"Why didn't you?" My throat was clogged and I tried not to dwell on how warm and comforting his palm felt engulfing my own.

"It was never the right time," Brock said.

Our gazes locked. A moment passed between us. Whether it was the connection over the loss of a parent or our mutual appreciation for how a house could provide so much more than shelter. Or maybe it was an acknowledgment that, like it or not, our friendship was growing. Morphing into something new. Whatever the cause, I didn't pull back the way I should.

I licked my lips and his gaze dropped to catch the motion.

"Brock," I whispered, not sure what I was asking.

He moved closer, eyes glowing with preternatural hunger. I could have pulled away. Should have run. Instead, I stepped closer needing more of his delicious scent.

"Hey, Alpha, what's for din—" A male voice, young sounding as he emerged from the living area, interrupting the moment. "Oops, sorry, didn't realize you had company."

I stiffened and withdrew from Brock, who cursed under his breath.

"My bad," The newcomer said. "But seriously man, I'm starving."

"You've got two hands, Nate. Try making your own food for a change."

He looked about seventeen. No Australian accent for this guy, he sounded like a born and bred New Yorker. He had short spikey black hair and dark brown eyes. His t-shirt was a mass of wrinkles and his jeans weren't much better. It was a good bet he had slept in those clothes and hadn't bothered to change. The glasses on his nose were held together by a piece of tape.

"But it's your turn. Besides, don't you want to show off for your lady friend? You know women dig guys who cook."

I couldn't help grinning at Nate and turned to Brock. "He has a point. Kyle sort of ruined my dinner. Let's see this fancy kitchen put to good use."

"I like her." Nate swung an arm around me. "She's a keeper."

Brock growled low in the back of his throat and the arm disappeared at warp speed. "Not for me. She's too old."

I flinched.

"Get. Out." Brock bit out the words and Nate beat a hasty retreat.

I offered him a tight smile. "You don't have to cook for me."

"It would be my pleasure." Brock's gaze searched my face. "But be warned that food will bring all the rest of them down on us. You sure you want to handle all that?"

My lips parted and I was about to say that, yes, of course, it was no big deal. It was simply a dinner with his people.

Yet, for some strange reason, it felt like more than that. I was still emotionally raw. Otherwise having some teenager call me old wouldn't have bothered me. At that age, I'd thought thirty was old. And Brock wasn't even there yet.

"Maybe some other time," I said instead. "But thanks for dragging me out and showing me this. It helped get me out of my head. I probably would have just spun my wheels otherwise."

His smile was soft. "I cook every Saturday and Wednesday. Consider the invitation officially open-ended. Come by whenever you like."

I turned to head back to the living room but Brock gestured toward the sliding glass door. "We'll go out that way. By now, Nate is spreading the word that I bit his head off."

"He called you Alpha," I remarked as we stepped out into the chill night once more.

The three females who'd been chatting in the gazebo paused to stare curiously at us. Brock lifted a hand in a casual wave and after a moment their conversation resumed.

"It's a term of respect. I'm the *de facto* leader of this motley little crew. Which basically means I get handed the bills and whined to when there's no food. As you just witnessed." He took my arm to help guide me down the steep incline and back to where his truck is parked.

"What's his story?" I asked when we were headed back to my place.

"Nate?" Brock put a hand on the back of his neck. "His parents were killed about two years ago. That's when I took him in."

Lots of dead parents going around. No wonder I looked old to Nate. "Are you related?"

"In a manner of speaking," he hedged. "We have common interests and I had the space."

If he didn't want to talk about it, I wasn't about to pry. I had too many secrets of my own bubbling away on the back burner.

"Well, it's a good thing you're doing. I'm not sure where I'd be if I hadn't had Aunt Jess to help me after my mother died."

"I'm sorry." Brock reached for my thigh, squeezed it lightly.

I nodded, accepting his condolences. It was silly, really. I'd lived more of my life without my mother than I had with her. Yet I still missed her every day.

We drove the rest of the way in silence.

Like a true gentleman, Brock escorted me to my door. It wasn't a date, despite that shared moment. Couldn't be a date. Even if the age difference didn't bother him, it bothered me. And I was technically still married. To a man-sized prolapsed anus. But still, I'd made a commitment.

Integrity didn't take a vacation.

"I'd kill to know what you are thinking right now." Brock

drew a finger across my forehead. "You look so woebegone, possum."

I looked up at him. "Did you ever wish your life was completely different?"

"That's what brought me here." That golden glow was back in his eyes, seeming to dispel the darkness around us. "I needed a fresh start so I gave it to myself."

The thought of my rapidly approaching birthday hovered in my periphery. "I'm not sure I have enough time for another fresh start."

"What do you mean?"

It was a risk, telling him this secret. Maeve and Sibby didn't even know what I believed. And it seemed like such a ridiculous thing, superstition. "My mother...she died the night before her fiftieth birthday."

Brock eased closer. "What happened to her?"

I let out a breath. "She went hiking. Alone. She fell and was trapped. She died alone."

He went still. "I'm sorry."

So was I. "It could have been worse. It could have happened before we found Aunt Jess."

"How old were you?"

"Ten." In a way that was the age, I always was, at least in the dark of the night. A scared ten-year-old along for the ride. "Before Aunt Jess took us in, it was...bad."

Brock didn't say anything which gave me the courage to continue. "We were basically living out of a station wagon, moving from place to place."

I closed my eyes, remembering the fear of that summer on the road. How I never felt clean, even after I'd washed up using some random person's outdoor hose. How I'd always been hungry because I wanted to make sure Maeve and Sibby had enough to eat.

How I could never trust anyone for fear that we'd be separated.

Gentle fingers stroked my face. "This is your truth, isn't it? The thing that drives you, that lives at the heart of you. You make beautiful homes for other people because you know what it is to be homeless."

The conversation had gotten way too heavy so I attempted a smile. "Well, it's not like I give them away."

Brock stepped even closer. "You don't fool me, Alys Stevens. I know you've donated both time and money to Habitat for Humanity. I know that you support local shelters and spend at least one Saturday a month volunteering at a food pantry."

My lips parted. "You really have been paying attention. I doubt Kyle knows that much about me."

He pressed his lips against my forehead. "Thank you for sharing this with me."

And before I could form a response, he walked back to his truck and drove off.

THE DREAM CAME AGAIN that night. I was trapped somewhere in absolute darkness. No stars, no light of any kind. Cold seeped into my skin where it was pressed into the bare ground. My nose was clogged with the scent of earth. My stomach growled. How long since I'd last eaten? Would it be the exposure that took me out? Starvation? Or would he come back to finish the job?

I curled up tight in a ball, helpless, utterly alone.

Would they ever find my body? Would they catch the one who'd put me here? What about my children?

*Jess will take care of them.*

But it wasn't right. That was my job. If only I had my magic....

The howl of a wolf jarred me from my troubled dreams and I lurched upright. The sheets were soaked in sweat. I closed my eyes and took a steadying breath.

Just a dream. Not real. My heart pounded as though I'd run a marathon and I couldn't seem to catch my breath.

Tossing the covers aside I got out of bed and moved to the window. The pane was fogged, the seals failed a long time ago. But old windows were better insulated than most newer ones, a secret most home builders kept to themselves. I unlatched the panes and pushed them wide, welcoming the cool breeze that swept through the space, dispelling the last lingering traces of the nightmare.

That hadn't been me in the dream. At least not the whole time. Thinking about children. It must have been talking to Brock about my mother that melded the past into the present and brought out my anxiety for the future.

Brock.

I rested my forehead against the glass. Part of me had badly wanted him to stay. Not for sex. Just to be with someone just a little bit longer. Someone who didn't ask anything of me or make demands. He would hold me if I asked. If I slept in his arms I was sure the nightmare wouldn't be able to sink its sharp talons into my mind. I didn't know where the certainty came from but it was absolute. Brock wouldn't let it take me. He would do everything in his power to keep me safe.

There was no way I was going back to sleep. My robe was lost in one of the random boxes on the floor, so I wrapped Aunt Jess's afghan around my shoulders and headed out to my laptop. Might as well get some work done.

A glance through my email showed that there were no estimates for the Mid-century Modern yet. Not surprising.

Most likely we wouldn't hear back until the demo was already underway.

I did what I did best. Made lists, checked the market for what homes in that area were going for, configuring a budget that would work and still give us all a tidy profit.

I checked my bank balances and my stock portfolio. Most of my money came from investing. Not just in the houses I fixed up but from back in my banking days. It was hard to walk away from that steady paycheck, but I'd been careful and frugal for my whole life. Kyle was the spendthrift, the one incapable of going without. In the beginning, I had indulged him. After all, we could afford it and it seemed to make him happy to buy cars and a boat and new golf clubs. He'd retired from his job as middle management at the same bank where I had worked right around the time Kal and Maeve were married.

I could have retired if I'd been so inclined. But I hadn't wanted to be alone with him all day with nothing to do.

That was probably a big red flag.

My stomach growled and I remembered that I'd had nothing to eat the night before. I put water on to boil and then turned to the cabinet to see what I could scrounge up. It really was pretty sad. All that money and I was squatting in the cottage like Old Mother Hubbard. At least there was no dog to starve along beside me.

Something thudded against the front door.

I whirled, my hand reaching for the knife block. The thud came again. And again.

Shit, where was my cell?

Bedroom. I'd plugged it into one of those portable chargers and had set the alarm.

I was halfway there, knife in hand when a vicious snarl ripped through the night. Heart in my throat, I waited. What the hell was out there? It sounded like a bear or maybe a mountain lion.

There was another thud and then all was quiet.

Pulse-pounding, I crept to the window and then peered outside.

My stomach dropped at the sight of what was on my porch.

# CHAPTER ELEVEN

## MAEVE

I woke to the familiar feel of a large, calloused hand cupping my breast. "Don't be angry, Evie," Kal whispered in my ear. He pulled me tighter to him and it was clear he wanted to do a whole lot more than kiss and makeup.

I rolled over and gave him a glare. "You've got to be kidding me. We just got them all to sleep."

Gimli and Grogu had come with a large basket filled with a down cushion for sleeping. Which they ignored in favor of Bella's canopy bed. They'd fit right in there, nestled among the mountain of stuffed animals. Not wanting to be separated from the dogs, Philip had announced that he was going to sleep in his sleeping bag on his sister's rug, in case the new additions needed anything during the night. I'd already resigned myself to washing dog hair and corgi piddle out of the sheets come morning.

Kal's hand moved lower, toying with the waistband of my pajama bottoms. "You're not really upset, are you?"

About the dogs, no. Having them around was a suitable distraction and gave me an excuse not to have the conversation I dreaded having with my husband and children. What was a little more laundry compared to that?

"I'm not mad," I breathed. "I just wished you'd talked to me about it first."

He nuzzled my neck. "Sorry."

"You are such a damn liar," I scoffed. "Better to ask forgiveness than permission, right?"

His lips trailed down the side of my neck. "Do you forgive me then?"

*Always,* I thought and gave in to the inevitable.

Kal slept naked, a fact that took me aback when we were first married. I'd asked all the practical questions. "What if there's a fire?" And later, "what if the kids want to sleep with us?"

Nothing seemed to faze the man though. He was the calm island in the sea of chaos. My safe harbor. He'd told me that he didn't care at all if our neighbors saw him in the raw because he would be too busy making sure I was safe. And as for the latter, it had never happened. Kal made it clear to Bella and Philip that our bedroom was our private space and they were always to knock and wait for an answer before entering. If the children had a nightmare one or both of us went to them.

"I hate these things," Kal muttered as he shoved my flannel pants down. He'd tried to convince me that I should sleep in the buff too, for easy access.

"They keep me warm," I protested, even as I struggled out of the fabric that had snagged somewhere around my knees. I couldn't bring myself to go to bed unclothed. Not wearing anything just felt wrong.

"Don't worry. I'll heat you right up." He yanked the fabric off and held the pants aloft like the spoils of war. A wicked grin flashed in the darkness. "What will you do to get them back?"

In answer, I parted now bare thighs and smiled.

"You win," he breathed. The pants hit the floor with a soft plop.

He made love the same way he did everything else, gently, sweetly, and with his whole heart. It always stole my breath that such a big man could be so incredibly gentle, even in the throes. Kal's childhood had been miserable and it had taught him to cherish every good thing that the universe saw fit to give him.

And he never failed to cherish me.

We knew each other well. There was nothing out of bounds when it came to the act of love. Nothing he wouldn't do to bring me pleasure. It took less than ten minutes for us to reach our peaks and two minutes after that, Kal was snoring in my ear.

I lay in his arms, knowing I wouldn't be able to sleep. Having Kal and the kids home, chasing after the dogs, the lovemaking, all of it served as a distraction. I hadn't been afraid while dealing with my family, which meant my magic —and I was still wrapping my head around the fact that I possessed magic—was locked down tight.

But with all that I had going on how long would it last?

Enchantress. What a ridiculous title. Kal was the only man who had ever made me feel beautiful and desired. What had happened at the Farmer's Market had been about as far from enchanting as a body could get.

Unsettled, I pried myself out of my husband's grip and headed to the bathroom to clean up. After retrieving my pants, I donned a robe and slipped from the bedroom.

I peeked into Bella's room and found her surrounded by corgis. Philip snored away from the foot of her bed. My smile was heartfelt as I shut the door.

The overhead light was on in the kitchen. I found Sibby there, bent over the fridge.

"You've got fuck-knots in your hair." My sister flashed me a knowing grin and extracted a container of eggs from the fridge. "Good for you, sullying that man like there's no tomorrow. I'm making an omelet. You want some?"

"Sure." I slid onto a barstool and watched with a bemused expression as Sibby opened every cabinet and drawer looking for God alone knew what.

She whisked the eggs into a frothy yellow mixture and added a little water to the concoction before tackling the spices.

"Why not milk?" I asked with a raised eyebrow.

"Milk works well for scrambled as it separates and fluffs. Water is best for omelets because it binds the egg and holds together." She added dill and salt, pepper and then started slicing a red bell pepper. "And how do you not know this?"

I shrugged. "I cook because people need to eat, not because I like it. Honestly, I hate the mess of it. Kal's the chef, not me."

"Gotta love a man who can cook." There was a sizzle as Sibby dumped the contents of the bowl into a sizzling pan. "What's it like?"

I snitched a slice of the Havarti dill cheese she was slicing. "Having a man who can cook?"

Sibby shook her head and half turned away from me to lay cheese across the omelet. "No, I mean, being with a man who loves you?"

My lips parted. "Haven't you ever been in love?"

She blew out a breath. "It's never gotten that far before...."

She trailed off. All her focus on folding the cooked egg over the cheese.

"Before what?" I pushed.

"Before things ended." She didn't look at me as she cut the omelet in half and then slid each portion onto a plate.

"Maybe because you're always on the run?" I offered tentatively.

Sibby's nostrils flared as she pushed one plate to me. "You sound like Alys."

"I'm not criticizing you. You live the way you want to. I admire the hell out of that." Picking up the fork she'd laid alongside the plate I twirled the tines in the melted cheese. "I wish I had been a little braver, done a little more."

"Are you effing kidding? Your life is perfect, Maeve."

I glared at her. "You know that isn't true."

"Kal won't leave you," she insisted. "He worships the ground you walk on."

"You don't know that." I pushed the plate aside, appetite gone. "And even if he stayed, would it be because he wants me or because he made a vow and feels compelled to stay."

Her warm hand closed over my fingers. "I know you're scared."

A pained laugh escaped. "Yeah, and now there's that too. I can't even be afraid without worrying over how it will affect everyone around me."

"I told you, you can control it. Proximity is probably a factor." Sibby released my hand and cut into her half of the omelet. We both watched the steam escape, curling up to the ceiling. "You had the whole Farmer's Market after you, not the whole town. So if someone gets that glazed look, send them away. Eventually, they'll be free of your influence."

She made it sound so simple. It wasn't just the proximity of strangers. "What about Kal? And the kids? I can't send them away."

"We'll figure something out," Sibby assured me. "I promise."

I wanted to believe her. Maybe I could harness my fear and find a work-around. But fear was something that could be overcome. Sibby had already proven that she could lasso her lust and even use it.

Alys was different.

Anger, especially considering the deep well of repressed emotion she had to draw from, was out of her control. And Alys didn't deal with things she couldn't control. Kyle was just the tip of the iceberg. If she tapped into all the things that she'd repressed for most of her life…

Her power would be fathomless.

"I'm really worried about Alys," I admitted.

"Me too," Sibby held my gaze. "Me too."

# ALYS

There was a wolf on my doorstep. He was lying on his side, his silver-gray muzzle matted with blood.

Frozen in place, I stared down at the creature. What had happened to him? And why was he on my porch of all places?

His eyes opened and our gazes locked.

My throat closed up. I knew those golden eyes.

"Brock?" I whispered. It couldn't be. Shouldn't be possible.

*Any more than the plants? And the lake? And almost hitting Kyle with a bolt of lightning?*

Deep down I knew it was true.

The wolf with Brock's eyes let out a pained whine. My hand shook as it reached for the doorknob. This was a monumentally bad idea. Worse even than drinking that stupid empowerment brew. I had no clue what had happened to him, and there was no guarantee that the wolf wouldn't attack me. But what were my options? I couldn't just leave him out there to bleed out. Whatever had done that damage might come back. Never mind that the scent of blood drew other predators.

With a final fortifying breath, I opened the door.

A quick glance told me that whatever had been thudding against my door had retreated. Brock had fought it off. I scrambled outside and knelt beside him on the porch.

I was no veterinarian, but the worst of his wounds seemed to come from his left shoulder. The fur there was matted and damp. The leg looked crooked, though thankfully no bone stuck out. There was blood on his muzzle but I didn't think that was his.

Prepared to lose a finger, I reached out to touch his head. "Hey, can you walk? We need to get you inside."

His eyes opened again and I shrank back, afraid he was about to go for my throat. He struggled upright, putting no weight on the injured leg. I retreated backward, keeping my eyes on the massive wolf as it staggered through the door.

His strength gave out and he collapsed again just inside the threshold. I had to nudge him clear with one foot so I could shut the door. After throwing the bolt, I dragged a chair over to it and shoved it beneath the handle for extra security.

Turning, I caught a white flash that enveloped the wolf's body. There was a shift and a crunch, a yelp of pain that ended in a man's cry of agony. It went on and on with me a helpless spectator.

Finally, after what felt like a lifetime but was probably more like ten minutes, the eerie glow retreated. Brock lay naked and panting at my feet.

"It really is you," I breathed as I knelt by his side once more.

He didn't answer. His breath tore out of him in ragged pants and his eyes were pinched tight.

"Brock," I reached for him, but hesitated, not wanting to hurt him any more than he already was. "What can I do? How can I help?"

I could hear his teeth grinding together and two words hissed out. "Touch me."

I wanted to ask where, since his whole body seemed to tremble in agony. Finally, I settled for gently stroking his hair.

"It's okay," I whispered reassuring words just as I had done for my sisters after our mother's death. "Everything is going to be fine."

Gradually, the trembling stopped and he seemed to relax. Sweat dotted his skin and I retrieved the fallen afghan and covered him up, making sure to avoid contact with the damaged shoulder. His breaths evened out and I thought he had fallen asleep when he whispered, "I'm sorry."

What was he apologizing for? Being hurt? Being a wolf? Showing up at my doorstep in the middle of the night? Whatever the case, he was in no shape for explanations. I made gentle shushing noises. "Hush now."

He shifted and I withdrew as he sat up. "I didn't want you to find out this way."

I studied his features. He looked better than he had after he first shifted, though maybe that was my imagination. "Are you alright? Should I call 911?"

He shook his head, wincing at the pain. "No, I'm healing. The shift accelerates the healing process."

"The shift," I said slowly. "As in you shifting from a wolf and into a man?"

His eyes met mine. "Go ahead and ask, Lys."

"You're a…werewolf?" My voice went high on the last syllable.

"I am."

I blew out a breath. Closed my eyes. "Okay."

"Okay?" Brock sounded skeptical. "Just okay?"

My lids lifted and I gave him a droll look. "How I wish this was the strangest part of my weekend."

Brock let out a bark of laughter that morphed into a cough.

"Easy," I soothed. "Can I get you anything? Water?"

He nodded, his eyes closed tight.

I scrambled up and over to the kitchen counter where Maeve had deposited the flat of water. It was room temperature, but after what Brock had been through, I doubted he would mind.

I cracked the seal and tried to offer the bottle to him. When he just looked at it, I moved closer and held the bottle to his lips. A little dribbled from the corner of his mouth and I used the cuff of my sleeve to wipe it clean before trying again.

He turned his head away and tried to get to his feet. "I'll leave—"

"Don't be stupid," I snapped at him as I caught a good portion of his weight. "You aren't going anywhere."

Those gold eyes turned to me, the brown totally gone. My heart sped up. "You don't need this. I didn't want this for you."

I had no idea what he was talking about. "Is...whatever you fought off. Is it dead?"

He shook his head. "No, I wounded it pretty badly, but no. It's not dead."

"Will it be back?" I wanted to believe that whatever it was, it was after Brock, but my gut told me otherwise. The thing had been pounding on my door and Brock had shown up and fought it off.

"Not tonight." He reached for a section of my hair that had fallen in my face. "I've never seen you so disheveled."

I snorted and readjusted my grip on him. "That's what happens when you show up at a woman's place in the wee hours of the morning. You see all sorts of unpleasant realities."

"Not unpleasant," Brock breathed. "Beautiful."

"No need for the smooth talk, pal," I grunted as I helped him into the bedroom. He was too big for the couch and I wanted him to be as comfortable as possible. "I already said I wasn't going to toss you out on your ear. Besides, you're not in any condition to try anything."

"Give me a few hours, possum," he murmured as he collapsed onto the bed in a boneless heap.

I laughed. It was such an odd thing to do considering our circumstances, but the sound just bubbled out of me.

"Love that sound." A smile curved his lips.

He was sprawled on top of the covers. I wasn't about to move him any more than I already had so I folded the comforter over the top of the afghan and then stepped back.

A werewolf. Was that why his eyes seemed gold at times? And what the hell was he doing hanging around as a wolf outside my house?

*And you're no longer mated."* His words from earlier drifted back. *"You aren't using him as a buffer anymore. You cut him loose.*

He'd been talking about Kyle. About my impending divorce. He'd used the term mated as though it meant something more than simply married.

Dear sweet dark chocolate, did that mean that Brock was interested in me as something more than a quicky?

*That means you're fair hunting.*

Fair hunting. I wrapped my arms around myself and stepped back.

The big bad wolf was in my bed.

And I'd helped put him there.

# CHAPTER TWELVE

The sound of a slammed car door and my sisters' bickering dragged me from sleep. The crick in my neck and twinge in my lower back informed me that curling up on the old sofa hadn't done me any favors. But since there was a werewolf in my bed I hadn't had many options.

Other than climbing in beside him.

Dismissing that thought, I peeked in to assure myself that said werewolf was still out cold before moving the chair away from the door to let Maeve and Sibby inside.

"What the hell is this?" Maeve flashed her phone screen at me too briefly for me to read, then proceeded to turn it around and read it herself. "Bring over some of Kal's old sweats, socks, and sneakers, ASAP."

"I'd think it was pretty self-explanatory," I said.

"It came in at five-thirty in the morning," Maeve bitched as she handed me a duffle bag. "Why the urgent rush for men's clothing?"

"It's not like you weren't up." Sibby yawned and put a take-out tray with three coffees and a bakery box on the counter. "Just what the hell were you and Kal doing at first light anyway?"

Maeve blushed to the roots of her hair. "You heard us?"

"Your bedroom is on the other side of my wall." Sibby yawned. "And to be accurate I mostly heard him."

Maeve was busy gnawing a hole in her lower lip. "Sorry. Maybe I should rearrange the furniture."

"You should have heard him," Sibby continued and then lowered her voice in a sad approximation of Kal's bass. "Don't stop Evie, right there, baby, oh yeah. Seriously, what had him in raptures?"

"Ssshhh," I said, my gaze darting to the closed bedroom door. "Sibby, mind your own business."

"You can't tell me you aren't curious." Sibby reached for the doughnuts and helped herself. "What could get that sort of response from a guy?"

I was curious but didn't want to admit it. "Listen, we have bigger problems—"

"We usually do," Sibby interrupted. "Come on, Maeve. You know I won't stop until I get answers."

From Maeve's wince, she recognized the truth of that statement.

"I suppose I could just ask Kal," Sibby remarked.

"It's Sunday morning," Maeve blurted. "We always do it Sunday morning."

"Do what?" I asked despite myself. "Are you talking about sex?"

But Sibby was shaking her head. "No, they did that last night. And there was a fair amount of headboard banging to accompany it. This was just Kal…." Her mouth fell open and a half-eaten piece of doughnut hit the floor.

"What?" I glanced back and forth between them.

Sibby let out a bark of laughter. "Oh Kal, you dirty, *dirty* boy."

"Ssshhh," Maeve and I hissed in unison. Me because I didn't want to disturb Brock. Maeve probably because she looked on the verge of panic.

Sibby wiped tears from her eyes and then looked at me. "You going to tell her or should I?"

Maeve mumbled something too low for me to hear.

"What?" I leaned in closer.

She mumbled again.

"Prostate massage," Sibby said with a hint of wicked glee. "Seems Kal is a big fan of backdoor action."

"It's medically recommended for some men," Maeve said defensively. "It lowers blood pressure and—"

"And gets his rocks off in a big way. So that's why you do it every Sunday morning," Sibby chortled. "No wonder he came home early. Some people go to church. Maeve and Kal go to booty town."

"Sibby," I warned.

"Do you use toys?" Sibby would not let it go. "Or are you more of a hands-on kind of girl?"

"Guys," I said, trying to get the mental image of all that Sibby was describing out of my head. How would I ever look my brother-in-law in the eye again after hearing this?

But my youngest sister was relentlessly curious. Either that or determined to humiliate Maeve. "Where did you even learn to do that? Did you just start playing around back there out of the blue or was it more planned?"

More mumbling from Maeve. I didn't want to add fuel to Sibby's fire but knowing Maeve, she would have researched the hell out of the dos and don'ts before embarking on anything new. I had a mental image of TED talks and demonstrations with Snapple bottles.

Sibby cupped a hand around her ear. "Say that again."

"We watched a video."

"Like *porn?*" Sibby sounded jubilant.

Maeve's chin went up. "It was a tutorial."

"Could you send me a link to this tutorial?" Sibby asked sweetly. "Because if I ever stumble across a guy worth keeping, I want to make sure to look out for his "*health*." She made air quotes around the last word.

"Guys," I said, desperately trying to rein the conversation in.

"Did you ever go in for that with Kyle?" Sibby's attention swung to me.

"Hell no." The words came out like a bullet fired from a gun.

Maeve flinched.

"Not that I'm judging you or anything," I stumbled to fix my thoughtless error.

"She's not," Sibby agreed. "Besides, there was probably no room, what with Kyle's head stuffed up his kiester."

"Stop it," I snapped at her.

"I was just trying to help."

"Well, you're not, okay?" I huffed out a breath and refocused on Maeve. "You guys are obviously in a healthy, committed relationship, so whatever it is you are doing for and with each other is cool, yes?"

Maeve had gone pale at the word healthy. "Can we please stop talking about this?"

"Yes," Sibby said. "It's time to discuss Alys's sudden urge to cross dress in the middle of the night."

"The clothes aren't for me," I huffed.

"Well, then who are they for?"

Both of them swung their attention to the closed bedroom door.

Sibby blinked. "Holy testicle Tuesday! Alys, do you have a guy in there?"

"It's not what you think," I said just as the bedroom door opened.

"Not a word," I hissed at my sisters as I carried the duffel bag over to where Brock stood with Aunt Jess's afghan wrapped around his hips.

"Sorry," Brock said. "I didn't mean to interrupt."

"How are you feeling?" His complexion looked better, less pale than it had all night. Though his shoulder was streaked with dried blood, the wound appeared completely healed.

"Better. Thanks to you."

I didn't have much to do with it, other than making sure he didn't die on my porch. "Maeve brought some clothes for you. They're Kal's."

Brock winced but took the bag. "Thanks."

A thread of unease wound through me. "You didn't hear us by any chance?"

His gaze met mine. "People like me have very good hearing."

Of course he did.

"I won't say a word, possum. Maeve looks about ready to jump out of her skin already. Mind if I take a shower?"

When I shook my head, he stroked his thumb along my jaw in a tender caress before disappearing back into the bedroom.

"Alys, you naughty, cradle-robbing cougar," Sibby spoke the second the door clicked shut.

I whirled on my heel and stalked to her. "Not another word or I will duct tape your mouth shut. I mean it, Sibby."

"No, you don't," she said cheerily as she extracted yet another doughnut. "No gathering clouds, no earthquake. You're not even remotely pissed. It's a huge tell."

I stared at her.

"Good sex is a mood elevator." Sibby pushed just a little bit more. "You and Hottie McNibblet must have worked out some serious pent-up aggression. Who ever thought I would be the boring one of our little trio? Could you tell me—"

I clamped a hand over her mouth. "Stop. Talking. Now."

Sibby mumbled something incomprehensible behind my hand.

"Get this through your thick head. I did not sleep with Brock."

"What's he doing here?" Maeve asked.

I released Sibby and reached for my coffee. Though I had no idea how good Brock's hearing really was, I didn't want to risk it. "Let's go outside."

My sisters followed me out onto the porch. Mist rose off the lake in ethereal trails making the trees on the opposite shore look like an oncoming army.

"What's been going on, Alys?" Maeve asked as she leaned back against the railing.

I blew out a breath and caught the two of them up on Kyle's showing up, going to Brock's halfway house and the assault on my door in the middle of the night that ended with a bleeding werewolf in my bed.

Sibby shook her head. "This is what happens when we leave you unsupervised."

"What did Brock fight off?" Maeve asked. "Did you get a good look at it?"

"No, and he was in no shape to explain." I swallowed. "I want to tell him."

Sibby was already nodding. "Yes."

Maeve looked between the two of us and then her eyes widened. "You can't be serious. You said yesterday that we can't tell anybody, not even Kal, who I am married to."

"Hear me out. Brock is a werewolf. And he's not new to this like we are. Maybe he knows something about what's going on with us."

"Or even if he doesn't, he might be able to steer us in the right direction," Sibby added. "It would make sense that the supernatural community would at least know one another."

"There's a supernatural community now?" Maeve's eyes were wide.

I reached for her hand. "We don't know. That's the point, we don't know anything yet. And judging from whatever was lurking around here last night, ignorance isn't going to do us any favors."

Maeve looked scared and I stiffened as I realized what that meant. "I should probably talk to him on my own."

Maeve closed her eyes and nodded. "I was going to go into town, to the office. Some samples got dropped off on Friday. Meet us there when you're done."

I nodded and pushed to my feet. "Hopefully, I'll have some answers."

～

"DID YOUR SISTERS LEAVE?" Brock came out of the bathroom dressed in sweats that were too baggy, but still an improvement over Aunt Jess's afghan. His feet were bare.

"The sneakers were too tight," he explained.

Seeing his naked feet was strangely intimate. Of course, I had seen all there was to see the night before but something about his unfinished state made me hot under the collar.

Dragging my gaze away, I depressed the plunger on the French press. It wasn't a one-cup kind of morning. "Want some coffee? There are some doughnuts too."

"Sure," Brock settled himself at the dining table. I set out the remainder of the doughnuts and then poured the coffee.

"I didn't think you ate doughnuts." He said as I set the mug down in front of him.

"Why would you say that?" I added two level teaspoons of powdered creamer to my mug and stirred.

"You always bypass them at the office. Or on a job site."

I stared at him. "You're right, I do."

"Why are you looking at me that way?" Both his eyebrows went up.

"You've been paying attention," I accused him, as though it were a crime. "This whole time, you have been observing all these habits and I never even noticed."

He shrugged as though his shirt had grown too tight at the shoulders. "It's instinct to track a mate."

Mate. He'd said that before. And he didn't mean it in the classic Australian way, like a good friend.

I'd been tempted to reveal the whole story to Brock. The empowerment brew, our abilities. But knowing he had been watching me so closely and I hadn't even noticed unsettled me.

"What was it at my door last night?"

Brock shook his head. "I'm not sure."

"But you fought it off."

"It gave me a bad vibe," he added. "Something about it didn't smell right."

I waited while he dunked his doughnut and finished it in two bites. "You know I have acute hearing. It's like that for smell and taste too. And when I'm in wolf form, my senses are heightened. After I dropped you off, I couldn't sleep." He looked over at me as though waiting for me to ask why not. When I didn't, he pushed on. "So, I shifted and went for a run in the woods. As soon as I reached the outer edge of your cove, I smelled it. The...wrongness. I knew you were alone here so I wanted to make sure that you were okay."

I leaned across the table, coffee and doughnuts forgotten. "What did it look like?"

Brock's eyebrows pulled together as he considered. "Man size and shape, but there were no distinguishing features. It was wreathed in shadows, like some sort of outer shell covering a dark heart."

His description made me shiver.

He tilted his head. "Do you know why it was here?"

I shook my head.

He reached across the table and covered my cold hands with his warm ones. "Alys, I know there's more going on with you than just your divorce."

"You do?" I whispered.

He nodded. "You took my shift way too stoically. Most women would freak out learning that werewolves are real and one happens to be her contractor."

He had a point.

"Also, your scent has changed. Between when I dropped you at Maeve's and yesterday morning when you called me in to help you look for Sibby. I didn't get a good scent from Sibby on Friday night, but Maeve's scent is altered as well."

I swallowed. "How is my scent different?"

"Hotter, wilder." His gaze met mine. "It calls to me. A song only I can hear. It's like when the full moon beckons and demands I shift for her. It's primal, ingrained, undeniable."

That was exactly how I had felt in the moonlight on Friday. Like I had tapped into something primal.

He released a breath and though admitting a personal failing murmured, "It toys with my control, Lys. I want to give you time and space to adjust. I told myself over and over that I would back off. But I can't seem to stay away for long."

I let out a breath I hadn't realized I'd been holding. "We drank something. On Friday night. It was called an empowerment brew. And it really did empower us. Sibby can teleport. That's where she went when we couldn't find her."

Brock's golden gaze turned thoughtful. "No wonder I couldn't pick up a scent trail. What about you? And Maeve?"

"Maeve almost caused a riot in town yesterday because she was afraid. And I," I swallowed. "You remember that thunderstorm that came out of nowhere? That was me."

He frowned and leaned back, releasing my hands. "You called the storm?"

"Unintentionally. When I get angry, nature responds. I almost killed Kyle with a bolt of lightning." Probably the worst time in the history of ever to go through a divorce. If things didn't go my way, someone could end up dead.

"Why did you do it?" Brock asked. "Why did you drink that brew?" He didn't look repulsed or as though he were judging me, only curious.

"I didn't want to, at least not at first. Sibby kept pushing for it. And then Maeve did it and Sibby did it and they went outside and started dancing and seemed so happy…." I put my head in my hands and laughed without humor. "I sound like the poster child for peer pressure."

There was a scraping sound and I peeked up to find Brock striding around the table. He crouched before me until we were at eye level. Those warm brown eyes ringed with gold seemed to devour the darkness within me. "It's not a crime to want to be happy, possum."

"No, but it was stupid. We had no idea what that drink would do and we drank it anyway." I should be glad that the only side effect was magic.

"Cut yourself a break. You don't always have to get everything right on the first go."

"I rarely get it right the first time. Just look at Kyle."

"The offer to bury him in the woods still stands."

Though he spoke lightly, a shiver gripped me. Brock meant it. And after that damn dream of being trapped alone in the dark…

A hand caressed my cheek. "Where did you go just now?"

I let out a shaky breath. "Nowhere good."

"Stay here with me." His thumb glided along my jawline. His steadying presence helped ease me back down from the precipice I'd been clinging to by my fingernails for over twenty-four hours. "Do you know what's happening to me? To us?"

He hesitated and withdrew his touch. "Not exactly."

"Tell me what you do know." I leaned forward. "Please, Brock. I'm scared for us."

He let out a slow breath. "Come on, let's take a walk. I think better when I'm moving."

"You're barefoot," I felt the need to point out the obvious.

He shrugged. "Won't be the first time and I doubt it will be the last. "

The sun broke through the clouds above as we walked down the steps and headed toward the path that wound around the lake.

"Magic is like energy. It can't be created or destroyed. It simply exists. It manifests differently in all living things, creating what is often times called an aura."

That sounded like what Sibby had read. "Go on."

He paused. "We all started out as human. But magic chose to…alter some of us. No one knows why. Except maybe the council of elders."

"Council of elders?" I repeated. "Who are they?"

"The ruling body that governs all the magically inclined. The fae, the shifters, the witches." He cut his gaze to me. "By council law, we are required to report any new magical people at the next council meeting. For your own protection."

I sucked in a breath. "Protection from what?"

"Magic hunters. Like the dark fae."

My lips parted.

"Their livelihood depends on siphoning magic off unregistered witches and wizards or made shifters before they find out about the council and register. Once the magic they possess is legally claimed, the magic hunters have to back off."

I frowned. "Could we just…give our magic to one of these hunters?"

Brock shuddered. "Don't even joke about that possum."

"Why not?" It sounded like an ideal solution to me. Get rid of the magic and move on with my normal life.

Brock paused and gripped me by the shoulders. "Because they will suck out your soul to get it."

## CHAPTER THIRTEEN

"Suck out our souls?" Sibby's eyes went wide. "Was he serious?"

"As a heart attack." I surveyed the inside of our office, glad Maeve was on the phone. The news was terrifying and I didn't want to trigger her magic while we were in the heart of town. "Apparently a magical sponsor, like Brock's pack, needs to bring us to the next council meeting and officially register us as users of magic."

With the toe of her sneaker, Sibby pushed the desk chair into a circle. "And when is that?"

"Spring."

The chair jerked to a stop. "Spring? As in, next spring. Two seasons and a dozen holidays from now?"

At my nod, she blew out a breath. "What you're saying is that until then, our magic and souls are fair game to one of these dark fae?"

Actually, what he had said was magic hunters, which led me to believe the dark fae were just one faction of magic hunters. But I kept that to myself. Who cared what sort of creature was jonesing for the soul-magic slushie at the end of the day?

"Pretty much. According to Brock, we can defend ourselves from them. Even kill them if they come after us. I got the impression that the magic hunters aren't well thought of by most of the magical community."

The way Brock described them were bottom feeders with no real power of their own and thought of as a necessary evil to keep magic from running amok.

"However, the more magic we use, the more likely these energy hunters will track us down."

Sibby put a hand to her neck and rubbed. "So, we're damned if we do and damned if we don't?"

"Yeah." I couldn't believe that this was my life. Two days ago, I'd been married—albeit not happily—and my biggest worry was a timeline for getting my Mid-Century Modern project done on schedule. And all of a sudden, I was headed to divorce court, living in a cottage with no electricity, being courted by a werewolf who was also my much younger GC, and in danger of having my magic along with my soul sucked out by dark fae. Whatever that was.

I blew out a breath. "We need to get Maeve back to the cottage so we can tell her. Without freaking her out."

"That won't be easy. She's in serious work mode." Sibby got up and moved to one of the rough sketches pinned to a corkboard. "Is this your new acquisition?"

"Yeah."

She looked at me. "Where's it located?"

I moved to stand beside her. "About six miles outside of town."

"In a remote area?"

I saw where she was going. "Pretty remote, yeah. What's your plan?"

"Tell her that you need to start demo on the place. We can

all head out there and work up a good sweat. That way she won't have enough energy to flip out."

My gaze slid to the closed door to the back. "I hate lying to her."

"It's not lying," Sibby insisted. "Think of it more like prioritizing. You don't build the house until you lay the foundation, right?"

She had a point. "Okay fine."

"I'll go get her." Sibby made to move but I caught her arm.

"Listen. I want to talk to you alone while we have a few minutes."

"About what?" One eyebrow popped up.

"Kyle. He said something yesterday and it got me thinking about my wedding. And how you told me not to marry him all of a sudden."

Sibby stayed silent.

My stomach was in knots. "Did he...do something to you?"

She held up both hands. "It's ancient history, Alys."

"He did." Anger bubbled up and I had to swallow. "Did he hurt you?"

If he had, I would kill him. Magic hunters be damned.

But much to my relief, Sibby shook her head. "No. He came on to me. Grabbed my ass and tried to kiss me. I kneed him in the junk for his trouble."

Frustration welled. "Why didn't you tell me?"

"Would you have believed it?" Both her eyebrows went up as she waited for my reply. The metal of her studs glinted in the overhead lights.

"Of course. You're my sister."

Her lips thinned. "Right. So it should have been enough when I told you that you should kick him to the curb sans all the gory details."

I wanted to retort that a statement like that needed verification or at least an explanation but the storeroom door creaked open and Maeve emerged carrying a cardboard box full of dove gray subway tile. She set it down by her desk. "What's going on?"

"Hey, we were going to head out to the Mid-Century Modern and get started with the demo." Suddenly, taking out my aggressions on that house's dated décor seemed like a most excellent idea. "You in?"

Maeve's teeth sank into her lower lip. "I should probably get started on those cupcakes."

"Buy the damn cupcakes," Sibby advised. "Better to conserve your energy for things that matter. Like hanging out and wrecking a house with your sisters."

Maeve met her gaze and then offered a slight smile. "Okay. Let me just text Kal."

Fifteen minutes later, we were loaded up in the Suburban. Maeve had wanted to take her minivan but I had told her honestly that the drainage on the road leading to the house wasn't the best and it was better if we had four-wheel drive.

Also better that she couldn't run away when we broke the news to her.

"This is so weird." Sibby popped the door and slid to the ground. She spun to take in the view. "I don't think I've seen another house of this style in the mountains. It screams suburbia."

"It's a beautiful spot though." Maeve circled around to the trunk to pull out our equipment. We had two sledgehammers plus a prybar along with helmets, gloves, and goggles. The demo crew starter kit.

"Other than that." Sibby chucked her thumb at the forty-foot construction Dumpster that had been deposited in front of the house.

"Trust me," I said as I hefted a sledgehammer. "We're going to need it."

We trooped inside and Sibby studied the house. "Where should we start?"

"The kitchen," I decided.

"Oh, let me get some before pictures for Instagram." Maeve, always thinking about our online presence, took her phone from her back pocket.

We waited while she took some pictures of the interior from a few different angles.

"Stand back-to-back," she ordered. "Let's humanize this."

I rolled my eyes but did as she instructed. Sibby made a snarly face and gripped her sledgehammer like she was headed into battle.

"Now one with all of us." Maeve perched her phone on the mantel and set the timer then scurried to pick up her crowbar. We stood and waited for the timer until Maeve instructed we could go.

"I should get video too," she insisted.

I caught her arm. "Save it for after the demo."

For a time, I lost myself in the steady rhythm of destroying soot-stained cabinets, warped countertops, and gaudy tile. Sibby cackled like a mad woman when I let her bust out the pantry wall. "Jeez, Alys. I can see why you are so into this. It's a great stress buster."

It really was. It had been too long since Maeve and I had gotten hands-on with demo. Sure, there were things we couldn't do anymore. Things that were too heavy to lift, like the ugly fridge and dated stove. But demoing out the old damage and making room for new possibilities was therapeutic in its own way.

We finished in the kitchen and moved on to the bathroom. Sibby made a face at the avocado-colored toilet with the obvious rust stain around the bowl. "I'm not dealing with that."

"Save it for Brock's crew," Maeve advised. "They all draw

straws for who has to deal with the toilets on each job. Speaking of which. Alys, did you learn anything from Brock this morning?"

Time was up.

I set my sledgehammer down and wiped my forehead with my sleeve. "Yeah, I did. Let's go sit outside and I'll tell you everything he told me."

Maeve took the news better than I would have imagined. Better than either Sibby or I had. She even seemed to understand why we had decided to wait to tell her about what I had learned until we were well outside of town.

"So that thing that was at your door last night. Did Brock think it was one of these dark fae?" Maeve asked.

I took a sip from my water bottle and shook my head. "No. He said the dark fae mostly resemble humans, just like the werewolves do when they aren't shifted. He didn't know what that thing was that he fought off. Or what it was after."

"Maybe it was another kind of magic hunter," Sibby suggested, proving that she had been paying attention. "You did say you called lightning down on Kyle."

"Not on purpose."

Maeve was wringing her hands. "I don't think that the not on purpose thing is going to be enough. You say we have two seasons before we can go to this council of elders and register our magic. Two seasons where we need to live our lives and deal with the stress of everything. We have to be able to control ourselves better. Otherwise, we'll call all of the magic hunters down on us."

"You're talking about controlling our emotions though," Sibby pointed out. "Anger, fear, desire. They're primal, ingrained emotions. We can't help how we feel."

"No but we can do our best not to give into those feelings," I said.

"You're talking about suppressing our emotions? How well has that worked out for you, Alys?" Sibby got up and began to pace. "Every time I open my mouth the ground trembles beneath my feet."

"Not suppressing," Maeve insisted. "Channeling. Like we did here with the house. I've been doing some reading online about energy budgeting. It's all about deciding where your priorities are and what is worth expending yourself for. Like you suggested earlier with the cupcakes, Sibby."

"What does that have to do with magic?" Sibby asked.

"Brock said magic is like energy. Our magic is fueled by our emotions. So maybe what we need to do is to channel our energies into productive ways to dial those emotions down. Meditation, hot baths, exercise, house demo. Whatever helps keep us on an even keel."

"You're forgetting about Kyle," I said. "I'm not sure I can even *look* at him without getting angry." Especially not after what Sibby had told me.

"You've got to try, Alys." Maeve took my hand in hers. "For all of our sakes, you need to try to deal with your anger over what he did to you."

She was right, I knew she was but I couldn't even fathom how to start.

"Come on," Sibby stood up and beckoned us back into the house. She handed me the sledgehammer and pointed to the ugly column. "That right there? That's Kyle. Have at him."

I huffed out a breath. "I don't know if I can."

Sibby stared at me a moment. "Tell me how you felt when you found him in bed with another woman."

"Tired." Just like I was now. My muscles were fatigued after all the work we'd already done. "Resigned."

"You can do better than that," Sibby urged. "He had

another woman in your bed. A prostitute, for the love of grief."

I shook my head. "It's not working."

Sibby looked at Maeve. "She's a tough nut to crack."

Maeve nodded in agreement. "Too much practice holding everything in."

"Guys," I huffed. "I'm standing right here."

"You can't tell me that you're not angry about what Kyle did to you. How he has been using you," Maeve said. "He retired on the back of your hard work and this is how he thanks you?"

A coil of disquiet rippled through me. I picked up the sledgehammer and gave it a swing.

"He used you," Sibby added. "For years he's been using you. Sucking you dry like a tick."

Another swing. This time the pillar cracked. I focused on that.

"And he'll keep it up if you don't stop him. He threatened your reputation," Maeve pushed. "Threatened to tell the town. Threatened our business."

"Aaaahhhhhh!" the primal scream tore from my mouth and I swung the sledgehammer with all my strength.

Plaster dust rained down as the pillar toppled over and landed on the floor with a dull thump.

"Good," Sibby's gaze was fixed on the pillar but she put a hand on my shaking shoulder. "Now we do Mom."

## CHAPTER FOURTEEN

I wasn't up for dealing with the vortex of emotions that swirled around my mother's death. Maeve must have seen it in my face. "I think we're good for today. She let out a big burst of emotion and there were no weather events. We'll give it a try tomorrow, maybe? After you meet with the lawyer?"

When I nodded and pushed my safety goggles up off my nose, she turned to Sibby. "You coming home with me?"

Sibby eyed me closely. "I think maybe I should stay with Alys."

"You do?" Maeve's house had cable, clean linens, and eventually, cupcakes. I didn't have food or electricity and the place smelled like mouse.

"If that thing comes back, I'm your best bet for getting out of there safely."

"And how are you going to activate your power?" I asked.

She shrugged. "Necessity is the mother of invention."

After collecting the pieces of the pillar, we tossed the stuff in the Dumpster and then headed back to the car. Tired, sweaty but feeling more in control, we dropped Maeve off at her minivan and then headed to the local pizza joint, aka *Tony's*.

"There's my favorite customer." The owner greeted us with his thick Brooklyn accent and a big smile. The hair on his head had gone completely white but there were enough dark tufts sprinkled across his forearms to proclaim him Italian by way of New York. "Where you been, doll? And who is this?"

"Tony, you remember my youngest sister."

"No kidding? Little Siobhan all grown up? And such a knock-out." Tony kissed her on both cheeks, a move she clearly wasn't expecting. "Are you seeing anyone?"

When Sibby shot me a panicked looked, I stepped in. "Now Tony, you know I won't let my sister anywhere near Angelo. Plus, she doesn't cook."

"Awe, that's too bad." Tony rolled his eyes heavenward. "God almighty help me, I love him dearly but that boy is the bane of my existence."

That "boy" was thirty-two and thought he was a real ladies' man. He wanted a woman to take care of him and until she came along, he was content to work at the gas station, tinker in his garage, and sponge off his grandparents. If you looked up the word mooch in the dictionary, you'd see a picture of Angelo.

Right next to Kyle.

"Come with me, ladies. I've got the best seat in the house for you." Tony led us to a booth in a dark corner. "What will it be, beer? Iced tea?"

"A pitcher of sweet tea. Any specials tonight?"

"Mama's been working on both a barbecue chicken pizza and a Margarita flatbread." Tony brought his fingers to his mouth and made a kissing sound. "*Bellissima*."

We ordered the flatbread plus some garlic knots and Tony insisted we try the fried calamari as well. It was a good thing

I'd been working like a demon all afternoon. Most of the time I couldn't afford the carbs that came with a trip to *Tony's*.

"I do too cook," Sibby said.

"I know that, but it was the nail in the coffin of Tony's matchmaking."

She rolled her eyes.

"So, why did you really want to come back with me?" I asked Sibby after Tony set the pitcher of tea and two red plastic glasses on the table in front of us. "Do you really think whatever that thing was will come back?"

"No, that was just an excuse." Sibby poured some tea into her glass. The ice cubes making clicking sounds against the plastic. "Maeve and Kal need to be alone. Well, as alone as they can be with the kids and the dogs."

"Dogs?" I took a sip of my tea, savoring the sweetness that coated my tongue and would probably send me into sugar shock later. "Since when do they have dogs?"

"Since Kal brought two corgis home last night."

I snorted. "That man is lucky Maeve loves him so much."

"He is." Sibby drew her finger down one side of the pitcher, making little patterns in the condensation. "Did you ever want that?"

"Want what?"

"What Maeve and Kal have."

I thought about it. My sister was happy in her marriage, anyone could see it but… "Did Maeve ever tell you about what she went through when she was trying to get pregnant?"

Sibby shook her head. "No. Why?"

I blew out a breath. "It was kind of horrible to watch. Her anxiety ratcheted up every month. She blamed herself, because of course in her eyes Kal could do no wrong. And he wanted a family so badly. She never said it but I think she was worried he would leave her if she couldn't have kids. Go back to his family in Canada."

"That's crazy," Sibby said. "Kal would never do that."

"I know that and you know that. I think deep down, Maeve knows it too. But fear isn't rational. So no, I don't want what they have. I never want to feel that sort of code-pendency. Like my life will fall apart without someone else. It's why I never had kids. I just can't…I don't know…extend myself that far. Not with anyone."

Sibby nodded but didn't say anything else. I wanted to ask what she was thinking but feared the answer.

Tony brought our dishes and we were quiet for a time, indulging in salt and fat and all things women our age were supposed to give up for the sake of looking good.

Life was too short to play by anyone else's rules.

I was done living on anyone's terms but my own. Aunt Jess and Mom had found each other. I had my sisters to grow old with. And while I enjoyed spending time with Brock and was grateful that he had been there last night and that he was going out of his way to help us, it couldn't happen between the two of us.

And why did that thought make me sad instead of resolute?

"What about you?" I asked to distract myself.

"What about me?" Sibby was busy tearing apart a garlic knot as though it had wronged her somehow.

"Do you want what Maeve and Kal have?" It occurred to me that it might have been the sort of question a woman asked because she wanted the other party to respond in kind.

"Doesn't matter what I want." Sibby threw the garlic knot down and then reached for the napkin dispenser. "I deal with the world as it is. This grease isn't coming off. I need to go wash my hands."

"Over there," I pointed to the door just outside the

kitchen, but it was unnecessary. Even if Sibby hadn't been in the pizza place for the last twenty years, she remembered. We all did.

*Tony's* was the first place we had ever been welcomed in Eckhart.

# SIOBHAN

I took my time washing the grease from my fingers and tried to calm my nerves. I'd wanted to tell Alys about my curse, one that had nothing to do with our recently developed magic.

It was nuts, how I could fall right back into the swing of things with Alys and Maeve but still feel like such an outsider. Tony hadn't recognized me. I'd been back for Alys's wedding and Maeve's, and when Philip and Arabella were born. But I'd felt like an outsider from the moment I walked into *Tony's*.

Not that anything had changed. Tony wasn't big on trying anything new. While the place was clean it still sported the faded black and white checkerboard linoleum, the same vinyl tablecloths, the same red caddies that held salt, pepper, dried red pepper flakes, and parmesan cheese.

It didn't matter what Alys said. She wasn't as closed off to the idea of a happily ever after as she pretended to be. Of course, a week ago she had been married to Kyle— that steaming turd—so why wouldn't she be against the idea of being in a committed, long-term relationship when that was her only experience?

It was the one thing in the world—other than my sisters and to find out what had happened to our mom—that I wanted.

The one thing I couldn't have.

But I could make a life here. Get a job. Demo'ing that house had been fun, even if my shoulders were sore. Before Alys had shown up, Maeve had walked me through her design concept for the Mid-Century Modern, showing me tile samples and asking my opinion on fabrics. She was going to need some help holding up her end of things. Maybe Alys would be willing to take me on?

As soon as the thought rose, I dismissed it. The last thing I wanted were my sisters treating me like some sort of charity case. I would have to find my own job and my own place to live, then I could help out with the business if Maeve asked.

I stalled in the bathroom long enough for Alys to pick up the tab and then pushed the door open.

Right into someone's face.

"Oh God," I said to the man who had been heading toward the men's room at the exact wrong moment. "I am so sorry. I should have pulled instead of pushed."

"Siobhan?"

I blinked. "Do I know you?"

He straightened and familiar odd eyes met my own.

"You," I breathed as I recognized the man from last night. "Sebastian, right?"

He was pinching the bridge of his nose but managed a passible nod.

"Is it broken?" I urged him toward the wooden barstools and pulled one out for him.

"I don't think so." He sat on the stool and delicately probed the area around his face.

"What happened?" Alys had been standing over by the register, check in hand, but she caught sight of us and hurried over. "Sibby?"

"I hit him with the bathroom door."

"Damn it, Tony," Alys muttered as she removed a fistful of napkins from the nearby dispenser and thrust them into Sebastian's hands. "I told him he couldn't use swinging doors on the bathroom. It's a damn code violation for exactly this reason. Bad enough he has it in the kitchen. At least there's a window to that. Can we get some ice down here?"

The last part was hollered and the teenager behind the register hopped to, probably afraid of what my sister would do if he didn't immediately obey.

Ice, I should have thought of that. But I was too busy feeling guilty over whacking the man in the face.

Tony bustled forward with ice in a plastic bag, which he'd wrapped in a clean towel. "I am so sorry, *Signore*. It is not too bad, I hope."

"It's bad enough," Alys muttered. "You'll be lucky if he doesn't sue you for the whole damn building. He has every right to if he can find a halfway decent personal injury attorney."

Tony went pale beneath his tan.

"No worries," Sebastian said to Tony. His voice sounded stuffy, which made sense because of all the blood clogging his nose. "I have no intention of suing you. I spend enough time with lawyers already."

"Let me see," I stood on my tiptoes so I could get a peek at the damage.

"I'm alright," Sebastian set the towel down and used some of the disposable napkins to clean off his face. It stood out horrifically against the white collar of his dress shirt.

"Do you need to go to the hospital?" I asked. Even if the door was at fault, I had been the one pushing it outward. I'd been so caught up in my own thoughts that I hadn't been paying attention to my surroundings. Not until disaster struck.

Sebastian's eyes met mine. "No. I thank you for your care, Siobhan, but I'll be fine."

"I didn't really do much good," I said, feeling mesmerized by his unusual gaze. Were those contacts?

"Somehow I don't believe that. I was hoping I would run into you again. It must be true what they say. Be careful what you wish for."

I cracked a grin at him. "Why?"

"Because I'd like you to have dinner with me."

My lips parted. "Really?"

"Truly," Sebastian dug in his pocket and fished out a business card, and handed it to me. "Call me any time, day or night. And can I get my bill please, Tony?"

"It's on the house," Tony spluttered.

Sebastian rolled his eyes. "That's not necessary."

"Please, I insist." Tony groveled.

Sebastian looked at me and my breath caught. There was something there between the two of us. Some sort of connection. He strode over to a corner table, fished his wallet out of charcoal slacks, deposited two twenties on the table. Then with a final wave, he took the suit jacket that matched his pants, casually flung it over his shoulder, and headed out the door.

"Do you know him?" I asked Tony as Sebastian's large shoulders disappeared into a sleek silver Lexus.

"I have never seen him before." Tony frowned at the money on the table. "He just had one slice and an ice tea. This is too much. Why would he leave so much?"

Alys was looking at me. "I think it's a message. Like that there are no hard feelings."

Tony's shoulders slumped. "That is good."

"It is as long as you fix that door." Alys shook her head. "And what did he mean that he spends enough time with lawyers?"

I looked down at the card in my hand.

*Sebastian Jones, attorney at law.*

I handed the card to my sister. "Probably because he is one."

Sebastian smiled to himself as he drove out of town and to the series of switchbacks that led to his rental. The house was large and imposing where it sat perched on the side of the hill overlooking the town below. He liked to think that he was watching over Eckhart from his perch high above.

Waiting for his chance to strike.

Louse lurked in the yard when he drove up just as the sun kissed the hill at a sharp angle. The shadows were plenty long for the creature to hide in and disguise his presence. He was an excellent nighttime spy.

"You were right," Sebastian acknowledged the creature. "The oldest sister has the magic as well. Good work, Louse."

"And the third sister?" the creature hissed. "Does she possess stolen power as well?"

"I'm almost certain of it."

Red eyes glinted. "Then let us go harvest them before other hunters arrive."

"Don't be so hasty, Louse." Sebastian strode to the garage door and punched in his code so the door would open. Inside all the tools of his trade were arranged neatly. The pot for brewing spells that would siphon the magic as well as the soul from one of the transients. His amulets for collecting and containing the powers he gathered. It had taken him centuries to learn that the best way to harvest magic down to the last drop was not to strip it from the soul it had attached itself to but to bind both soul and magic into a stone. The soul died a little with each direct use of the magic, which negated the price that most magic wielders had to pay.

In essence, Sebastian borrowed the powers the thief had stolen and made him pay for it again and again.

He removed his hated contacts and looked in the scrying glass. He used it to hunt his empowered prey. Contacts muted the telling amethyst color of his eyes that marked him as a natural-born fae but also his vision. Then he studied his nose. Tender and the skin beneath his eyes were beginning to blacken, but so worth it to draw two of the sisters so near and verify that they possessed what it was he sought.

He could have used one of the amulets to fix the damage but decided against it. Siobhan had felt so guilty that he knew just a little persuasion would convince her to give in to him.

"I don't understand." Louse hesitated at the edge of the garage. The creature knew it wasn't permitted into his personal space and dared his wrath from coming so close. "Why aren't you stripping them of their souls even now?"

Sebastian lifted an eyebrow. "Since when do I explain myself to you?"

The sound of gravel crunching under tires alerted them. Louse hissed as the headlights shone right through him.

"Worry not, Louse. I know exactly what my next move will be." Sebastian closed the garage and went out to greet his visitor.

## CHAPTER FIFTEEN

### ALYS

Another rough night filled with terrifying dreams led to me feeling stiff and cranky on Monday morning. I'd showered the worst of the demo off before falling into bed, but headed into the bathroom anyway for another shower to help loosen up sore muscles and work out the kinks in my neck.

Sibby was up and dressed and had that damn book open beside her coffee mug.

"The electrician should be here around ten," I said by way of greeting. "If you are going to hang around, would you mind letting him in?"

She shrugged. "Not a problem. Are we going to talk about what happened yesterday?"

"Which part?" I was having trouble keeping up with all we had going on. "Be more specific. The part where your new boyfriend is Kyle's divorce attorney." A fact that it had taken Google all of thirty seconds to burp up.

Sibby rolled her eyes. "First of all, I only met the guy once, so no, he is not my boyfriend."

"Doesn't stop you from teasing me about Brock," I muttered as I poured the rest of the French Press into a travel mug.

"McNibblet is obviously interested in you, even if you are too damn stubborn to admit it," Sibby shot back.

"The guy asked you out, probably just to get dirt on me for Kyle's case. Did you ever think of that?"

Her lips parted. "Oh, so you're saying it's impossible that he's interested in me?"

"Did you see him, Sib? That suit was worth thousands. The car was easily fifty grand, with all the bells and whistles."

She put her hands on her hips. "So, what you're saying is I'm not worth his time. That me and my crazy hair and tats and big mouth are too wild and wooly for a classy guy like that."

"Money does not equal class," I snapped. "And quit changing the subject. He's in bed with my ex, just like the last hooker."

She shook her head. "We don't know that he's Kyle's lawyer."

And she called me stubborn. "Except he's new in town and Kyle was bragging about scoring some big-shot lawyer who was going to get him everything he wanted and then some. Put two and two together and tell me what you get."

Sibby opened her mouth but I held up a hand. "I can't afford to mix it up with you. I need to keep as calm as possible so nothing freaky happens today. If you like the guy, that's fine. But please, can you just wait until we know more about him before you go falling in lust with him?"

"Too late," Sibby quipped. "Did you see him?"

"I did." Even covered in blood there was no denying that Sebastian was attractive, though I personally preferred Brock's rugged earthiness to the lawyer's urbane polish.

"I've got to go," I said and snatched up my briefcase, laptop bag, and keys.

"Alys," she called out.

When I turned back, she gave me a tight smile. "No matter what happens, you still have us."

"Thanks," I said and meant it. Sibby and Maeve were in my corner and no high-priced lawyer could compete with that.

I headed to the office first. Lora was at her desk, and she flashed me a smile as I walked in.

"How was your weekend?" I asked as she handed me a stack of messages she'd already transcribed from our answering service.

"Great, right up until Aston fell on our hike."

"Is he okay?"

She nodded. "Nothing broken thankfully. I'm not sure what I would have done if he had. He's getting too big to carry."

"You would have called me and I would have sent Kal and Brock and any other number of the big strong men in our orbit into the gorge to help you." I put a hand on her shoulder. "It takes a village, right?"

She covered my hand with hers and squeezed. "Thanks, Alys."

"Your mom doing okay?" Her mother had stage four bone cancer and last I had heard, was refusing another round of chemo.

"The best we can expect." Lora blew out a breath. "Why does adulting have to be so damned hard?"

"Wish I knew." I blew out a breath. "Speaking of which, I'm headed out in a few."

"Another project house?"

If only. "It's personal business."

Lora studied me, her dark eyes assessing. "Are you okay?"

I hadn't planned on telling her but Lora was so open about everything going on with her mother and son it felt almost selfish to keep the news to myself. Like I didn't trust her, which was not the case.

*Put your money where your mouth is, Alys.* "Kyle and I are getting a divorce."

She sucked in a breath. "Woah."

"Yeah. I have a feeling that he's going to be difficult about everything because that's his way. I would appreciate it if you kept this to yourself."

"Of course." She nodded and reached across the desk and took my hand. "And whatever you need, I'm here for you."

Well, that was easier than expected. A cakewalk compared to a conversation with Sibby. I headed to my desk and scanned the stack of messages. A few were inquiries from real estate agents interested in selling me property or finding a buyer for my home in progress. One was from my doctor, reminding me that my annual visit was coming up. And the last one was from Brock marked urgent.

My stomach did a little flip as I punched in the number. He picked up on the first ring. "Lys."

"What's going on?" I asked wondering why he hadn't just called my cell.

"Were you at the Mid-Century project house yesterday?"

"Yeah. Maeve, Sibby, and I got started on the demo."

There was a pause. "What time was that?"

"Mid to late afternoon. We headed out around six. Why?"

He blew out a breath. "Because someone has completely trashed the place."

BROCK WASN'T KIDDING. I stared at the house with dismay. Every pane of glass had been broken. The siding had orange paint thrown up against it and the lawn had been torn up by what looked like ATV tracks.

"Shit," I breathed. "Shit, shit, shit."

Brock's face was grim. "This is bad, Lys. The windows alone will close to double the estimate I sent you."

"Do you have any idea who could have done this?"

Brock hesitated and pulled me away from where the rest of the crew worked on cleaning out the garbage. "It was made to look like kids. That's what the four-by-four tracks are about."

I stared up into his golden gaze. "But it wasn't."

He shook his head. "No. It was too deliberate. Sometimes drug addicts will break in and try to steal anything of value. But they don't stick around to make a mess. They're in and out. This feels more like the work of someone who has an axe to grind."

I swallowed past the lump in my throat. "You mean Kyle."

He hesitated and lowered his voice even further. "I can smell him here."

I looked up at him. "Seriously?"

He nodded. "I know his scent. It's like baby powder and sweated onion."

"But why destroy a project I'm working on?" I asked. "The more it costs me to fix the damage, the less money I pull out of the business?"

"I don't have any answers for you." He blew out a sigh. "Should we call the police?"

I considered it a moment and then shook my head. "No, they would want proof beyond your stellar sense of smell. And I doubt Kyle was stupid enough to leave a calling card."

Brock reached out and stroked my cheek. "Are you alright?"

I shook my head and as much as I wanted to curl into his

touch, forced myself to step back. "I have to meet with my attorney. Maybe she'll have some advice."

"How do you want to proceed here?" Brock asked.

The windows wouldn't just be an added expense. Ordering the necessary custom panes would delay the renovation. There was no way I was going to put anything of value in the place until it was sealed up tight. "Finish the demo and salvage what you can. Board up any entrance with plywood. I'll see about getting security up here to monitor the place at night and ordering the glass."

Brock nodded. "I'll get you exact measurements by this afternoon."

I headed back to my SUV and called my lawyer's office to let her know that something had come up. Her secretary told me she had to head to court in a few minutes but she would reschedule the meeting for one o'clock.

I hung up and, not knowing what else to do, headed back to the office.

Thousands of dollars, gone. It was one thing to run into a problem that needed to be remedied mid-construction. But such blatant vandalism was entirely different.

Kyle's little message wasn't lost on me. He would go out of his way to make my life difficult unless I gave him what he wanted. The bastard wanted to have his cake and eat it too.

I headed back to the office. Lora was gone but Maeve was at her desk, looking at something on her computer screen. Her eyes rounded when she saw my face. "Alys?"

"Kyle trashed the Mid-Century Modern." I paced in front of her desk, too agitated to keep still.

"What?" Maeve blinked.

"The whole house. Sometime between when we left yesterday and Brock's crew showed up for demo this morning. All the glass broken, the lawn torn up, paint everywhere…." I ran a hand through my hair. "I'm going to lose it, Maeve."

Maeve shook her head. "You can't."

I let out a bitter laugh. "It's almost like he wants to see me lose my temper."

"Maybe he does."

I turned to the doorway and spotted Sibby, book in hand, her face pale.

"What do you mean?"

She set the book down on Maeve's desk. "I was reading about these magic hunters. Oftentimes they need to ferret out the magic users they are hunting. Beat the bushes and see what shakes out. You said you almost hit Kyle with a bolt of lightning the other night, right? And then later that dark thing showed up and tried to break down the door."

"What are you getting at, Sibby?" Maeve asked. "You think Kyle is being used by a magic hunter?"

Sibby's gaze met mine. "Or maybe he is one."

"Kyle?" Maeve shook her head. "No. No, I can't believe it. He's a bastard-coated bastard with bastard filling, but he's not some power-hungry dark fae."

"Think about it," Sibby insisted. "He's been trying to get Alys's goat for days now. Pushing her buttons, the way only a vindictive ex can. He's trying to get her to unleash her magic."

"There's just one problem with that theory," I told her. "Kyle was screwing a hooker in my bed *before* we drank the empowerment brew. He has no idea that I have magic."

"But it follows our line," Sibby insisted. "Any decent magic hunter worth his salt would be able to trace magic running in a family. What if Kyle married you just to see if you would manifest magic? What if he came onto me for the same reason?"

"Kyle came on to you?" Maeve blinked. "What's she talking about?"

I slumped into my desk chair and put my head in my hands and uttered a phrase I had never spoken before. "I can't deal with this."

"Alys," Sibby began.

"I need to get out of here." I had hours until I met with the attorney and found out what I could do about my problematic ex.

"You can't drive, not in your state." Maeve insisted. "I'll drive."

There was no arguing with her when she got that look on her face.

"Fine," I snapped. "You drive. Let's just go."

"Where to?" Maeve asked once we were all seated in the minivan. It smelled like cheesy crackers and sunscreen.

"I need to blow off some steam." My insides were seething as anger writhed like a pit of snakes. "Any suggestions?"

"We could go to a bar," Sibby suggested.

"It's ten-thirty in the morning," Maeve said.

"And your point is….?" Sibby raised a brow.

"No booze." I was barely hanging on to my control as it was.

"I know," Maeve said and then backed out of the space. She headed out of town in the opposite direction from Witch Way, out past decrepit barns and overgrown pastures until she came to a run-down pole barn.

"Where the hell are we?" I asked as we got out of the car.

"Glen Hanson's old place," Maeve said. "He's got ninety acres just sitting here."

"But what are we doing here?" Sibby asked.

In answer, Maeve went to the rear of the vehicle and extracted a large case with a combination lock.

She set the case down, spun the combination, and stepped aside letting us peruse the contents.

"Holy shit," Sibby breathed. "Do you always carry a handgun in the back of your minivan?"

Maeve shook her head. "No. Kal and I used to do target shooting at the range before the twins were born. I was intending to sell it, but things have been a little hectic lately so I haven't made it to the pawn shop yet. And if we can't use magic to defend ourselves, we ought to have something else. What do you think, Alys?"

I studied the weapon. "Can I use it on Kyle?"

"The scary thing is," Sibby said out of the corner of her mouth. "I'm not sure that she's joking."

Neither was I. "Okay."

"Atta girl." Maeve grinned and closed the case. "This way."

We headed out to a field where a half dozen tin cans were set up on the posts of a split rail fence.

Maeve set the case down, spun the lock again, and extracted the weapon. It was a revolver, sort of like you would see in an old detective movie. "Where did you even get that?"

"Present from Aunt Jess," she muttered.

I grimaced. "Of course."

"So why get rid of it?" Sibby asked.

"Having it in the house with the kids makes me twitchy." We watched as she checked to see if it was loaded, then placed bullets into each chamber before snapping the thing back into place.

She stood confidently, feet shoulder-width apart, disengaged the safety, pulled the hammer back, aimed, and fired.

One of the old cans took flight.

"You make it look so easy," Sibby breathed.

"This is a single-action revolver." Maeve re-engaged the safety.

"You say that like either of us has a clue what it means," I reminded her.

"It's more accurate than something like a Glock because it's easier to aim and pull the trigger. You ready, Alys?"

I let out a deep breath. "It's worth a shot."

"If the magic hunters don't kill me," Sibby muttered. "The puns might."

# CHAPTER SIXTEEN

## MAEVE

Neither Alys nor Sibby took to the revolver, but the impromptu target practice helped diffuse Alys's temper. By the time we headed back into town neither one of them had shot a can, but they had each given the split rail fence what for.

"Thanks," Alys said as I parked beside her car in front of the office. "I think I can handle going to the lawyer's now without risking any natural catastrophes."

"Anytime." The lie about bringing the gun to the pawn shop had been worthwhile. I would never sell that old revolver. It had been Aunt Jess's and she had cherished it up until the day she had passed it on to me. I'd worn it, unloaded of course, in my garter belt for our wedding. The memory of Kal's reaction made me grin.

Being armed made me feel safer, especially when we had magic hunters on our six. My sisters deserved to have that same feeling of safety, that they could take care of whatever might show up, at least until help arrived. I'd decided last night that they ought to learn and had been trying to figure out a way to bring it up.

Alys headed off to meet with her attorney and Sibby and I headed back inside.

"Do you really think she'll be okay?"

I settled at my desk and shook my head. "It's Alys."

"Meaning what?" Sibby lowered herself into Aly's chair.

"Meaning that even if she's not okay, we won't know until it's too late."

Sibby thought about it for a beat. "Okay then. Do you think Alys will mind if I use her computer?"

"Of course not." I was glad of anything that would distract my youngest sister from more talk of magic. I had tasks to accomplish before I headed out to that freaking bake sale.

Lora had returned and I called her back to study the orders I was considering for the Mid-Century Modern. Our assistant had a hell of an eye and I was grooming her to take over my spot in the business.

"Not that one, it's two brothel-esque," Lora said as I indicated a rug done in bold jewel tones.

"Hmm," I said even though I had come to the exact same conclusion. "Well, I want to stay in this price range. Any suggestions?"

The main living room space was huge and if Alys had her way, would look even bigger when it was all done. And because we'd already decided on bamboo for the floors, we needed a large rug to help muffle the echo and make the space feel less cavernous.

Lora scrolled down the listings, her delicate nose wrinkling as she studied the selections. "Why not pick something with geometric patterns? Something that speaks to the early style of the house?"

I thought about it for a beat. We were updating all the old tile and dated décor but having a single piece that harkened back to the era when the house was built made a lot of sense. Especially if we tied it in with a necessary object.

I did another search and came up with something like she had suggested. Gold burgundy and purple octagons made a unique display. "Like this?"

"Perfect." Lora gave me a thumbs up.

Sibby had rolled her chair over to look as well. "Wow, that's intense."

"It's what a space that big needs. We're going to keep the rest of the room neutral, including the furniture. It'll be a blinding sea of white and dark, but this will add a much-needed pop of color."

"You could get accent pillows in the same pattern," Sibby suggested. "Or maybe just one of the colors to tie it all in."

"She thinks like a designer," Lora said and Sibby beamed.

I saved the link. Yes, the rug we had chosen would work well in the house, but we needed to see what our budget looked like after Brock estimated the new repairs. I couldn't spend what we didn't have.

"I better get going." I got to my feet and my leg went numb from the hip down.

*No.*

My hands went out and I caught myself on the desk so I didn't crash to the floor. I'd been feeling so good, so power-ful, and much more like my old self after the target practice. I couldn't be dealing with this now. *It's too soon.*

But that's how chronic illness worked. It struck like a viper hidden in the leaves.

"Maeve?" Sibby moved to my side. "Are you okay?"

The panic eased and I nodded. "Yeah. It wasn't...you know."

Sibby didn't look convinced.

"Really, my leg is just asleep is all." And it was, thankfully. I eased back into the chair and met Sibby's eyes as I rubbed my leg. "I'll be okay in a minute."

Sibby knelt before me but was pushed out of the way by Lora. "Hey, what the hell?"

My mouth went dry when I saw the glazed look in her eye. "Oh no."

From her position on the ground, Sibby blinked. It was the first time she had seen my magic in action. "She looks like she's sleepwalking."

The fear that had been slowly dissipating spiked once more as Lora hovered over me, her eyes unseeing. "What the hell do I do?"

"Where does she live?" Sibby asked.

"Three blocks over, in a condo next to the park. Why?"

Sibby got up and circled Lora, making sure not to come between her and me. "Tell her to go home."

I shot my sister a poisonous glare. "What?"

"You need to tell her to go home. Give her some distance and let her come back to herself."

"She has a son." I swallowed. "I don't want him to see her like this."

"I'm sure it will fade as soon as she is far enough away from you."

I licked my lips. "Only if you go with her until she comes back to herself."

"I'm not going to leave you." Sibby appeared insulted that I would even suggest doing such a thing.

"Oh yes, you are." When she looked over at me, I leveled my gaze at her, doing my best Alys impression. "I am not sending a mindless woman who I consider a friend out in public alone. What if she walks in front of a car?"

Sibby shut her eyes, the internal struggle visible in her tight jaw and clenched fists.

"I'm going to go lock myself in my van and wait for you to come back. The office is officially closed for the day because the Silver sisters have personal matters."

Sibby's eyes opened and she pointed a finger at me. "You will stay right where you are until I get back. And the second she wakes up I'm doing a one-eighty. Are we clear?"

Apparently, I wasn't the only one who could channel Alys. "Agreed."

Turning my focus to Lora. "Hey Lora, we're good for today, so I want you to head home now. Gather your things and we'll see you tomorrow." I spoke slowly and clearly, not sure if she would remember any of the conversation. If she did it was better if she thought I'd been doing her a solid and letting her cut out early.

Sibby and I watched as Lora pivoted on her heel and strode purposefully to her desk. Her movements weren't super smooth as she collected her purse and coat. But then she headed to the door.

"Sibby," I pleaded

"Don't move a muscle until I get back," Sibby said and then followed after the blank-faced Lora.

I put my head in my hands and tried to do some deep breathing exercises. *Focus on your inner self, all the little lights, and shadows that make you you. See that energy rise and fall.* Guided meditation was supposed to be rejuvenating and right now that was what I needed to fix my damaged calm. Because Sibby's words had hit home.

The ability to move my muscles was what caused this mess in the first place.

# ALYS

Glenna Feinstein was waiting in the entry to her office building beside the courthouse. She was a trim woman in her fifties who ran marathons. I had sold her a refurbished chateau Maeve and I had tackled a few years ago.

"Alys. It's good to see you, though I am sorry about the circumstances." Glenna's soft southern drawl washed over me.

We shook hands and she inquired if I would like anything to drink, which I politely refused. She led me into a conference room which was done in soothing shades of green and set off the cherry table and chairs.

"So, I've already heard from Kyle's lawyer and his list of demands are utterly ridiculous. I want to know how you wish to proceed. Do we fight, or do we settle? It's your call."

I'd been all ready to fight to the bitter end but with the possibility of magic hunters and worry over exposure, I couldn't risk it. "I already told him he could have the house and the car. How much does he want?"

Glenna flipped open a file folder and spun it around so I could see.

My jaw dropped. "That's half the value of my business."

"Like I said, ridiculous."

I shook my head. "What gives him the right to go after so much?"

"He said you've been hiding money from him for years. Claims he supported you while the business was growing and he deserves his cut."

I snorted. "Kyle only ever supported one person—Kyle. And he gladly gave that up as soon as possible."

"Do we fight? With the infidelity, you have a solid case, even without a prenup."

One a judge would have to hear. More waiting, more wondering, more stress with the likelihood that I would lose my temper and endanger my sisters. Acid burned in my stomach. Considering what I suspected he had done to the Mid-Century Modern project he didn't deserve a dime, but I forced the words out. "How about a counter offer?"

"Like what?"

I knew he wanted money, he'd said as much the other night. "Palimony. A monthly sum until he remarries."

Glenna considered. "You want to tempt him. If you really want to keep this out of court, you need a decent amount."

A decent amount for an indecent man.

She wrote down a figure. "Does this look appropriate?"

*No,* I thought. "Yes," I said.

It was money well spent if it would make Kyle go away.

She flipped the folder closed and tapped it on the table twice to settle all the papers within. "I'll send it over to his lawyer immediately."

She showed me back out and I hesitated as I asked, "What do you know about him? The attorney Kyle hired."

"He's ruthless," she said immediately. "A real barracuda. I'm shocked your husband was able to retain his services on such short notice. Why?"

I made a face. "Because my sister might have broken his nose yesterday."

Glenna gave me a level look. "You're kidding."

When I shook my head, she sighed. "Intentionally? I can refer you to a personal injury defense attorney."

"It was an accident and he seemed to understand." I worried my lower lip. "It's just that he seems interested in my sister and I was curious about who he was."

Her piercing gaze bore into me. "If I were you, I would tell your sister to steer clear. Not only would it be in your best interest, but from what I've heard, it would be in hers as well. He's ambitious and will annihilate anyone who gets in his way."

I blew out a breath. "I'll tell her. Thanks again, Glenna."

I headed down to the parking lot and was surprised to see Brock standing beside the Suburban. "How did it go?"

"About how I expected." I pinched the bridge of my nose.

"Did you ask your lawyer to confront him?" Brock's tone was hopeful. "Or call him out on what he did to the project house?"

How much I wanted to do just that. "No. I essentially paid him to go away."

Brock stood there, not saying anything.

"He's such a sleaze. What did I ever see in him?" It was meant as a rhetorical question.

Brock didn't take it that way. "You're asking me? Do you really want to know what I think?" He stepped closer until all the small hairs on my arms lifted.

Did I? "What the hell."

"I think you were looking for someone to take care of."

I blinked up at him. "What?"

Instead of answering my question, he asked one of his own. "When did you marry Kyle?"

"When I was twenty-nine." His age, though I didn't say so.

He would have been nine. Had he already been a were-wolf? I wanted to ask but didn't want to derail the conversation.

"Was that before or after Maeve met Kal?"

"After. They weren't married yet but they were dating. She brought him to the wedding."

"So, Sibby was grown, and Maeve had met her mate. You needed someone to tend, to devote your energy to. Guys like Kyle can sense that need and take shameless advantage of it. He insinuated himself into your life. And he's been bleeding you dry ever since. Emotionally, financially. Tearing you down to build himself up."

My lips parted. I wanted to refute the charge but hadn't I had the same thoughts? That somewhere along the line I'd picked up a two-hundred-pound parasite and didn't know how to remove it?

Brock wasn't done. "You work all the time. Day and night. Non-stop. Why?"

"Because I love my job." I'd think the insightful man who saw so much would understand that fundamental truth.

His smile didn't reach his eyes. "I know you do, possum. I also know that it gives you back some of the life Kyle habitually drained out of you. You would head home for the night, eyes sparkling and a bounce in your step, and come to the job site the next day utterly depleted.

"Don't give him anything, Lys." Brock ran his fingers down the side of my face. "He's already stolen so much from you. Your life energy, your heart, and soul, moments that are gone forever. It's been agony to watch and not do anything. Stand up for your life. You're worth so much more."

Unsettled by how much he saw and by the clear yearning in his eyes, I retreated. His hand fell to his side.

"It's not that simple. I have to stay in control of myself. I told you what happens when I lose my temper."

"You did," he said not sounding at all upset. "I also know that trying to control your emotions is futile."

"But what about the magic hunters? This isn't just about me. I have to think about Sibby and Maeve, plus my niece and nephew. A protracted legal battle is just asking for trouble."

Brock didn't have any answers for me. Not that I'd expected him to. "Come to my house tonight. The pack is dying to meet you. They're planning a big cookout."

I shook my head. "I can't. My nephew has a soccer game."

"Stop by after. Bring your sisters," he pushed. "It would be good for them to meet some of the community. For you all to see that what you've gained isn't all bad."

He tipped my face up and my breath caught as I stared into those glowing gold eyes. Was he about to kiss me again?

I wanted him to, almost desperately.

"You aren't alone, Lys." He traced my lower lip with the pad of his thumb and then stepped away. "Never forget that."

He walked back to his truck and I watched as he drove away.

The glint of a reflection caught my eye and I turned fully to see what it was.

A camera. And the lens was pointed right at me.

CHAPTER SEVENTEEN

SIOBHAN

L ora came back to herself halfway to her condo. It was obvious in the way her gait changed from determined to almost hesitant. She paused as though she had forgotten something.

"Have a good night," I called.

She started at the sound of my voice and then lifted a hand and turned away.

I blew out a breath and then hustled back to *Silver Demo and Design*. Maeve sat still in her chair, her gaze unfocused.

"She's fine," I answered her unspoken question. "Really."

She closed her eyes and nodded. "Good."

Nothing about this situation was good. "Should we call your doctor?"

She shook her head. "There's nothing else she can do."

"Another doctor then," I insisted. "If you tell Alys she has contacts all over the state."

"Back off," Maeve growled.

"No." I reached out a hand to help her up. She looked at it for a long moment. "No, Maeve. You called me, begged me to come. You needed someone to talk to because you were afraid that Kal and Alys would pity you and take over and suffocate you and you knew I would let you handle this in your own way. You were smart enough to ask for help and I responded. So no, you aren't going to run me off now. I'm in it for the long haul, sister, no matter how much you snap and snarl. So just suck it up and deal."

She made a frustrated noise. "You are such a pain in the ass."

But she took my hand and allowed me to pull her to her feet.

"I hate this," she whispered. "I hate being so unsure. So scared all the damn time. Here Alys is all worried about losing her temper and bringing the magic hunters down on our heads. But I'm the one who is putting us at risk every minute."

I didn't say anything as I helped her out the door and then got her settled in the passenger's side of her minivan.

"Where to?" I asked as soon as she was buckled.

"I need to pick up those damn cupcakes. I was supposed to set up Philip's soccer game fundraiser."

Driving the minivan felt like operating a tank after riding my motorcycle, but I managed to back out of the space without carnage. "Okay, so I'll peddle the damn cupcakes so you can go home and rest before the big game later."

She swallowed. "I don't know if I can risk going out in public like that."

"You can."

She closed her eyes and reached out a hand. "Thank you."

I took her hand and squeezed. "You would do the same for me. It's more important that you de-stress. Listen to one of those meditation videos, take a hot bath, unwind for a spell. We'll get you to the soccer complex on time."

The sound of frantic yipping and whimpering greeted us as we walked into the house. I settled Maeve on the couch and then released the G&G wrecking crew from their crates and shooed them into the backyard. Kal never would have saddled Maeve with those ridiculous dogs if he knew what was going on with her. But it was Maeve's own fault for delaying the inevitable. It was her news to tell.

I just wished she'd tell it soon.

The store-bought cupcakes were sitting on the island. I took them out to the minivan and loaded them in the cargo net then headed back inside.

Maeve was settled on the sectional with her laptop open in front of her.

"Creatures in or out?" I asked.

"In," she said. "Kal will be home soon. Besides, I can always put them back in the crates if they get to be too much."

Oh, she might threaten, but I knew my sister. Those dogs had made early parole and there was no way she would lock them up if she didn't have to.

I let the wee beasties in and they scampered and thudded down the hall, never more than four feet between two dogs on the ground at a time.

I shook my head and then poured Maeve a glass of water and hid a smile as I found her on the couch surrounded by corgis.

"They aren't supposed to be on the furniture," she griped even as she scratched Grogu behind the ear. Gimli circled three times and then plopped down on the keyboard of her laptop.

"Have you told them that?" I set the water down on the side table within Maeve's reach but out of the line of corgi antics.

"It's like you and Alys in dog form. They don't listen to a thing I say."

I frowned at her. "That's not true."

She shrugged. "Thanks for taking care of the bake sale. Watch out for Missy Hargraves. She's a real pain in the ass, but don't piss her off because I'm not convinced, she won't get in her husband's ear and have him bench Philip if we get on her bad side."

"No one could be that petty."

Maeve snorted. "Trust me, they can be, especially the power trippy sorts like Missy. She's a real harpy."

I blew out a breath. "Okay, don't piss off the harpy. Got it. Call me if you need anything."

"Will do. And Sibby? Thanks."

I winked and headed for the door, leaving my sister and her furry attendants to rest. Which I hoped she would actually do.

Kal was pulling into the driveway just as I settled in the van. He frowned when he saw it was me instead of Maeve behind the wheel. "What's up?"

"I volunteered to do bake sale detail so Maeve could get some work done at home." The fib fell handily from my lips. If I was a better person, I probably wouldn't have been such an accomplished liar. "I still can't believe you brought those dogs in without telling her. You, my friend, like to live dangerously."

Kal flushed. "We'd been talking about it for a while, how having pets would teach the children responsibility, but she never seemed ready to pull the trigger. The guy who sold them to me made me an offer I couldn't refuse."

I barely stifled a grimace. Knowing Maeve, she hadn't wanted to commit to the pet until she knew what she was dealing with regarding her health. Because even if the intention was to teach Bella and Philip responsibility, we both knew Maeve would be the one who made sure the dogs were walked and fed and taken to the vet on time.

"Just make sure the kids pull their weight with the dogs." I cautioned him. "And you too."

Kal nodded. I half expected him to step back but he hesitated. "Is everything okay, Sibby?"

I paused. "What do you mean?"

"I don't know. The three of you have been kind of secretive lately. And I know something is going on with Maeve but she won't talk to me about it."

Perceptive man. "You know about Alys getting divorced, right?"

When he nodded, I threw my oldest sister's personal issues out as a distraction. "Well, Kyle is being a real asswipe about it. He showed up at her place the other night making all kinds of bullshit threats."

"Threats?" Kal stiffened. "Should I kick his ass?"

Oh hell no. That was the last thing we needed. "Not physical threats, but he screwed up the project they are working on and hired a lawyer to go after her assets. We're trying our best to be supportive, but you know Alys. She will only let us do so much. Feels like she has to handle everything herself."

Kal glanced to the house. "She's not the only one."

"Hey," I put my hand on his forearm and squeezed. "Just give her time."

His jet-black brows drew together. "Time for what?"

"To sort through things her way." I let out a breath. "Trust me, Kal. She'll open up when she's good and ready. Just be patient."

"Thanks, Sibby. We'll see you later?"

When I nodded, he stepped back and I rolled up the window and let out a slow breath.

"Maeve, you better get your head together soon," I muttered and headed off to tackle the bake sale harpy.

# ALYS

"Hey," I shouted and the creep in the bushes jerked back as he realized I was talking to him.

I took note of his face—unfamiliar—and his clothes. He was wearing a brown trench coat and slacks the same sandy color, along with a Yankee's ballcap that looked ridiculous.

"Who are you?" I called out.

He bolted. I gave chase, though I had no idea who the guy was or why he'd been taking pictures of me without my knowledge.

Of course, I was dressed all wrong for hot pursuit in slacks and heels and frustration mounted as the camera creep easily outran me. I hopped on one foot as I yanked off one heel and then the other and his lead increased.

Some of the townspeople called out but I ignored them, singularly intent on catching up.

He ran behind the library to a small alleyway that I knew dead-ended with a five-foot concrete wall that listed the names of Eckhart's town heroes. If my brain had been work-ing, I might have realized that following the guy into a one-way alley was a dumbass idea. What if he was armed with more than just a camera?

But my adrenaline was up and I dashed headlong into the alley.

He hung from the wall, camera dangling across his back, obviously trying to haul himself up and over the obstruction. He was about my age and not in the best shape because the pull-up was beyond him.

"Who are you?" I asked again.

He made a strangled sound and fell to the ground, camera first.

"Fuck." He rolled over and immediately checked the camera. "Oh. fuck me sideways."

"Not gonna happen." I had no sympathy for this foul-mouthed couch potato idiot. "Tell me who you are and what you were doing?"

He didn't answer, too distraught about his camera. "Do you know what this thing cost?" He ripped the Yankees cap off and threw it on the ground, displaying his balding head.

"Then maybe you should have taken better care of it." I was winded but at least I wasn't sucking in oxygen like he was, as though the stuff was on a two-for-one clearance special.

He just shook his head. The picture of dejection. Judging from his reaction, he couldn't afford to replace the camera.

I crouched down in front of him. "I'll replace it if you answer my questions."

He looked at me through narrowed eyes, then nodded once.

"Who are you?"

"Joe. Joe Barnes."

"And why were you taking pictures of me, Joe Barnes? I'm not a celebrity or anything."

He blew out a breath. "I'm a PI."

I blinked. "Seriously?"

He nodded.

"So someone hired you to take photos of me?" That didn't make sense.

Unless….

"You work for that lawyer, don't you? The one Kyle hired?"

He shook his head. "I'm not supposed to talk about it. That's what they said in the course."

My brow furrowed. "What course?"

"The one I took on becoming a private investigator."

"Was it free online or something? Because I hate to break it to you, pal, but you kind of suck at it."

"I know," he sighed, obviously resigned. "But I lost my job and I need the income. The others have gotten much better stuff on you."

My blood chilled. "What others?"

He eyed me warily. "I don't think I should tell you anything else."

My hands clenched into fists. "That's fine, you told me enough."

I leaned down and yanked the broken camera out of his hands so fast he yelped. Popping the bottom section, I removed the sim card and then tossed the broken thing back to him.

He fumbled it and it hit the ground with another crack.

Heels in my left hand and sim card in my right, I stalked from the alley. Dark-bellied clouds scudded across what had been a clear blue October sky.

"Wait? You said you would replace my camera!" Joe Barnes called out.

"Bill your boss," I called over my shoulder. Sebastian Jones could afford it.

I stalked back to the Suburban, threw open the door, and

heaved myself inside. Then I sat, clutching the wheel in a white-knuckled grip. Fury bubbled through me like magma in seawater as all the crap Kyle was putting me through ran on a carousel through my hand. The cheating. The using. The insults and threats to my sisters, my business, my reputation. And now some bottom-feeding lawyer had multiple PIs tailing me.

A bolt of lightning touched down against the ground, blinding me. People ran for cover as pea-sized hail began to rain down. I was losing. It wasn't going to stop. He had nothing better to do than spend my money to make my life a living hell. Because he was a petty person, he would devote himself to it. The sniping, the games. There was no easy way out. No quick and dirty fix.

I had to fight.

In one shaking hand, I picked up the phone and dialed the last number I called.

"Have you sent the offer we discussed over to Sebastian Jones?" I asked my attorney.

"Not yet," Glenna said. "Did you change your mind?"

I closed my eyes and took a deep breath. "He gets nothing. Not the house, not his car, not anything from me or my business ever again."

"Understood," Glenna said. "I'll be in touch."

"And Glenna, there's one other thing," I said and leaned back against the headrest. "I want to have him arrested for destruction of private property."

*Take that, Kyle.* I thought.

"You should go to the police. File a report," the attorney advised. "They'll question him and it will go on record."

This felt good. It felt right. The magma inside my belly cooled and the hail stopped pinging off the metal roof.

"I'm headed there right now."

The sky cleared as I drove to the police station with a small smile on my face.

I was done letting that damn energy vampire bleed me dry.

And I couldn't wait to tell my sisters. Or Brock.

# CHAPTER EIGHTEEN

"Go, Philip!" I shouted from the sidelines as my nephew ran toward the goal as fast as his chubby little legs could take him.

Maeve was sitting in the camp chair next to me and raised her arms up over her head as her son took his shot and missed the goal by a mile. "That's okay, bud," she called. "You'll get it next time."

"Will he?" Kal asked from where he sat on the ground with Bella in his lap. She was hard at work making him a crown out of spent dandelion stems, which I knew from past experience, he would wear until it fell apart.

"Hush," Maeve swatted at his shoulder. "We're supposed to be encouraging his interests."

"That's why we're here," Kal said. "But there's a fine line between encouraging his interests and making him think he's got a future in sports. Poor kid couldn't hit the broadside of a barn."

Maeve made a disgusted noise. "Okay, Papa Reality Check. How about you go see how the bake sale is going?

Sibby's been there for over an hour. I'm sure she needs a respite."

"Why can't Alys go?" Kal winked at me, letting me know his complaint wasn't serious.

"Because say it with me now, Alys is *supportive*," Maeve said. "She brings good vibes."

I snorted. "Yeah, besides, you'll have more luck peddling sugar and carbs to all the soccer moms than I will. They want to have them anyway. Just tell them they don't need to diet and that men like well-padded posteriors in that deep, reassuring voice of yours, and those cupcakes will evaporate."

"I feel so used." Kal shook his head, just as Bella placed the crown on it, but got up. "Come on, peanut. Let's go rescue Aunt Sibby."

Once he was gone Maeve turned to me. "Before Sibby gets here and rats me out, I need to tell you something. I lost it in the office earlier. Enchanted Lora."

"What happened?"

She shook her head. "It was stupid, but it doesn't take much."

"No, it really doesn't." I plucked a piece of dried grass and began wrapping it around my finger. "I had a close call too. Even though I tried to avoid it."

"What are we talking about?" Sibby jogged up and plopped down on the ground. "What did I miss?"

"Our earlier mishaps," Maeve answered. Her gaze was on where Philip stood staring off into space. "Our control techniques aren't working."

"Ironic, isn't it?" Sibby sprawled out flat on her back and folded her hands behind her head.

"What?" I asked.

"You two with your orderly lives get magic and you're falling apart. Where me and my chaotic one is sitting pretty."

"It's the trigger," I complained. "It's a lot easier not to feel desire than it is to hold your temper or keep fear in check."

Sibby was wearing dark sunglasses to protect her from the evening rays but I knew she rolled her eyes at me. "Tell yourself that, Alys. Like you wouldn't have been hopping around like a horny bunny when Brock showed up naked in your living room."

I was about to tell her that I'd been worried about his injuries not ogling his body but pressed my lips together. She was right, I had been thinking about Brock differently, allowing myself to notice him. Was it really fair that I claimed her magic trigger was somehow less volatile than my own?

She'd been able to use it when it counted, to get Maeve out of the Farmer's Market. Though it left a bitter taste in my mouth, she was right. Out of the three of us, Sibby was managing her power best.

"Speaking of Brock, he invited us to meet the pack tonight. Officially."

Sibby sat up. "Really?"

I nodded. "I think it would probably be a good start in getting to know what this new supernatural community is all about."

"But they're werewolves, not witches," Maeve said.

A woman walking by with a large pink cupcake paused to stare at us.

"My screenplay," Sibby called out. "I'm hoping to sell to one of the streaming services. Kinda like a *Twilight* for adults."

"Good luck," the woman called out.

"You are such a good liar, Sib." Maeve took an unsteady breath. "That's Jeannine McFee, and she's the biggest gossip in town. That could have been a disaster."

"Practice makes perfect," I quipped.

Sibby threw a clump of dried grass in my lap and then turned to Maeve. "You're giving this town too much credit. Mom and Aunt Jess flew under the radar here for years."

"She's right," I added and both of my sisters started. "Plus, Brock and his wolves have been around awhile, too. Until we drank the empowerment brew, we knew nothing about any of them. People see what they want to see and take the easy way out when you give it to them."

"So, we're going, right? All of us?" Sibby looked back and forth between the two of us.

"Maeve?" I asked.

Her head bobbed. "Yeah, okay. I don't know what to tell Kal though, why I'm gone all the time. He'll get suspicious."

"He already is."

Maeve shaded her eyes and looked down at Sibby. "He told you that?"

"He's your husband and, in case you missed the memo, not an idiot. Relax," she added when Maeve looked about to hyperventilate. "I told him Kyle is being a tool and we are trying to help Alys out as much as she'll let us."

Maeve picked at a loose thread on the arm of the camp chair. "I hate lying to him."

I put a hand over hers. "I know. But honestly, do you really want to dump all this on him?"

"Especially if there's nothing he can do except worry about you," Sibby added.

Maeve shook her head but her lips were pressed into a firm line as if she were biting something back.

The game wrapped up with a zero to one and Coach Hargraves invited everyone out for pizza. Sibby and I waited by the Suburban while Maeve spoke with Kal. He nodded and kissed her on the forehead before heading to the minivan with Bella and Philip.

"We'll have to swing back by here later and get Kal's car," Maeve said when she climbed in next to me.

"My bike is parked at your office, too," Sibby added.

"Let's do the vehicles first. Maeve, drive Kal's car home and then we'll go get Sibby's motorcycle and she can follow us to Brock's place."

"In case Alys wants to spend the night going down under," Sibby snickered.

I glowered at her in the rearview mirror. "It's just more efficient."

In reply, she made the okay sign and then did something lewd with her other hand. Maeve snorted and then popped the passenger's side door and headed to Kal's Toyota.

I followed her to her house and then waited as she went inside to let her dogs out.

"You sure you don't want to bring them?" I asked.

"To a werewolf barbecue?" Sibby sounded incredulous. "As what, the appetizers?"

Maeve wrinkled her nose at her and then answered me. "No, the kids will be eager to get home to them."

I backed out of Maeve's driveway and then headed into town. I needed to tell them about the PI who had been photographing me for Kyle's lawyer but wanted to wait until we'd cleared the town limit in case Maeve freaked.

One close call a day was enough.

We passed the Farmer's Market, the town hall, the VFW, and the library as well as many other closed-up businesses. People had been busy putting out fall decorations. With a start, I realized that Friday was Halloween.

Two days after my birthday.

"Do you guys remember our first Halloween here?" Maeve was obviously thinking along the same lines. "Aunt Jess brought us to town and we hit up every single business along the main streets and then did the houses too."

"I was too young," Sibby sounded sad.

"We dressed you like a frog." I grinned. "And Maeve was the fairy princess who had to kiss you."

"And what were you?" Sibby sounded eager.

My tone was quiet as I said, "I was the wicked witch who cursed you."

"The more things change…" Sibby said and Maeve snort laughed.

"Are there any pictures?" Sibby asked.

Maeve frowned. "I know Aunt Jess had some albums."

I swallowed. "I took them out of the cottage after she passed." Though I'd fully intended to scan the photos and go digital so our memories wouldn't be lost, I'd never gotten around to it.

Maeve was worrying her bottom lip. "You don't think that Kyle would do anything to them, do you?"

I cut a glance at her. "Honestly? I don't know what Kyle would do anymore." His behavior had been so erratic and spiteful.

Sibby leaned over the back seat. "Okay, so let's go get them."

I glanced at her in the rearview. "Now? What about your motorcycle?"

She shrugged. "No time like the present. I can pop back by and get it another time. Come on, let's get in there and snag anything worth snagging before it occurs to him that he can hurt you that way."

*Don't give him anything, Lys.* Brock's words rang in my ears. *You're worth so much more.*

I squared my shoulders and nodded crisply. "Let's do it."

≈

THERE WAS no sign of the Corvette in the driveway. I looked up at the house and made a face. "I really hate this soulless place."

"Then why did you live here for so long?" Sibby asked.

I shrugged. "Honestly? Kyle wanted something new and easy to maintain. It wasn't worth the fight."

My sisters both looked at me. I replayed my words and flinched. What I really was saying that I hadn't believed my own wants and desires were worth the fight.

"The only place I've ever really been happy is at Aunt Jess's."

"Me too," Sibby said, surprising me.

Maeve reached out a hand to either of us and squeezed. "It's a special place. I love my house and my family but when I think of home, the first thing that comes to mind is Aunt Jess's cottage and you guys."

And yet somehow, we'd let it sit empty and alone for years while we were busy doing other things. No checking on it, no updates. Tears burned at the back of my eyes and I sniffled. "Okay, enough of this mushy stuff. We need to get while the getting is good."

We popped the doors and Maeve and Sibby flanked me as we went up the stairs. I was half expecting that my key wouldn't work but the lock turned with ease. "I guess he hasn't gotten around to calling a locksmith yet."

"His lawyer probably told him he shouldn't make any changes," Sibby said.

The place smelled musty and a little rancid. My sneakers squeaked over the wood floor. My yellow orchid sat on the half-moon table and I picked it up, heading to the kitchen for water.

Empty beer cans and pizza boxes were scattered over the island and tumbled onto the floor. My aloe plant looked a sickly yellow. On closer inspection, I saw cigarette butts stabbed out in the soil.

"It's true what they say," Sibby shook her head. "Men turn into slobs without a woman around to keep them in line."

"That's not true," I said, thinking of Brock's beautiful kitchen.

"That's just Kyle," Maeve added. "Kal would die before letting the kitchen look like this."

I measured out water for the orchid, added it to the poor flower, and moved on.

The living room was no better. The Persian rug was stained and there were chips mashed into the sofa. Three used condoms lay abandoned on the hardwood floor, despite the wastebasket that sat in the corner.

I turned away in disgust. It was impossible not to recall the clean homey scent of Brock's place, the neat and welcoming atmosphere, sounds of laughter and comradery. Who'd have thought the werewolves were more civilized than the humans?

Sibby swore. "This is repugnant. I've been to less gross frat houses."

"What's he trying to do?" Maeve shook her head at the mess. "Relive his misspent youth? If he keeps this up, he'll have a heart attack or a stroke."

"Couldn't happen to a nicer guy," Sibby grumbled.

I shook my head. "It doesn't matter. I'm not his mother and soon I won't be his wife anymore. Let's do what we came here to do and get the hell out."

"Where are the photos?" Sibby asked.

"My office. Upstairs." I kept my eyes on the ground less I step in any nasty surprises.

But there was no avoiding them.

My heart sank as I saw the open office door.

"No," I breathed as I rushed forward and looked at the disaster that had once been my refuge.

The neat and tidy white desk that I had painstakingly refurbished lay broken in several pieces. My bookshelves had been tipped over, all the books and magazines I had saved lying in the pile.

And the albums….

I knelt on the floor beside the torn photos, the pages ripped out with a cruel viciousness I couldn't even comprehend.

"He trashed them all?" Sibby knelt beside me and picked up a ripped image that had been taken on her third birthday. She wore a pink sweater and a crooked party hat, her face smeared with blue icing.

She reached into the mess and found the other half of the image. Our mother, beaming down at her with pride.

"Maeve you really do look like her."

My eyes misted. "I never knew. That he hated me this much. What did I do to make him hate me this much?"

He knew what I'd been through as a kid. More than anyone other than my sisters Kyle knew how my life had been and what these memories meant to me. And he had intentionally destroyed them.

"You didn't do anything." Sibby put a hand on my shoulder. "My guess is, he's got a drug problem."

I wiped my eyes. "Really?"

She nodded. "I've seen it before. I used to work at a women's shelter and it all fits. The erratic behavior, his plea for money. He doesn't hate you because of anything you did, Alys. He hates you because of what he can't do."

"At least he didn't burn them." Maeve knelt on the other side of me and began picking up the pieces. "We might salvage some of these."

We collected the pieces of our past in silence until I heard the sound of a car door slam. Followed by a woman's laughter.

I handed my stack of photos to Sibby, who had retrieved a shoebox from my closet. Drug problem or no, Kyle would pay for what he had stolen from me and my sisters.

Our past, our history.

My hands clenched into fists and outside, thunder rumbled.

*It's not smart to piss off mother nature.*

CHAPTER NINETEEN

MAEVE

"What's she going to do?" I whisper-hissed to Sibby as Alys left the room.

"Not a clue." Sibby's blue eyes were wide.

Alys had been too quiet since Sibby had mentioned the possibility of Kyle having a drug problem. I hated when she turned inward. The silence she radiated was deafening. In the wake of Kyle's devastating betrayal, she would lash out. The question was, how?

Thunder rattled so loud that it shook the windows.

"Come on." Sibby picked up the box of destroyed photos. I grabbed the orchid and we hastened after Alys.

She stood on the landing, straight-backed and poised when Kyle staggered through the door. He wore wrinkled kakis and a beer-stained black polo shirt strained over his belly. His thinning baby-fine hair was disheveled. He was with a woman in her late twenties wearing a pleater micro-mini and way too much makeup for a small mountain town. Another prostitute? Where the hell did he get them, *Hookers-R-Us?*

Kyle's eyes were red-rimmed as he looked up at his wife. "What the hell are you doing here?"

Alys didn't speak. Her silence was more damning than any word shouted in anger. She surveyed him slowly from head to toe, her face neutral.

Through the open door, I saw the enormous pines that lined the drive bending, bowing to a mighty wind.

She was past anger, beyond fury. Alys was wrath incarnate. And the world around us responded to her rage.

"I see you've brought the whole family," Kyle smirked at me before his gaze settled on Sibby. He winked at her. "Want to join us?"

"Only if she's planning to fry your balls over an open flame," Sibby said sweetly. "Oh wait, my bad. You haven't got any balls."

I put a hand on her arm in silent warning. This wasn't about scoring points off of Kyle, even though I appreciated how he turned an unhealthy purple at the insult. The danger was a lot closer to home.

Kyle nodded to the box in Sibby's hand. "I see you found my little art project. That was my lawyer's idea."

Sibby turned pale at his words. Lightning hit one of those pines and there was a deafening crack as the wood split. Then a groan and a crash as half a tree landed across the driveway.

"Alys," I begged, scared to touch her, scared to let her stand there on her own and react. "Alys, don't lose it."

"He said that I shouldn't destroy anything of value." Ignoring the woman, the weather, everyone but Alys, Kyle headed up the stairs, a smirk on his unshaven face. "But I read between the lines. Of course, I didn't tear up all the photos. I saved a nice one of your mom. Something to jerk off to."

The whole house shook. I was thrown into Sibby as the earthquake rattled the house. We caught the banister and held on for dear life. Kyle wasn't so lucky. He tumbled down the stairs like a doughy bowling ball. Outside, the driveway began to crack under the strain. The hooker screamed and clapped her hands over her ears.

"Alys stop," Sibby shouted but her cries were lost as the windows around the house shattered. I pulled her down so she wouldn't fall.

As quickly as it had started, the quaking stopped.

"Goodbye, Kyle. I'd say it was nice knowing you, but I'd be lying." Alys turned and helped me and Sibby to our feet. She took the orchid from my trembling hands and guided us outside.

"That's it?" Kyle hollered. The fool was winded and blood streamed down his face but he chased after us. "That's all you've got?"

Alys climbed up into the Suburban and Sibby and I hastened to follow.

Once the doors were closed, Alys put the car in reverse and drove past where the Corvette was parked, and then onto the lawn to avoid the downed tree.

She braked and then turned to look out the back window.

Just as a sinkhole opened right beneath Kyle's car.

He screamed and darted back toward the house.

I blinked at Alys. A slight smile stole over her lips. "Gotcha where it hurts, didn't I?"

"What. The. Hell?" Sibby breathed.

Alys looked at her in the eye. "Money is the only thing Kyle values. And I just took his easiest source of cash from him. He won't have a way to pay his fancy lawyer now. Or the damn PIs."

"PIs?" Sibby and I asked in unison.

"I caught one this afternoon and took this off him." She

reached into her cupholder and pulled out a sim card. "He said he was one of several hired by Kyle's lawyer."

I clamped a hand over my mouth, afraid I was going to vomit. "Do you think they've seen anything…witchy?"

Sibby was the one who answered. "Hell no. If they had, they would have posted it on the internet. PIs follow the money and no lawyer could pay what a tabloid could if they had proof of magic."

I blew out a breath. Her argument made sense. "What about the house? Can't Kyle sell it?"

"Worthless. After that quake, the foundation will crumble soon enough. It'll cost more to fix the damage than the place would go for on the open market." She shook her head. "Kyle has no recourse now. And he'll be too busy scrambling to do more damage to our project."

"But he knows something," Sibby insisted. "He was baiting you. The house, the photos… He wanted you to react that way."

"What if he's looking to sell you to the tabloids?" And the nausea was back.

"What way?" Alys shrugged. "He had a witness who will state she didn't see me do anything but wait out an earthquake and then leave with my sisters. Even if there were cameras pointed at me, they didn't see anything. Kyle doesn't have a leg to stand on."

"What about the magic hunters?" I asked quietly. I couldn't blame her for reacting the way she had. Kyle had lashed out at her viciously and Alys had fought back. I probably would have done the same. But the potential repercussions from this were like ripples in a pond.

Alys blew out a breath. "Let's not borrow trouble, Maeve. Right now, I just want to see what a werewolf barbecue looks like. Are you still up for it?"

I exchanged a glance with Sibby, who nodded.

We drove in silence for a time. I stared out at the dark waters of the lake and tried not to panic over what had just happened.

There would be plenty of time for that later.

ALYS

I'd been checking my rearview mirror to make sure I wasn't being followed. The last thing I wanted to do was bring a clump of PIs down on the werewolves. It was tempting to drop my sisters at home and skip the event. We needed answers. Because what I had just done….

I'd controlled it. Used the magic to express myself. It had felt amazing. Cathartic even.

And I wanted to do it again.

Full dark had set in by the time we reached Brock's halfway house for wayward werewolves. Maeve looked pale and even Sibby was quiet, proof that I had scared them.

Maeve swallowed and met my gaze. "Maybe this isn't the best idea. I'm not feeling all that steady."

"All the more reason to be around them instead of regular people." I'd been thinking about it all afternoon. "You're worried you're going to enchant Kal and the kids by accident. If that happened, how would you explain it afterward, especially if someone else saw you?"

She swallowed.

"If you do it here," I gestured up the slope to where

orange lanterns crisscrossed between trees, "it doesn't matter."

"What do you mean it doesn't matter?" Sibby stepped forward.

"Because they already know about what we are. Just like we know what they are."

"Mutually assured destruction," a softly accented voice called from the shadows.

I turned and felt something inside me ease at his approach. "Brock."

"I'm glad you came. All of you." He stepped forward and took Maeve's arm, urging her up the slope. "Come on, I have some friends who are dying to meet you."

I was about to follow but realized Sibby hadn't moved. "You okay?"

She nodded too quickly to be believed. "Fine. I just need to make a phone call."

"You might want to head down to the boathouse," Brock hollered over his shoulder, making Maeve jump. "For privacy."

"Werewolves have excellent hearing. As you just saw." I touched her arm. "Come find us when you're finished."

She forced a smile and turned to the water and I jogged to catch up with Brock and Maeve.

The night was turning cool and the breeze off the lake made me shiver. Brock caught the gesture and raised his voice so the people on the patio could hear him "Nate. Bring some blankets out for our guests."

Nate had been sitting on the stone wall by the fire pit. He jumped up and disappeared inside the house.

"That's the first time I have ever seen a kid that age do what he was told without complaint," Maeve's tone was full of awe. "What's your secret?"

"He knows I'll eviscerate him if he embarrasses us in front of you," Brock spoke in a deadpan tone.

Maeve's jaw dropped.

"He's kidding," I said as Nate returned with the blankets. "Tell her you're kidding, Brock."

"Oh, he's not kidding," Nate said as he draped a green and purple blanket over Maeve's shoulders. "We all got the speech earlier today."

"Go man the grill with Devon and Alex," Brock ordered.

Nate vanished.

"Thank you," I called out as I wrapped the red and blue checked blanket around myself. Then smiled at our host. "We appreciate it."

"I should have thought of it before." Brock folded the last blanket, a yellow and black one most likely for when Sibby returned, over his arm. "Cold doesn't bother us. Our metabolisms are on average four times faster than a human's. We forget what it's like to feel its bite."

"Must be nice." The blanket was warm and soft and smelled like Brock. I tucked in tight and took my first deep breath, coming down off the high of using magic.

"Better?" When we both nodded, he started forward again. "I'll introduce you to the ladies, first."

He headed toward the gazebo. The same three females I had seen the last time sat there, though more strands of fairy lights had been wrapped around the railings and spindles. Probably for the benefit of our human eyes. A toddler in a brown suede Sherpa coat and pink jeans toddled between them. The little girl couldn't have been more than eighteen months old. Her big brown eyes latched onto me as we approached.

"Debbie, Ana, Simone, this is Alys Stevens and her sister Maeve Silver." He gestured for us to sit on the unoccupied section of bench. "Can I get you ladies anything? Wine?"

There was a collective agreement that wine would be amazing and Brock touched my shoulder in a gentle caress before heading to the kitchen.

"Silver?" The oldest of the three, a woman in her mid to late thirties, frowned. "Like the design team in town?"

Maeve nodded. "That's us. Silver was our mother's name. My husband is Inuit and his people didn't believe in family names. He actually legally changed his name to Silver when we married."

"Brava." The smallest of the three, a dark-haired beauty with a rich Latin accent, clapped in appreciation. "I wish more men would take their wives' names as a show of respect to the female line."

"Or how about everyone keeps their own identities and let the paperwork go hang?" The last woman, a buxom redhead with a Southern twang that indicated Texas more than North Carolina reached down to pick up the little girl who had been toddling toward the step. "Stay here, Lia."

"Debbie, are you saying you won't take my name when we are married?" The brunette raised an eyebrow.

The redhead—Debbie—hefted the baby up. "I'm saying I still haven't agreed to marry you, mate or no mate. You're a bossy pain in the ass most of the time, Ana."

"You know you love me." Ana made a theatrical kissy-face and took Lia from her and began murmuring to the girl in Spanish.

"You two are mates?" I blurted. "How does that work, exactly?"

"Brock hasn't told you yet?" Simone raised a brow.

"There's been a lot happening in my life." It was a crummy excuse but a valid one. I didn't think I wanted to know before. But curiosity got the best of me. "Is it much different than being married?"

All the women threw back their heads and laughed.

"What's so funny?" Maeve asked.

Ana rocked Lia back and forth even as she explained, "There is a world of difference between being mated and being married. Mated means you're emotionally bound to one person. Devoted to only that soul. Debbie was married to a real jackass and was pregnant with Lia when we met. But as soon as we saw each other for the first time we felt it."

"It?" I asked.

She nodded as Lia reached for the shiny pink barrette in her hair. "The connection. The bond. It's immediate for our kind. Unbreakable and it's eternal. Ow, *niña,* don't pull my hair."

Maeve was frowning at Debbie. "So, you left your husband to be with your mate?"

Debbie flinched and Maeve immediately retrenched. "Sorry, I didn't mean for it to come out all condescending. I'm not judging your choices. I want to understand."

"The problem is, you don't leave a werewolf," Ana said quietly. "Our kind needs a pack to survive and a female who abandons her male, even for a mate, is considered an outcast. Her family, her friends, all of them shun her."

Maeve made a growling sound in the back of her throat and I knew she was thinking about Kal.

"We're very fortunate that Brock took us in," Debbie added.

"We all are," Simone said. "He is the best Alpha I've ever known. And he even brings us wine."

That last bit was said a little louder and I turned to see Brock carrying a tray with five glasses in one hand and two bottles in the other. He stole my breath, standing silhouetted in the moonlight. So considerate, so gentle, and caring to those around him. Yet I'd seen the aftermath of his viciousness on Sunday morning. He asked for so little and gave so much.

No man could ever be sexier.

"Food should be ready in a few," he said as he set the glasses and bottles down and withdrew a corkscrew from his back pocket. He looked at me first. "Red or white?"

"Yes," I replied and he grinned down at me, the skin around his eyes crinkling with amusement.

It was there, just the way Debbie and Ana described it. A connection. Our special bond.

*Mate.*

Had it been between us all along? Maybe I had been too blind to notice. Set in my ways and driven to succeed. But he'd been paying attention.

Kyle had betrayed me in the worst way. I'd brought precious pieces of my past into my home and he'd defiled them. I knew Brock would have treasured them, would have asked questions, and laughed at some of the funny stories attached to my memories. He was aware of my moods, my needs, helping where he could, and never pressing for more than I could give.

He leaned down so Simone could whisper something in his ear. His gaze slid to me and our eyes caught and held.

Connection. Devotion. All there for the taking.

The question was, what was I going to do about it?

# CHAPTER TWENTY

## SIOBHAN

The sound of laughter and talking drifted down to where I sat huddled in the damp boathouse. Moisture seeped through the seat of my jeans, making the back of my thighs cold. I stared down at the white rectangle in my hand, wishing I knew what to say. That was the only reason I hadn't dialed his number. Who knew what would come flying out of my mouth?

Bad enough he worked for that asshole Kyle. But he'd encouraged the bastard to hurt Alys.

To hurt me.

And then the PI thing…. Were we being followed even now? When had it started? And why?

I thought of the terrible show of Alys's power. There had been a moment when I was sure all her pent-up rage would bring the house down on top of us. It was the first time I had cursed the source of my magic. Kinda hard to get turned on when I was afraid for our lives.

But just thinking about Sebastian, even after what I had found out. It got the ol' hormones firing. Knowing that pissed me off even more. Damn it, I shouldn't want him when he was actively hurting my sister. I barely knew him and what I knew wasn't a ringing endorsement.

What could I say to a man who I didn't even know? That I was angry and hurt? Would he even care? We had met twice and he'd indicated that he was interested. That was reason enough for me to keep my distance.

But the truth was, I was drawn to Sebastian. Intrigued by him. He radiated a sort of strength and surety I envied, even as I wanted to curl up closer to its source. Sebastian knew exactly who he was and what he wanted. And the way he looked at me made my heart race and my palms grow sweaty. I missed the feeling.

So where did that leave me? Back where I started. Needing to talk to him and not knowing what to say.

"Fuck it," I muttered and dialed. Plans were for people like Alys and Maeve. I always did better when I just let 'er rip.

He picked up halfway through the second ring. "Siobhan?"

"How did you know it was me?"

"I didn't," he murmured. "I was just hoping it was you."

His voice was a low purr and that accent felt like an auditory stroke. A sigh escaped before I remembered that I was supposed to be chewing him out.

"You told Kyle to destroy Alys's photos," I snapped.

There was a shifting sound. I squeezed my eyes shut, doing my best not to picture him reclining in a chair or, chocolate help me, lying back on a bed.

"No, I didn't. I intentionally told him not to damage anything of value." Sebastian sounded confident.

"Well, he didn't listen. He practically destroyed Alys's current project house. Smashed windows, threw paint, tore up the lawn."

"What are you talking about?"

"I'm not sure if that was before or after he tore up all of

the photos. The only pictures in existence of our mother." My voice trembled but I soldiered on. "I'm not like my sisters. I don't have a ton of memories of her. Hell, most of the time, I don't even remember what she looked like. Those pictures were all I had."

"Siobhan," he breathed. "I didn't want this. Kyle is…difficult. Irrational. If I knew he would do this, I would have told your sister's lawyer to suggest removing her mementos from the house. Please believe me. It was an accident."

My grip on the phone tightened. "And the private investigation? Why are you having us followed?"

He was silent.

"Am I under surveillance too? Or Maeve?" Her husband or her *children*?" My voice went up an octave on the last word.

"Just Alys," Sebastian said. "And Brock."

"Brock?" An icy tendril snaked through me and I looked around as if a surveillance team was going to scurry out of the woods. "Why would you be having Brock followed?"

More silence.

A laugh bubbled up but there was no humor in it. "I don't even know why I called you. It's not like you're going to own your part in this."

"Siobhan, try to understand. Your brother-in-law is my client. What he tells me is protected under attorney-client privilege. Hell, I shouldn't even be discussing this with you."

"Then why are you?" I shot back. "Why did you give me your card?"

"I don't know," he sounded genuinely puzzled.

He was a liar though. Capable of a great deal more than I would have believed.

"You knew who I was when you first approached me. Don't bother to deny it. What, were you hoping to get the inside scoop on Alys? Maybe try and seduce a little information out of me? Spill my sister's secrets over some pillow talk?"

"No, I would never do anything like—"

"Well guess what, pal? Alys doesn't *have* any secrets worth investigating. What you see is what you get with the women in my family." That was a huge lie, but I was hoping it would make my point if I added a genuine truth. "Even if you did manage to get me into bed, I would regret it for the rest of your life. Both minutes of it."

"Siobhan—"

I shut the phone before he could utter another word and then powered it down. I doubted he would call back but if he did, I didn't want to know about it.

Sebastian had been a sexy distraction, a bump in the road. Nothing more. It was time to move on with my life.

Sᴇʙᴀsᴛɪᴀɴ sᴛᴀʀᴇᴅ at the silent phone, unable to believe how quickly he'd lost control of the conversation. He checked his incoming calls, found her number, and dialed.

Right to voicemail. What could he say?

"Siobhan, I'm sorry for what happened." He was sorry that things were escalating. He wasn't a cruel being, not like his mother had been. He didn't want to cause needless suffering.

He couldn't give her answers, so he went with a request. "Please, call me back when you get this."

He'd had Siobhan on the hook, he'd sensed her interest. But then this call combined with the shocking news from Alys's attorney that she wasn't willing to settle.

Why had he given her his card so soon? It had been a foolish impulse. He should have asked for her number instead, brought her in closer before the truth was unveiled.

Sebastian had miscalculated, badly.

He always liked leaving himself a second way in with his targets. Part of what made him such an effective hunter was his attention to detail, his backup plans in place in case of unforeseen variables. Courting Siobhan, gaining her trust, had been riskier than playing the enemy lawyer. He thought he'd considered all the angles. Believed that he knew enough to bait his hook and reel her in. She was the outsider in her family, the wandering wild child. A rebel. Setting himself up as part of the enemy camp should have intrigued her even as it drove a wedge between her and her sisters and added pressure to all three.

Stress and strain led to magic use. And that was the ultimate goal, to harvest the magic at its ripest.

An enemy lawyer or romantic interest, it didn't matter to him. It was all a façade, a false face that would allow him to investigate the sisters more thoroughly, to develop a plan of attack regarding their abilities and how best to negate their powers when the time was right.

So why did Siobhan's accusation that he was courting her to help that idiot Kyle bother him? And what about that final cryptic statement?

*Even if you did manage to get me into bed, I would regret it for the rest of your life. Both minutes of it.*

"Master?" Louse called from outside.

Setting his phone down, Sebastian strode out the front door to where the shadows blended into the lawn. "What is it?"

"I need blood. Let me hunt the witches. Tonight," the sibilant voice hissed.

"It's not time yet." He turned back to the house, irritated that he'd come outside to turn down an idiotic request.

"But—"

Sebastian paused and glanced over his shoulder. "Need I remind you what happened the last time you disobeyed me?"

The shadow shivered.

Sebastian kept his tone low and smooth as he spoke, knowing the effect it had. "If you need blood, hunt an animal. Do not approach the witches."

No need to lay out the consequences. Louse knew what he meant.

His phone vibrated where he left it on the counter and Sebastian quickened his step. Had Siobhan called back?

But it wasn't Siobhan on the other end of the phone. "She's nuts! She destroyed my car! I want that bitch arrested."

Sebastian let out a breath. "Calm yourself, Kyle."

But Kyle was on a roll, his voice a few octaves higher than normal. "You came to me. Made promises. You said you would get me all her assets because I could sue the contractor for alienation of affection and get his money too. Those were your words and here my car is at the bottom of a sinkhole!"

Sebastian turned to stare out the window. "These things take time."

"You said if I got her riled enough that you would take care of Alys for me," Kyle sputtered. "Well, I've done my part. When are you going to do yours?"

"I specifically told you not to destroy her property," Sebastian growled. "And yet I hear you wrecked her project house as well as some of her personal keepsakes."

"Just get me my money," Kyle snapped. "Or I'll tell the cops everything."

And Sebastian was left staring at a silent phone for the second time that evening.

He let out a breath and rubbed his eyes. His contacts were bothering him. He went to the bathroom and took them out and then stared at his reflection. The brilliant Amethyst color glowed against the mirror. The only marker left of his heritage.

He set the contacts in the little case, added the saline solution to cleanse them, and then headed into his bedroom. The curtains were pulled back and he stared down at the lights of Eckhart and thought of his plan.

Kyle would need to be dealt with. The man was unstable and had quickly gone from being an asset to a liability.

Sebastian turned back to the front room and walked outside. "Louse, I have a job for you."

Time to retrench.

# ALYS

"Can I talk to you for a sec?"

I looked up from my plate of delicious barbecue to see Sibby approaching.

"You can use my office," Brock volunteered. "It's sound-proofed for privacy."

But Sibby was shaking her head. "No, I need to talk to both of you. Now."

I bristled at the tone but paused. Sibby's eyes were red-rimmed, a good clue that she'd been in tears.

Brock blinked once and looked to me for direction. At my slight nod, he got to his feet. "This way."

We followed him into the house through the open kitchen door. How they didn't have a million bugs inside was beyond me, but I quickly dismissed the thought as Brock held open a thick oak door and turned on the light. He held the door and Sibby marched past him into yet another beautiful space.

A fireplace sat in one corner and a leather couch was pressed back against one wall. A laptop was closed on a polished oak desk that was devoid of any other clutter and an oversized office chair sat opposite what must be a spectacular view of the lake.

I settled on the sofa and Brock leaned against his desk. We both watched Sibby pace. She was chewing on the corner of her left thumbnail, a habit she had since we were kids. It only manifested when she was reluctant to tell someone something because she knew it would upset the listener.

She'd done it on my wedding day.

Brock's gaze darted to me as if asking if we should prompt her. I shook my head slightly. She'd come to whatever her point was eventually.

Her hand fell to her side and she whirled on her heel. "Sebastian is having you followed. *Both* of you."

"You talked to him?" I barked.

"I had to," Sibby insisted. "I had to know if he knew anything about us."

She meant the magic.

Brock looked between the two of us. "Who's Sebastian?"

"Kyle's lawyer," I told him, but my focus remained on my sister. "And? Did you find out what you wanted to know?"

She ran a hand through her blue tresses. "Yes. No. I'm not sure. He said he's had people tailing both of you. He didn't mention anything supernatural but it's only a matter of time if they keep going. I thought you should know."

Air rushed out of my lungs and I looked at my GC. "I'm so sorry. I didn't mean to bring this to your doorstep." Fucking Kyle.

"I'm not worried," Brock put a hand on my arm. His touch was reassuring as he murmured, "The pack would sense anyone who came too close to our territory. We have precautions in place meant to keep werewolves at bay. I'm just not sure I understand why he would bother."

The sim card that I had lifted from the inept PI was still in my pocket. "Let's find out."

I pulled it from my pocket. "Do you have anything that can read this?"

Brock went to his desk and pulled open the top drawer. He pawed through a few items and brought out something that looked like a flash drive. "Smart card reader. Plugs right into a USB port."

I gave him the card and he loaded it into the device and then opened his laptop. Sibby and I flanked him on either side as he opened the files.

The first photo was from this afternoon, as I exited the attorney's office. Brock and me standing by my Suburban. Him putting a hand on my arm. You could tell we were deep in conversation. My shoulders were slumped and I appeared dejected and unhappy. The next was a series of slow-motion stills that ended with Brock driving off.

"That was right before I spotted the guy," I said.

Brock clicked to the next row that was dated three days ago. The first was a shot of Brock's truck, with Brock standing beside it, balancing three cups of coffee. It was parked in front of *Silver Demo and Designs.*

I frowned. "That's from Friday morning. Right after the closing. You stopped in to get your check and brought coffee."

There was nothing untoward about it though. He was my subcontractor and he brought me and Lora coffee. So why bother to photograph it?

"Wait, Friday morning?" Sibby looked at me. "You mean before you caught Kyle cheating?"

My stomach cramped. "Let's see what else he got."

I clicked on the next photo. It was of Brock's back as he headed into the office.

The next one he was opening the door. "I'm not sure what this has to do with anything," I muttered. Brock clicked to enlarge the next shot.

It was me, dressed in the clothes that I had worn to the closing, but looking less than daisy fresh. So that was after I caught Kyle. I had my head down as I disappeared into the office. The next was Brock's truck pulling up again. He looked over his shoulder, right at the camera.

"Did you know someone was there?" I asked.

He nodded. "I saw a guy with a camera but since we were downtown, I figured he was just a tourist doing some leaf-peeping."

The next shot was of Brock and me standing out in front of the office. The photographer had captured us in profile and I was looking up at him with my lips parted.

Then him helping me into the passenger's side of my car. The last shot from that day was the car heading out of Eckhart.

"I don't understand this." I straightened and winced as a muscle in my lower back sang out.

"Alienation of affection," Sibby murmured.

"What?" I asked.

"In North Carolina, if a spouse is having an affair, alienation of affection allows the other spouse to sue the other person for causing harm to a marriage."

My stomach dipped. "Wait, you're saying that Kyle is going to try and sue Brock even though he was the one buying hookers?"

Sibby's lips were compressed in a thin line. "Probably."

"Unbelievable." It was my turn to pace. "I should have opened the sinkhole under him instead."

Brock got up and looked at Sibby. "Thank you for bringing this to our attention. May I have a moment with your sister?"

Sibby nodded and then headed for the door.

Brock didn't get in my way as I strode the length of his

office. So many emotions warred inside me. Anger, humiliation, frustration.

"He'd been planning this." I bit out. "The bastard already had a lawyer and they had a strategy. It's not enough that he wants everything I have, he's coming after you too."

"It's okay, Alys."

"It's not okay. You haven't done anything wrong." The injustice of it was like a punch in the gut. It stole my breath and made me want to vomit all at the same time.

"I'm in love with another man's wife," he said quietly.

The words froze me in mid-step.

His gaze was intent on me, focused. "I knew you were my mate the moment we met. You were so strong, so sure. By turns demanding and generous. I have never met a more driven soul. But you were married. And human. Oblivious to the instinct that I had to fight all the time when I was with you."

"What instinct?"

"It's a niggling feeling right here." He put his hand over his chest, over his heart. "An urge to be near you. To be the first to help when you need it. To sate my curiosity about who you are, what you like, and what exactly it is that makes me crave more. I knew wanting all that was wrong because you could never be mine. But it didn't stop the longing."

On impulse, I covered the hand over his heart with my own.

"It's stronger now. And not just because you're done with Kyle." The gold in his eyes seemed to outshine the light in the room. "Whatever was in that empowerment brew, it has awakened more than just your ability to wield magic. I'm as drawn to you as I am to her."

My brows drew together. "Her?"

He gestured to the night sky, where the moon waned. "Your pull is greater. Constant, day and night. I'm caught in your orbit. I want so much from you. So much more for you. More than I have any right to ask. I want to heal your wounds and build you up so you could get back in the fight. I want to spend time with you without an excuse, but just because I crave your company and you enjoy mine."

That sounded amazing. And completely doable. But he moved closer and tilted my chin up to meet his.

"I want to make love with you. For hours, days, weeks on end. I want to pleasure you in a way a woman like you deserves and to leave you utterly spent and totally satisfied. But it's not enough for me to want all this, Alys. You need to want it, too."

And at that moment, I felt it. A sensation I thought was long gone, never to be experienced again. Desire. It burned hotter than my anger toward Kyle. Hungrier than that time Maeve and I had done a cleanse with nothing but lemon water for a weekend.

I licked my lips and stepped closer.

Someone started pounding on the door. "Alpha, come quickly."

Reluctantly, Brock pulled away and moved to the door. "What is it, Devon?"

The guy on the other side of the door looked a few years older than Brock. He had dirty blond hair cropped short and sleeves of tattoos etched over his well-muscled arms and peeking out beneath his white t-shirt. His gaze was a piercing gray. He looked past Brock and focused his attention on me. His words chilled my blood.

"There's something wrong with Maeve."

# CHAPTER TWENTY-ONE

"**M**aeve?" I pushed past Brock and shoved the werewolf ahead of me, urging him to show me where to go. "What happened?"

"We don't know."

"Where is she?" Brock barked.

"In the living room. Ana thought it better if we put her on the couch since she seemed unable to walk. That way we could tend to her wounds."

"Did she fall?" I asked as we sped down the hall and out into the great room.

I have no idea if Devon answered as I spied Maeve's green and purple blanket past the clustered werewolves. "Get them out of here, Brock," I ordered. "If she's scared, she'll enchant them all." If she hadn't already.

Sibby sat on the leather couch beside Maeve. There was glass embedded in her hands, which Sibby was picking out with tweezers and placing in a large salad bowl that sat on Maeve's lap.

"What happened?" I knelt next to my sister. She seemed

211

embarrassed and irritable but not frightened. That was something at least.

"I fell." She shook her head. "It was an accident. Too much wine. I was carrying the glasses to the kitchen. My foot must have snagged on a root. Or maybe a rock."

"Maeve," Sibby looked pained.

"It was an accident," Maeve repeated and then winced as Sibby plucked another shard of glass from her palm.

Sibby carefully removed the last piece of glass and then dabbed iodine onto the cuts with a cotton ball. "You need to tell her."

"Tell me what?" My head whipped back and forth between them. "What's going on?"

Maeve's face had lost all color and, as her eyes met mine, I knew that whatever she was about to say was going to change everything.

"I have MS."

I stared at her, uncomprehending.

"Multiple Sclerosis," Sibby said.

There was no sound but the ticking of a cuckoo clock.

*Say something.* "You're sure?"

Maeve shut her eyes. "It's not actually official yet. It's a pain in the ass to diagnose. The doctors need to rule a bunch of other stuff out first. But it's coming."

"How long?" I wasn't sure exactly what I was asking. How long had she suspected? How long had she been having symptoms?

How long had she and Sibby been keeping it from me?

"About six months," Maeve whispered. "I was having trouble with my eyes. Thought it was just middle-aged. It was Dr. Hagerty who suggested MS."

Dr. Hagerty was our optometrist. Six months. I turned to Sibby. "And how long have you known?"

Sibby finished bandaging Maeve and then looked me square in the face. "From the beginning."

I swallowed my hurt, swallowed my fear. Couldn't let them see.

"So, what's the treatment?" Multiple Sclerosis. I knew nothing about it, something I would change by morning. "What are they doing for you?"

"I need to be diagnosed first," Maeve said quietly. "Officially."

"Have you been to a specialist? Is our insurance coverage, okay? I should look into the policy for—"

"Just stop," Maeve barked. "Damnit, Alys. Stop trying to control everything! This is why I didn't want to tell you!"

Her face was mottled red and purple and her eyes were bright with unshed tears.

"Maeve," Sibby breathed. "Don't."

But Maeve wasn't listening. "This is what you do. You don't let yourself feel anything. You lock it down tight, ignore the pain. You've been doing it since Mom. Well, some things can't be fixed. Feelings can't be fixed like one of your houses. You can't fix me, Alys, because I'm not fucking broken!"

I stared at her, not knowing what to say. My whole body trembled. Maeve put her head in her hands and started sobbing. Sibby stroked her back and made soft murmuring sounds.

I stood up and backed away from them. Brock was hovering by the door. He'd heard every word. "Alys—,"

"Do me a favor. Get them back to Maeve's. I can't—" I swallowed and forced the words out. "I can't be here right now."

And I ran. Ignoring Sibby calling my name and chased by Maeve's ragged sobs that tore big bloody chunks out of my heart, I fled past the werewolves and out into the yard to the

Suburban. I fumbled the keys and cursed when I dropped them in the gravel.

After scooping them up, I turned the engine over, reversed out of the driveway, and then sped down the road.

I wasn't alone. Maeve's accusations rode shotgun. *Stop trying to control everything. You don't let yourself feel anything. You can't fix me because I'm not fucking broken.*

If that was how my sister—who I was closer to than anyone on the planet—saw me, then that's who I was.

A control freak. An emotional void. A fixer who over-stepped so she needed to be kept in the dark or she would make the sick person worse.

My vision blurred and I had to slam on the brakes so I didn't miss the turn to Witch Way. The Suburban fishtailed and gravel flew from tires as I pounded on the gas. I bumped down the road, uncaring of being jostled about, the car's undercarriage or anything that crossed my path. I just needed the serenity of Aunt Jess's place and time to regroup.

A lamp was lit inside the house. Had I ever thanked Sibby for waiting here for the electrician? I couldn't remember. But I wouldn't be in the dark any longer and it was because of my youngest sister's insistence that I should know.

A humorless laugh bubbled out of me. I'd told Brock that Sibby was the bad one. I should have had him check with Maeve first. Maeve and I worked together. I spent most of my free time at her house, with her kids. And she hadn't said a word.

I got out of the suburban, remembering at the last second to collect the shoebox of picture scraps and my orchid and carry them inside. I plugged in my laptop and waited impa-tiently for it to boot up. Research. I needed to see what the monster looked like. Needed to know what Maeve was facing. Forewarned and forearmed.

An hour later I sat back, left with more questions than

answers. Multiple Sclerosis was a chronic autoimmune neurological disease. The body attacks nerve coverings called myelin that disrupts the messages sent to the body from the central nervous system. There were different courses the disease could take, and from the dozens of accounts I'd read, it was highly individualized to each person it touched. Some people had trouble walking, others talking. Still others small motor functions, like writing. Some ended up in wheelchairs and needed constant care.

I sat back and rubbed my eyes. I had hit a wall, both physically and emotionally. I needed to talk to my sisters. I was afraid to talk to my sisters.

Someone knocked on the door, making me jump. I hadn't heard a car. Not that I had been paying attention.

"Who is it?" I called. Not my sisters. Would a soul-sucking magic hunter respond?

"It's me," Brock's reply was soft.

I opened the door and gestured for him to come in. "What are you doing here?"

"Are you kidding?" His jaw clenched. "I came right here after I brought your sisters back."

"Thank you for that."

Brock's brown eyes were hard, the gold muted. "You can't take off like that, Lys. Not after the display of power Sibby described you using earlier. You might as well have sent up a flare for the magic hunters."

Funny that I had forgotten all about magical dangers until he knocked. "You're right. It was stupid to take off on my own that way. "

He opened his mouth as though he were ready to continue arguing but then my words penetrated. "It was?"

I nodded and wrapped my arms around myself. "I'm not used to this."

"Used to what?"

215

"Any of this mess." I gestured at the laptop with the MS blog and the tattered box of photos and then over to the greenhouse. "When did this become my life?"

Tears filled my eyes. It was wrong, all of it. I had magic I couldn't use to fix problems that grew bigger with every heartbeat.

He studied me a moment and then pulled me into his arms. "Come here, possum. Let me hold you."

I went willingly into his arms. My tears were silent as they ran down my cheek in a steady stream.

Brock held me close, not asking for anything in return. He offered comfort and his solid, reassuring presence slowly seeped into the cold dark places inside me and allowed me to draw a shuddering breath.

And then I said what I had meant to say before my world had collapsed in on itself. "Kiss me, Brock."

MY MOTHER USED to read romance novels. Dirty ones filled with tawdry sex scenes. When I was about fourteen, she caught me reading one. She whisked the book away from me but the next day after school the bodice ripper was waiting for me on the counter. Several paperclips had been inserted between a few of the pages.

"Now Alys," she'd said, her honey-filled accent thick. "I think you're too young to be readin' these sorts of books. But seeing as I was about your age when I picked up the habit, I can't very well deny you. So here's the deal. The clips mark the sex parts. If you feel you are ready to read them, you can just remove the paperclip. If not, skip on to the next bit. Either way, it's still a fun story."

Consider this your paperclip warning. You can skip on to

the next chapter and I will catch up with you there. But I have a werewolf to shag and I intend to do it thoroughly.

Because I *always* removed those paperclips.

"Are you sure?" Brock's eyes glowed in the low light. "There's no rush."

In answer, I tugged him toward the bedroom. "Speak for yourself."

A deep chuckle rumbled through him. His hands moved to my face. I leaned into the touch, enjoying the heat that radiated off of him, the gentleness. No man had ever touched my face the way Brock did. The tender caress was somehow even more intimate than the act of sex itself. He conveyed so much with a look, a touch, silent, stoic support.

We didn't bother with the lights. His hands moved to my hair even as I slid my palms up over his chest. There wasn't a bit of him to spare. All lean muscle stretched over long bones. I'd seen him shift and change and part of me still wondered how exactly that worked.

The other part was too busy rediscovering the way desire could pool in the pit of my belly. Sensation zinged through my limbs, awakening a trembling need I had all but forgotten.

And then he kissed me.

His lips brushed over mine once, then again, coaxing, beckoning. My own mouth parted in invitation. He took me up on it, deepening the kiss. Our tongues touched and danced until I broke away, needing air.

"Lys," he breathed while trailing kisses down the side of my neck. My hands snaked around his back. I tugged the cotton shirt out of the waistband of his jeans. I needed to feel the smooth warmth of his skin.

Heat and connection radiated through me. My touch sparked something in him too. The gold in his eyes glowed brighter and he attacked my clothing as though it were an enemy. One he was hell-bent on defeating because it was the only thing keeping us apart.

Fabric ripped and fell away under the onslaught. I shivered.

He paused with his hands on my bra. "I'm sorry."

"What for?"

"I frightened you."

A laugh burst out of me.

Those glowing eyes narrowed. "You aren't afraid."

"No, Brock. I'm not afraid of you. I never have been."

He shook his head. "How is that possible?"

It occurred to me that this might have been a problem for him. "Have women been afraid of you before?"

I heard him swallow. "No woman I've ever been with knew me. What I am. They never saw the monster."

"But the werewolves—"

"Pack is like family to me."

He'd never been with a werewolf. Or anyone who knew he was one. I considered what that must have been like for him, holding himself on a tight leash. Seizing control of the baser instincts because his partner wouldn't understand. Would be afraid of him.

He'd been right there, under my nose the whole time. We'd both been alone, unsatisfied. So much time wasted. Anger mingled with the desire inside me at the unfairness of it.

A gust of wind pushed open the unlatched windows filling the room with the cool scent of the night.

"I've seen the monster that lives in you. You won't hurt me. I know that you will do whatever you can to keep anything from harming me." I took off my bra and then reached for him. "Don't hold back, Brock. Not with me. Not ever."

His hands cupped my breasts fingers sliding over my

nipples. They responded to his touch as much as the cool night air, pebbling tight as though asking for more.

He shook his head even as he caressed my breasts. "You don't know what could happen. *I* don't know what could happen."

I pushed closer and reached for him, stroking him through his jeans. "Let's find out then."

His eyes shut leaving me in total darkness. After giving him one final caress, I withdrew far enough so I could make quick work of my shoes and socks, pants, and underwear. When he opened his eyes once more, I stood before him, my skin reflecting the golden glow of his gaze.

I'd expected him to lunge for me. Wanted it even. It had been years since any man had seen me naked and even though I knew Brock wanted me, it was strangely vulnerable to be naked before him.

The old insecurities surfaced. I remembered who and what I was. Almost fifty. Sagging breasts, silver hairs, not so trim hips and thighs. He was young, fit, perfect. Why would he want to be with me?

He took his time perusing me. I could feel his gaze the same way I had felt his touch. Slow, taking in every detail that my eyes couldn't see but knew that he could.

But Brock wouldn't judge me the way Kyle had. The little digs about arm flab or cellulite were part of what had shut me down years ago. Why share yourself with a person who didn't appreciate everything you were? Who actively tried to make you feel bad instead of good?

I forced my shoulders back, lifted my chin. I wouldn't let a man make me feel less than. Not ever again. My body had served me well and I was damn proud of it.

The wind swirled around me, lifting my hair up, and splayed it out like a banner.

JENNIFER L. HART

Brock went to his knees and pressed his face to my belly. He inhaled deeply, as though scenting me. "I'm not worthy."

My fingers threaded through his thick hair, enjoying the soft texture that was in direct contrast to the rough stubble pressed up against my abdomen. "I think you are."

"Lys," he breathed me in again, and just that, the idea that he was desperate to fill his lungs with my scent made me wet. Made me ready for him.

I lifted my right leg and placed it over his shoulder. I was open completely. He fell on me then the way I had anticipated. Control gone, replaced by rabid hunger. His hands gripped my ass, holding me in place, even as his mouth went for my core. The first stroke of his tongue sent shockwaves through me. The second went even deeper. I cried out as he licked me. Had anything ever felt as good as Brock exploring my female flesh?

Hail pounded down on the roof and thunder rumbled in the distance, but I was barely aware of it as he devoured me, consumed me.

The leg on the floor began to shake as my release drew nearer. I was tempted to let him finish me off. He seemed more than happy to keep going.

But I wasn't ready to lose control yet.

I tugged him away from my sex. He growled at me and kept going.

"Brock, stop," I commanded.

He paused. His shoulders heaved as he fought for control.

I lowered my leg to the floor and then sat back on the bed.

There was something no longer human about him as he rose to loom over me. His face glistened from my wetness and I almost orgasmed on the spot.

"Lose the pants." I nodded to his groin.

He tore them free from his body, uncaring of the damage.

The sound of material being shredded made me grin. No, Brock wasn't being careful anymore.

He prowled up the bed, hovering over me. He was hard everywhere and I had to do a doubletake at the size of him. Having Kyle's bait and tackle as my most recent frame of reference hadn't prepared me for Brock in all his glory.

His gaze was on my face and he must have sensed my hesitation because instead of falling on me, he rolled onto his back. His chest rose and fell in those great, heaving gasps as though he were still fighting with himself not to lose it.

I appreciated the reprieve. Brock was a whole lot of were-wolf. I appreciated his wildness. Craved it. Even though I was no blushing virgin, some things a woman had to take at her own pace.

He jumped when my fingers caressed his arms. I touched him lightly, gently. It was instinctive as though I were trying to soothe his inner beast. And he did relax as I made my way over his pectorals, down the eight pack of cut muscle. A puff of air escaped when I found his length and stroked just as teasingly, enjoying the way he shifted and twitched.

*Mine.*

The thought belonged to me and it didn't. It was covetous, greedy, and claimed ownership. Past the point of nerves, I rose up until I could straddle him. Then slowly lowered myself onto him.

At the first contact, Brock threw his head back. Tendons stood out as he arched beneath me even as I slipped down his shaft.

I moved slowly, enjoying the feel of opening for him and taking even more within. My eyes would shut and then snap open because I adored looking at him. As I rose up those gold eyes locked on mine. He breathed my name as I slid even deeper onto him.

Connection.

One more lift and then a sharp plunge and he was in as far as he could go.

The shutters banged against the house. Lightning flashed and I arched back, lost in the feel of our mating.

Brock sat up, wrapped his arms around me as though afraid that I would vanish. The move drove him even deeper. A groan tore from me. His lips fastened on one nipple as I writhed in his lap.

"More," I whispered, not sure what I was asking for, but positive that I needed it.

In response, he lifted me from him long enough so he could kneel. Then he eased me back down. His arms ran along the length of my spine, one slightly higher than the other, bracing my back. The position changed the angle of penetration slightly and gave him the leverage to thrust.

A tear tracked down my cheek. Another followed it. Brock didn't ask about them, just kissed them away even as he made love to me.

It was all too much. His tenderness and strength and the way he used his body to pleasure mine. His whispered words pushed me over the edge.

"I love you, Lys."

It all froze. The wind, the banging shutters, the tears, our bodies. I clenched up tight on him and let it all go.

Distantly, I heard him groan. My release must have triggered his. Good thing because I was tapped out. We clung to each other in the aftermath of the storm. Trying to recall who and what and where we were.

Not that it mattered. We were together. And that was enough.

# CHAPTER TWENTY-TWO

The sound of a buzzing pulled me from the deepest sleep I could remember. I woke warm and sated with my head on Brock's chest. Outside the window, birds twittered their early morning greeting. It would have been perfect.

Except for the damn buzzing.

"You awake?" Brock's fingers trailed the length of my spine.

I turned my face to look up at him. "Hi."

He smiled at me. "Hi yourself."

He didn't call me beautiful and I found that I was glad. Being called beautiful meant that others were less so in his eyes. I didn't want to be compared to any woman. I didn't want to feel like I had to compete. I wanted to be seen as I was and valued for myself and what I could contribute.

"What are you thinking?" Brock asked.

"You can't tell? And here I thought you could read my mind."

He chuckled and pulled me tighter into his arms. "No, I guarantee that you are still a mystery to me."

I snuggled back into him, enjoying waking up with him, lazing with him for a few moments before we started our day.

Then winced as I thought about all that was waiting for me. "I wish we could just stay here all day."

"Who says we can't?"

I sat up. "Well, there's this little thing called work, in case you've forgotten."

"I haven't." He stretched out, looking utterly scrumptious in my bed. "But until the numbers for the replacement windows come in, there isn't too much more we can do on the house."

"Frigging Kyle." I gritted my teeth as I recalled the damage. "I swear if he costs me my whole design plan, I will have his guts for garters."

Beside me, Brock set up. "Can I make a request, Lys?"

When I nodded he said, "Your ex isn't welcome in your bed again. Not even his name."

I laughed. "That is a rule I can live with." But my amusement faded fast. "I need to talk to my sisters. Especially to Maeve."

He nodded. "Yeah, I figured you would. That was ugly last night. I have never seen you two fight."

"We usually don't." I let out a sigh. "It's Sibby who I fight with. Maeve avoids conflict."

He stroked a hand down my arm. "You're scared for her."

It wasn't a question but I answered as though it had been. "And Kal and her kids. There's just so much they don't know about that disease and each case is as individual as the person who has it. She must be so scared…."

I trailed off as the light dawned. "No wonder she is having so much trouble controlling her magic. Her power comes out when she's afraid."

Brock frowned. "What triggers yours?"

"Anger."

He blinked. "So should I be worried about what happened last night?"

I grinned at him. "Not even a little bit."

"Explain it to me." Brock leaned back in the bed again. "I'm curious about how this works for you."

"I think...I think it's not just being angry. I think that it's just that anger is the emotion I stuff down the most often, so it's like I have a well of it ready to tap into. But after what happened last night, I think it's probably any strong emotion that calls it to me."

He tucked a lock of hair behind my ear. "Well, that's good to hear, since I plan on making you as not angry as I can for as long as you will let me."

I wanted to ask what he meant but the buzzing, which had paused, started up again.

"I better get that." Brock slid out from beneath me and strode naked to where what was left of his pants remained. "Two calls before six AM is never a good sign."

I admired the view as he opened his phone. "What's up, Nate?"

Whatever Nate said changed his entire countenance. His shoulders squared with military precision as he barked, "When was the last time you saw her?"

I got up and snagged my bathrobe. My intent was to give him privacy but he caught my arm as I passed him. Those gold-rimmed irises pleaded for me to stay.

So, I stayed.

"We'll be there soon to help with the search." Brock disconnected.

"Search? What's going on?"

He let out a breath and started gathering what was left of his clothing. "Debbie and Lia are missing."

"What? Are they sure?"

He nodded. "Ana woke up and said they were both gone. She figured maybe Lia was being fussy and that Debbie took her out for some fresh air. But they've been gone for over an hour. Debbie's Chevy is still in the garage and there was no note which is unlike Debbie. She knows Ana worries."

I recalled what the werewolf women had told me the night before about the pack Debbie had belonged to and the husband she'd left because she found her mate. "Do you think her ex might have something to do with it?"

"At this point, I'm not going to rule anything out." He looked helplessly at the scraps of clothing in his arms. "Damn it."

I took the garments from him. "You'll get there faster if you run."

He blinked at me. "My truck…?"

"I'll bring it when I come by to help. I want to talk to my sisters first. Sibby has the most knowledge about magic. Maybe she can find something that will let us help you."

Brock grabbed me and pulled me to him. His lips covered mine in a kiss that was as different from the ones we shared the night before as night was from day. There was passion, but also gratitude.

"Thank you," he pressed his forehead to mine and then stepped back. "I'll change in here so you don't have to watch. Just open the doors to let me out in about two minutes."

I left him to it and went straight to my phone and dialed Sibby's number.

"Alys?" Her voice was filled with early morning frogs.

My knuckles were white as I gripped the phone. "I need you here. Now. Both of you. As soon as possible."

No hesitation. I heard fabric rustling and the creek of a floorboard. "We're on our way."

## MAEVE

"So what exactly did Alys say?" I asked Sibby as we headed back out to Witch Way in my minivan.

"Just that she needs us." Sibby eyed me carefully. "You look like shit."

Appropriate since I also felt like shit. Being wracked with guilt until the wee hours in the morning will do that to a girl. "I'm fine."

"Liar."

I blew out a breath. "Sibby, for the love of chocolate, let it go."

"Didn't anyone ever tell you that confession is supposed to be good for the soul?"

It hadn't been a confession though. It had been an outright attack. My leg had frozen up and I'd tripped on nothing and gotten two fistfuls of glass. Between the pain, the shame, and the fear which had been doubled because I'd been worried about enchanting the werewolves with my fear, I'd lashed out at Alys. And now I had to figure out a way to apologize for being a turbo bitch.

"Isn't that Brock's truck?" Sibby asked as we pulled up in front of the cottage.

Since she'd ridden in it just last night, I figured that was a rhetorical question. I parked behind Alys's Suburban and we slid to the ground. Alys must have been pacing the living room because she flung open the door the second my feet hit gravel. She wore skinny jeans and an oversized sweatshirt and sneakers on her feet.

She greeted us with an announcement. "Lia and Debbie are missing."

"Shit," Sibby said even as I asked, "Was it the ex?"

Alys shook her head. "No. Brock called a few minutes ago and said they verified he's still in Texas."

"Doesn't mean he didn't hire someone to take them." Sibby's tone was dark.

I wondered what my youngest sister had been through that made her so cynical, but it wasn't the time to investigate. Instead, I turned to Alys. "What can we do to help?"

"The pack is combing the area around the lake, trying to pick up their scent. I thought maybe there was something we could do." Her gaze slid to Sibby. "Some witchery."

Under normal circumstances, I knew Sibby would make Alys squirm and admit that she'd had been right and Alys had been wrong. But a little girl's life might be on the line so all my youngest sister said was, "Are you sure that's smart? Intentionally using more magic?"

Alys looked at me. "I used it yesterday out of spite over some old photos and vandalism. I think it's worth the risk to find Debbie and Lia. But this isn't just my decision."

"Yes." If it had been Bella or Philip missing, I wouldn't have hesitated. I could do no less for little Lia. "I say we do it."

Sibby nodded as well. "Let me check the books. There might be something about different ways to use our magic."

Sibby went into the greenhouse and I made to follow her. Alys's hand touched my arm lightly, causing me to pause.

"I'm sorry," she said.

My lip trembled. "Alys, you have nothing to be sorry for. I ambushed you with the news. It was a shitty thing to do and I'm the one who is sorry."

"I wish," Alys took a deep breath and then released it. "Damn it, Maeve. I wish you could have talked to me about what was going on. I wish I didn't have my head so far up my ass that I missed all these things about people who matter to me."

The hurt in her gaze gutted me. There was only one thing I could say that might make her feel even a little bit better. "Kal doesn't know either."

"What?" She blinked at me.

"It wasn't just you. I didn't want to tell anyone that was a regular part of my life. People I look in the eye every day. People who would feel sorry for me. I thought…if I could just keep a lid on it for as long as possible, then maybe I could have a normal life. At least until I knew for sure."

I couldn't meet her eyes as I told the heartfelt truth. "Telling you, or Kal…it makes it real. And if it's real, I don't know what I'm going to do."

Suddenly, her arms were around me. I hadn't been prepared for the embrace and my nose bumped her shoulder. Alys hugged me the way she did everything else—fiercely.

"It will be okay," she whispered. "We will find a way forward together."

I hugged her back, fighting the tears that threatened. My body trembled from all the raw emotion coursing through me. I hadn't realized how much I had needed her support until she offered it freely.

"I'm glad you had Sibby to talk to," she mumbled into my hair.

229

"She's been amazing," I admitted. "A pain in the ass of course, but amazing." My sisters were the best people I knew. I didn't deserve them. Either of them.

Behind us, Sibby cleared her throat. "I think I found something."

I pulled away, rubbing the sore spot on my nose where it had connected with Alys's collarbone.

Sibby set the massive tome on the table. "It's an enchantment to find someone who is lost. I don't know if we have all the necessary plants. But it will take all three of our powers to activate. Plus, we need something that belongs to the missing."

I read over her shoulder and raised my eyebrows at the list of ingredients. "I think we have most of that here. And Alys and I are always raring to go. It'll take a little bit of time to steep. Otherwise, we should be good to go. What's the problem?"

"Me," Sibby said. "To find the missing, mother nature needs to scry, the enchantress needs to dose the items and the traveler needs to invoke the spell. But I can't access my magic without—"

"Without desire," I said grimly.

Alys looked thoughtful. "Maybe not."

We both turned to face her and I was shocked to see that she was blushing.

"Brock…well he and I…that is last night…"

Sibby made an impatient noise. "You got it on. And?"

"And I sort of tapped into my magic from a different angle."

"A different angle," I repeated.

"You mean you went all mother nature when the two of you got freaky with it?" Sibby summarized.

"Yeah. I think that maybe we can call our magic with any strong emotion, not just the one that triggered it."

The idea of that scared the hell out of me. I was already worried about enchanting Kal when I was frightened. But if I could do it when we were making love….

"Maeve sit down," Alys ordered. "You're staggering on your feet."

I leaned against the counter and closed my eyes. Counted to three. "Okay."

"Do you need a paper bag to breathe into?" Sibby asked.

I shook my head. "I'm good."

"Liar."

I glared at my youngest sister. "You really are a pain in the ass."

She refocused on Alys. "I hear what you're saying but we don't have time to experiment and see what trips my trigger right now. We have to go with desire."

Alys nodded grimly. "Then there's one more ingredient we need."

# CHAPTER TWENTY-THREE

### ALYS

"Ma'am, you can't go in there." The busty blonde secretary tried to block me from my destination.

I gave her a look of pure withering disdain and she shrank back even as she said, "He's in a meeting,"

Ignoring her, I shoved the door open with my shoulder. Sebastian's office was much fancier than my attorney's office. It was sleek and modern instead of old and musty. The aesthetic was austere in the extreme. Chrome and glass, black lacquered bookshelves, track lighting. Everything screamed cold and competent.

Just what I would have expected from the man.

Sebastian emerged from a door to the left. I heard the telltale sound of flushing. He paused when he caught sight of me.

"Mrs. Stevens." His smile was not all that pleasant as he eyed me.

"I'm sorry, sir." The blonde apologized from behind me.

"It's all right, Brandy," he murmured. "Shut the door."

Sebastian didn't return to his desk chair. Instead, he

leaned against the glass table and crossed one ankle over the other.

"I don't like you," I said to him.

He raised a brow but didn't comment.

"And I'm onto your little plot to help Kyle sue Brock. It won't work."

"And why not?"

"Because the only person responsible for alienating affection between me and Kyle is Kyle. I have bank statements and witnesses that will back up my claim. You could drag this out just to be a bastard, but in the end, you will lose."

Something sparked in his eye. "I never lose."

"Everyone loses. But that's not why I'm here." Sibby was going to kick my ass up and down Main Street. "My sister needs you."

I'd shocked him. Sebastian wasn't the type to overly emote. But the way his lips parted told me what I needed to know.

"Your sister won't return my calls," he murmured.

"That's because you hurt her. And Sibby runs when people hurt her. You do it again, and I will eviscerate you."

His lips turned up. "I like you, Mrs. Stevens."

I didn't give a shit. "Listen, a mother and child are missing. And I am asking you, for Sibby's sake, to join the search party. We're gathering at Brock's place. Your PIs have the address. If you really want to prove yourself to my sister, you will come and help us."

I turned and stalked out, not waiting for his answer.

SEBASTIAN STARED at the empty doorway where Alys Stevens had exited. She was so incredibly strong. The magic had been weaving itself through her soul until the two had almost become one. That sort of power would sustain him for years.

But he didn't want just one sister. He wanted all three.

A missing mother and child. A werewolf, if they were meeting at Brock's. Sebastian frowned. The weres had excellent senses. It was why he had ordered the PIs to only follow Alys and the Alpha in town, where their scents would mingle with other people. Nothing and no one should have been able to abduct a mother and child out of their midst.

Except….

Sebastian got to his feet and retrieved his coat from the hook. Brandy glanced at him as he strode by. "Mr. Jones, where are you going?"

"Out," he replied. He waited until the elevator doors closed behind him and then called his magic and traveled to the property he had rented.

"Louse!" he called.

No answer.

He searched the slim shadows, hunting for the wraith. Nothing. Sebastian let out a disgusted breath and went inside to change into something more appropriate for stalking through the woods.

It was time to hunt.

ALYS

I parked Brock's truck in the drive behind Maeve's minivan. I hoped I was right about Sebastian Jones. That the attorney would show up for Sibby to give her the lust-filled jolt she needed.

Sibby didn't have to forgive him. In fact, I hoped she wouldn't open her heart to the cold man who'd been ready to destroy my life and Brock's for a paycheck. But that was a worry for another day.

The air at Brock's was much different than it had been the day before. People were running in and out of the house and over toward the gazebo. Brock was there. So were Ana and Simone. Simone had her arm around the younger woman. They were staring down at something, a map most likely. No sign of Maeve or Sibby.

I spied Nate hurrying up the hill and called out. "Have you seen my sisters?"

"In the kitchen." He barely slowed his pace, his motions preternaturally quick.

I headed inside and spied Maeve perched on a stool, her bandaged hands plucking orange flowers off a plant and dropping them into a mortar. Sibby stood at the stove stirring something that smelled like the cesspits of hell."Holy crotch-rot, Batman. Ugh, no wonder they're all outside," Sibby turned her face away from the fumes. "I don't ever remember Mom or Aunt Jess brewing something that smelled this nasty."

"Are you sure you did it right?" I moved to the window over the sink and cranked it open.

"I'm doing the best I can, Alys," Sibby snapped. "And where is whatever you had to get in town?"

"It'll be here." I hoped. "Is there anything I need to do?"

"Open these," Maeve pointed to a pot of plants with white buds tightly closed. "The recipe says they need to be in full bloom."

I hesitated, unsure of how to go about funneling magic so precisely. I never had before. Even creating the sinkhole that swallowed Kyle's car had been a major expenditure of power. The difference between throwing a bucket of paint at the broad side of a barn and writing calligraphy. One took brute force and strength, the other skill and discipline.

"Maybe I should take it outside."

They were too focused on their own tasks to pay me any heed.

I plucked up the plant and then moved to a picnic table overlooking the lake. After setting the plant down, I cupped my palms over the top of it and tried to tap into those feelings that seemed to bring forth my magic. Anger, fear, desire. I'd felt them all acutely.

My lids drifted shut and I pictured Lia's chubby cheeks. Imagined her scared and lost. Debbie might be hurt. My heart rate increased my palms grew damp. I felt it then, the trigger.

I didn't grip it with both hands and pull as I had done

with the sinkhole. I touched it, lightly, barely scraping a mental nail over it.

I reached out with my mind to the plant, could feel it turning toward me. Almost there…

There was a crack and I jerked back instinctively.

"Lys." Warm hands settled on my shoulders.

My gaze went from Brock to the plant, which had busted out of the little clay pot and crept over the picnic table and down to the ground below. "Does that look like full bloom to you?"

He didn't smile but the hand on my arm squeezed.

I turned to face him. "Any news?"

He shook his head. "We're heading out to search."

I bent down and began plucking several of the flowers off the still-growing plant. "I need to stay here. Finish the potion with Maeve and Sibby. Once I do, we can help with the search."

"Nate's coordinating the teams." He pointed his thumb to the gazebo. "Check in with him before you go. And make sure you have your cell with you, fully charged and on before you head out."

I turned into him and wrapped my arms around him. "I will. We'll let you know if our magic uncovers anything."

He squeezed me tight and did that thing where he just breathed me in for a moment. As though my scent gave him strength.

I watched him move back over to the gazebo and then plucked another few flowers before heading back inside.

"Is this right?" I dumped the flowers on the cutting board beside Maeve.

She blinked down at them. "You got all these from that one little plant?"

"Er, I sort of grew them into Brock's picnic table."

She picked up two blossoms and added them to her

mortar and pestle. "This is more than enough. Would you grind these down in a clockwise motion? I need to go find something of Debbie's and Lia's for us to enchant."

"The more personal the better," Sibby added.

My hands wrapped around the cool ceramic and I took over for her.

"I don't want her going out into the woods," Sibby muttered once Maeve was out of earshot. "She's had a few too many incidents lately. Having her out there searching is a bad idea."

I felt the same way but didn't know how to broach the topic with Maeve. "And how do you propose we keep her here? Tie her to a chair?"

She shook her head. "All I know is that I have a bad feeling about all of this."

"Sibby, I doubt anyone has a good feeling when a child goes missing."

"At least she and Debbie are together. That's enough." Sibby nodded at my mortar and pestle. "Add the mixture to the brew."

I moved to stand beside her, trying to breathe through my mouth. Maeve returned carrying a stuffed doll and a gold necklace that read Debbie.

"Here goes nothing," I said and added the contents of the mortar to the brew.

The change was immediate. Instead of the bubbling stink of green glop, the pot now contained a pinkish liquid that smelled of honey and cloves and something else that I couldn't quite define.

"Wow, talk about a makeover," Maeve stared down into the pot in awe. "So, what's next?"

"Next, you're supposed to douse the items with the potion. Then Alys can scry for their location."

"Only problem is I have never scryed before," I said.

"It's pretty simple. Mostly we need your connection to the Earth. Plus, a map and this."

Sibby reached into her pocket and pulled out a transparent crystal. It caught the light streaming through the kitchen window. "I found it in a drawer in the greenhouse. I think it was Mom's."

I took the delicate chain from her hands. "It was. I remember her wearing it."

I cleared my throat and then said, "Okay Maeve. Get to work dipping the items. Nate has a map at the gazebo."

Nate had his back to us as we approached and I saw that he was on the phone.

"Any news?" I asked when he hung up.

There was news. I could tell by his pallor that it wasn't great. "They found Debbie. About five miles from here, in wolf form. Something messed her up pretty badly."

"A bear?" I asked. "Or maybe a mountain lion?"

He shook his head. "Nothing like that could take on a werewolf and live to tell the tale."

"Any sign of Lia?" Sibby asked.

Nate bowed his head.

And that was the moment that Sebastian Jones arrived.

# CHAPTER TWENTY-FOUR

## SIBBY

"What the hell is he doing here?" I looked to Alys who sagged in relief. How could she possibly look relieved after the news Nate had just relayed. Unless…

Her gaze met mine. "You needed a jolt."

My jaw dropped. "So you called him?"

"No, I went to see him. We need your powers active if we want to find Lia. It's the only way."

I couldn't fault her logic, cold and calculating as it was. "He's Kyle's lawyer."

"He owes us for those photos. And he's another body to help us look for a little girl. Use him and discard him. He deserves nothing else from you." She put a hand on my shoulder and squeezed. "I'm going to go bring Maeve up to speed."

Sebastian approached cautiously as if he knew none of us were happy to see him. He wore dark jeans and a red button-down shirt and hiking boots. Clearly, he had come to help with the search.

My arms went around myself. Alys said I was the one

who always concocted the harebrained schemes. But I didn't feel any desire for the man in front of me, not after what he had allowed to happen. What he had inadvertently encouraged.

"Siobhan," he said, that oddly muted gaze of his roving over my face. "Where is everyone else?"

"Out looking." I was aware of Nate behind me, trying really hard not to stare and that didn't help with my lack of desire. "Follow me."

I led Sebastian down the hill toward the boathouse.

"I brought bottles of water and protein bars for the searchers," Sebastian said as we walked. "They're in my trunk."

"That's thoughtful of you."

"Have the police put out an Amber Alert yet?"

Shit. Alys hadn't thought this through. Of course, a normal guy like Sebastian would be expecting us to follow the conventional procedures for locating a missing child. But werewolves had better noses than even the best K-9 unit. And the mortal authorities weren't equipped to deal with something that could severely incapacitate a mother werewolf.

We'd reached the boathouse. I turned and looked up at him. "I want to hire you."

"What?" His blond brows drew together.

"As my attorney." Because I needed that whole attorney-client privilege thing to work for me rather than against me.

"Siobhan—"

"How much?"

"My standard rate is two hundred dollars an hour."

My jaw dropped.

He shrugged in an *I'm that good* kind of way.

"How do you even sleep at night?" Grumbling, I reached into my jeans pocket and pulled out the contents. "All I have is a twenty. What does that get me, about six minutes?"

He shook his head. "Siobhan, I don't want your money."

"Too damn bad." I clapped the mangled bill into his palm. "You are mine for the next six minutes."

Then I gripped him by the front of his shirt and kissed the living hell out of him.

It hadn't been my intent. I wanted to use those well bought minutes to explain about the werewolves and why I needed him. But Sebastian didn't deserve my explanations.

I tasted his surprise. I'd caught him with his mouth open and used it to my full advantage. I may not be able to have sex without dire consequences but kissing was a different matter. And I knew all the tricks.

I swayed into him, pressing our bodies together. He was hard everywhere. It didn't take long for the low-level buzz that signaled my arousal and the potential trigger of my magic to run through me.

That ought to be enough to invoke the spell. I started to pull away.

Sebastian's hands gripped my hips. He spun us until my back was pressed up against the side of the boathouse. If I thought I had been turned on before it was nothing compared to the way he wedged his knee between my legs and pressed into me. His hands moved restlessly up and down my sides, mapping me, memorizing me. His lips moved on mine hungrily. I'd expected smooth seduction that matched his outward countenance. Instead, I felt as though I had thrown myself into the heart of a volcano and was being steadily consumed.

"Siobhan," he growled my name as he kissed down the side of my neck. "Gods, Siobhan, how I crave you."

This was more than I'd bargained for. Much more. I

needed to tell him to stop. Needed to get back to the kitchen before….

It happened in an instant. I traveled. From the boathouse to the kitchen.

Maeve squeaked as I appeared beside her. She held a basting brush, the bristles covered with the enchantment goo she was using to coat the doll and necklace.

I staggered, the wall behind me gone and my head spinning from that encounter.

"Are you all right?" My sister asked me.

No. I had just traveled in front of Sebastian. He was still on the property and he would be wanting answers.

But I had what I needed from him. "I'm juiced. Let's do this."

## ALYS

"It's pretty simple, meh, meh meh," I mimicked Sibby's voice to ease my mounting frustration that I couldn't scry worth shit. My mother nature mojo just wasn't working. Was I doing something wrong?

"Siobhan!"

I turned and spied Sebastian running up the hill. He appeared frantic. Which meant Sibby must have done a literal love him and leave him.

"Alys," he ran up the hill to me. His eyes were scanning the whole area and his breathing was labored. "She's gone. Disappeared right in front of me."

"Sebastian—" I began.

He gripped me by the arms, shaking me. "You don't understand. She just vanished. Someone must have—"

The ivy from the gazebo lashed out and wrapped around his wrists.

He yelped and even Nate retreated from me.

"Sibby is fine," I said.

"Let him go, Alys," Siobhan called from the patio.

Sebastian's face changed as he watched her and Maeve come up the hill to us. His brows pulled together and his lips parted. He shook his head, obviously trying to come to terms with what he saw.

I made a face at Sibby, but there would be time to berate her later. My fingers wiggled and the vines loosened.

Sibby looked at Sebastian. "You're still on the clock, yes?"

He frowned and then, for whatever reason, held out a crumpled twenty to her.

"Okay, so the thing is, we're witches."

*"Sibby,"* Maeve hissed.

"Cool your jets," she said. "Attorney-client privilege. He can't repeat this."

I snorted. "You hired him? With a twenty?"

"It's all I had. And we're burning time here." All her focus was on Sebastian. "We're fairly new to this whole having magic gig and there are some very bad people hunting for us. So you can't say anything to anyone about us. *Capeesh?*"

He blinked as though he didn't know what to make of her. I knew the feeling.

Sibby took a step closer to him. "You have the chance to be on the right side here. Hold our secret and I will overlook the thing with the pictures."

His lips parted. "And the private investigators?"

"All of it," she nodded. "I know that Kyle going nuts wasn't your call. I'm offering you a one-time pass. I will forgive you for everything."

He stared at her for a long moment and then nodded.

Sibby smiled up at him and then refocused on me. "How's the scrying going?"

"Badly." I turned back to the map. "Are you sure this thing works?"

Sibby took a breath and then touched the crystal. It hummed and cast beams of light all across the map.

"Maeve," she called. "You need to get in here."

Maeve set the doll and the necklace on the bench and then touched the crystal. The hum grew louder. A few of the beams faded, while others grew stronger.

Sibby's gaze met mine. "You too, Alys."

I reached out a finger and touched the crystal. The prisms of light all receded inside. Sibby and Maeve moved away and the crystal tugged out of my hand. I let it go.

It landed on the map, standing straight up on its tip.

Nate looked down at the map. "That's clear on the other side of the lake from where they found Debbie. No way could Lia have gotten there on her own."

"What do we do?" Sibby bit her lip. "Do we call Brock and let him know? Do we trust this?"

"Can you travel there? Maybe check it out?"

She shook her head. "I can't travel to map coordinates. I need to picture the terrain where I'm going."

I stared down at the map, then turned to Maeve, decision made. "I need you to stay here."

She opened her mouth to argue but I didn't relent.

"Brock is bringing Debbie out. Someone needs to be here to show him this spot."

"Nate can do that," she protested.

But Nate shook his head. "I should go, too. As a wolf so I can scent Lia's trail."

I cut a quick glance at Sebastian but he appeared to be lost in thought.

"Please, Maeve." I put my hand on my sister's shoulders. "Someone needs to stay. It makes sense that it's you."

She didn't like it. Her lips compressed into a firm line but she nodded once.

I picked up the doll. "What is it I need to do with this?"

"Nothing," Sibby said. "It will start to glow when we're near its owner."

247

Handy. I looked at Maeve and then at Sibby, Sebastian and Nate. "Let's go."

We took Sebastian's Escalade. Not only did he have room for all of us, but the back held protein bars and bottled water as well as a first aid kit. Nate shifted in the third row as Sebastian drove around the lake.

Sibby sat behind me, poring over the spell. I winced as Nate made a pain-filled sound. It took all my willpower not to turn around and look at him.

I eyed Sebastian whose expression could have been carved from stone. "You're taking this better than I would have expected."

He didn't look at me as he murmured. "You don't know a damn thing about me, Mrs. Stevens."

Fair enough. I turned and looked out the window.

There was no direct route to drive to the spot on the map. The gravel road turned to rutted dirt and then dead-ended.

Sibby opened the door and wolf Nate hopped out ahead of her. "Do we know whose property this is?"

I shook my head. "I think it's state land. There used to be a gemstone mine around here somewhere, but it's been boarded up for years."

I sent a quick text to Maeve to tell her where we were starting out and received a thumbs-up reply. I stashed a few protein bars in my back pocket and grabbed two bottles of water. Sebastian stuffed more water, protein bars, and the medical kit into a backpack and Sibby took the map, the doll, and the scrying crystal.

We walked for several miles. The sun was strong and leaves fluttered down around us. The doll did nothing, but Sibby pointed out that the range on the enchantment was probably limited.

Someone had taken Lia. It became obvious with every

mile we traveled. There was no way a toddler could have made it so far from home on her own. Someone that could mess up a werewolf in a fight.

But why bring her out here, to the middle of nowhere? I checked my phone, hoping to see a message from Maeve saying that Brock was on his way, that Debbie was going to be all right, that Lia had been found. Anything.

But there was no news.

We came to a trailhead. It was poorly marked, the sign weather-beaten with only a few chips of white paint left.

"Which way?" I asked Sibby.

She stared down at the doll, held it to the left. Then to the right. Shook her head. "I don't know."

"Nate?" I asked the gray wolf. "Any insight?"

He sniffed the air then looked back at me.

I let out a breath. "Then we split up."

I didn't want to. In fact, it was the last thing I wanted to do. "Sibby, give me the map and the crystal. You go with Nate and use the doll."

Sebastian stepped forward. "Siobhan should stay with me."

"Why?" I narrowed my eyes on him.

"Because," Sebastian held my gaze. "You came to me for a reason. I have something to do with her magic use, correct?"

"He's right, Alys." Sibby touched my arm. "If I get into trouble, I can jump us both back to the car. Or to Brock's."

Acid churned in my gut at the thought of leaving the two of them alone together. But Lia was out there. Scared and in the clutches of something that could mess up a full-grown werewolf.

I hugged my sister tightly. "You be careful. I don't trust him."

"You don't have to," she whispered back. "Trust *me*."

"I hate it when you say that," I told her.

She winked. "That's why I say it."

I watched them walk away and then turned to Nate. "Come on, wolf. Let's put that nose of yours to good use."

# MAEVE

I was pacing the gazebo, feeling like a useless lump when the Debbie necklace began to glow with a purple light. I whirled around just as Brock came out of the woods. He was naked and carrying a limp wolf over one shoulder. Brown fur was matted thick with blood.

He ran past me to the house, but I was hot on his heels. More wolves streamed down the hillside, though they didn't come into the house. With a start, I realized they were all shifting, as a unit.

Brock set the injured wolf on the big dining room table. She didn't appear to be breathing. He leaned over her and I could see that his back and shoulders were covered with vicious red gouges.

"Change, damn you, change," he snarled at the inert wolf.

"Medical supplies?" I asked. "Or a doctor?"

Brock didn't take his eyes off the wolf. "No doctor. Medical kit is in the hall closet in the large duffel bag."

I ran for it and by the time I returned, Ana stood by Brock's side. She was reaching for the wolf, tears running down her face.

Brock caught her hand before she could make contact. "She'll tear your arm off. Don't you see what she did to me?"

My gaze went back to the bloody rips in his arm. Debbie had done that.

The wolf on the table thrashed and yelped. I started but Brock and Ana both relaxed.

"She's shifting," Brock said on a sigh. "As long as she has the strength to change, she'll make it. You keep an eye on her, Ana."

Without waiting for the reply, Brock pulled me from the dining room and slid the pocket doors shut behind us.

"What about Ana?" I asked.

"She's Debbie's mate. She'll be safe enough. And Alys would kill me if anything happened to you." Brock strode to the hall closet and yanked a pair of navy sweats off a hanger. I tactfully turned my back instead of ogling my sister's werewolf lover the way I know Sibby would have done.

"Where is Alys?" Brock touched my arm, letting me know it was safe for me to turn back around. "And Siobhan?"

"They're with Sebastian and Nate, out looking for Lia."

"Sebastian?" Brock's brow furrowed.

"The lawyer. Sibby needed him to make her magic work." I wasn't going into any more detail than that.

A yelp of pain came from behind the dining room door and Brock's jaw tightened.

"What happened to her?"

"I'm not sure," he said. "Hopefully, she'll be alert enough to tell us when she's done shifting."

I studied the massive scratches across his chest. "You're going to need stitches."

"I can't leave. Not until we find Lia." His jaw was set in a stubborn line.

The bag of medical supplies was at my feet. I bent down

and scooped it up. It was well equipped and contained dissolvable stitches.

"Want me to do it?" I asked Brock.

His brows popped up. "You know how?"

"I used to be a nurse. That was how Kal and I met. Idiot broke his leg snowboarding. Ugly compound fracture. He still has the surgical scars." The memory made me smile. "Come into the kitchen. The light is better in there."

Brock sat on a stool and I went to the sink to wash my hands thoroughly before donning gloves and reaching for the antibacterial ointment.

"Can I ask you something which may sound weird?"

Brock hissed as I touched a cotton ball to one oozing scratch. "Go ahead. It should help take my mind off of things."

I hesitated. "Do I…smell different than before?"

"Different?" He looked down at me.

"Alys said you scented the change in us after we drank the empowerment brew." I prepared to stitch the wound closed, my focus on the task so I wouldn't meet his gaze. "It made me wonder if anything else was different."

He winced as I went to work. "What exactly are you looking for, Maeve?"

"Do I smell sick to you?"

"No," he said and I relaxed a bit. But then he added, "We can't smell diseases, not really. Maybe advanced forms of cancer or other things, but to us, people just smell like people."

"Oh." I wasn't sure why I had asked. Some dogs could scent diseases. I guess I wanted to know if Brock could tell for sure if I had MS. Guilt blossomed in my chest. It seemed shitty to be thinking about myself when Debbie was so badly hurt, Lia was missing and who knew where Sibby and Alys were at the moment.

I finished closing his wound and then applied gauze over the top.

"Maeve?"

I turned back to face him. "What?"

"If I had known, I would have told you."

I smiled at him. "You're a good guy, Brock. Alys is lucky to have you."

"I'm the lucky one," he said and I could see that he meant it.

The pocket doors banged open with a crash. I was expecting to see a frantic Ana looking for help. But it was Debbie who stood there, naked and coated in blood.

"It's a wraith," Her gaze found Brocks.

He paled. "You're sure?"

She nodded, eyes blazing. "It inhabited me. I don't remember all of it, but it used me to get to her."

"What's a wraith?" I looked between them.

"A vengeful trapped soul," Brock said. "You said it inhabited you. What does it want with Lia?"

"It doesn't want Lia." Debbie's eyes met my gaze. A shiver coursed through me as she said, "It's after the Silver sisters."

# CHAPTER TWENTY-FIVE

## ALYS

The trail was more of a goat path full of switchbacks that cut across the steep terrain. Trees grew smaller and sparser as we traveled up and up and up. Nate had no problem with the treacherous route but I struggled more with every step. I was in decent shape, but there was a difference between a little manual labor and endless hours of hiking.

I paused at times for water breaks and to check the map. The luminescent crystal showed we weren't far from our goal. If we were getting closer, Sibby and Sebastian would be moving farther away. I'd tried to text Sibby but my phone had lost its signal. I couldn't go back for them until I found Lia.

I gave Nate some water by pouring small amounts into my cupped palm and then into his mouth. The first bottle went dry. The sun made its slow progression across the bright blue October sky. We would need time to descend with a toddler in tow. Nate could always shift back to help me but he would be naked with no shoes.

I decided that if we didn't find Lia by the time we reached

the halfway mark on the second bottle, we would have to turn around.

Suddenly the path ahead leveled off and led to the opening of a cave. Nate looked at me and I shrugged. "It's too steep for bears. Go check it out."

He trotted inside. A moment later he returned, tail twitching lightly as though saying all clear.

I followed him inside.

It took several moments for my eyes to adjust after the bright light of day. I blinked and looked around, waiting for the dark shapes to resemble something familiar.

The first thing I spied was a pick-ax. Then a dented metal pail.

And beyond that… glittering gemstones lined the walls.

"It's a mine," I said to Nate. My voice echoed off the stone walls.

From somewhere deep within came a child's wail.

"Lia!" I called out. I rushed forward, wishing I had were-wolf eyesight or at the very least, a flashlight.

I picked up the pickax, praying I wouldn't have to use it. The weight was considerable, but I was used to worse. *It's not much different than swinging a sledgehammer with a point.*

I was so full of crap.

Another breath and then a prolonged wail. I had to get to her, get her the hell out of here. Using the wall for guidance, I made my way forward.

A growl from Nate. I rounded, searching for the threat.

But Nate was growling at me. His eyes were glowing red.

I backed up a step. "Nate, what are you doing?"

He ran for me. I screamed and swung the ax, praying I would stop him and in the same breath hoping I wouldn't hurt him too badly.

He landed on top of me. The ax clattered away into the darkness. I flailed backward and toppled. There was nothing behind me, the floor falling away. I plummeted down down down into darkness knowing that this was the end.

The day before my birthday. Just like Mom.

SEBASTIAN HAD PLAYED his role perfectly. He'd witnessed Siobhan's traveling, had acted upset as a normal male would have, and had even stuck around to help with the search.

And he had been rewarded. Because now he was alone with one of the witches in a dark part of the forest.

He could do it right now. Cast his net, drain her magic and her soul. Her magic was a little under ripened, but Alys had grown so powerful. He needed to incapacitate the older witch by taking out the younger one.

*Do it.* His instincts whispered. *Do it now.*

"That's funny." Siobhan was staring down at her phone, her back to him. She trusted him enough to turn her back on him. A deadly mistake, one she wouldn't ever be able to make again.

His heart pounded as he judged the slender column of her throat. His hands remembered the feel of her. The look in her eyes when she had *bargained with him for his time.*

Him, a dark fae.

Something was stirring in him. It wasn't the curse, at least not yet. Whatever the odd sensation was, it had something to do with her. The youngest witch, the most vulnerable.

The most trusting.

*You have the chance to be on the right side here.*

He'd wanted to laugh when she'd said those words. He had never, in his entire wretched existence, been on the right side of anything.

Poor, naive Siobhan wouldn't have the chance to learn. Sebastian called his soul net in from his personal vault. It was thin, light as a cobweb. One trapped beneath it would never escape. The strands would drain the soul dry, absorbing the magic along with it.

He tensed, eyeing the distance between them. She tipped her head back, her eyes closed. The breeze blew strands of bright blue hair away from her face.

*You are mine for the next six minutes.*

*I crave you.* Sebastian could lie, but keeping the truth in was much more difficult. Especially when her kiss rearranged everything he had ever known.

His jaw clenched.

Enough of this madness. It was her or him. He was a survivor, against all odds, Sebastian had lived when he had been left to die. A magicless changeling that no one wanted.

He needed to do this. He had to drain her. Now. And then with her power go after Alys. They were thieves, all three of them, possessing that which didn't belong to them. He had never hesitated at the thought of watching one of their ilk wither to a husk beneath his net. He hadn't flinched.

Not once.

His hands fisted on the unbreakable net. His muscles tensed for the throw.

*I will forgive you for everything.*

Siobhan began to turn back to him.

He threw the net.

It vanished an instant before it touched her pale skin.

He doubled over, his hands gripping his stomach. He wanted to laugh, wanted to weep. He couldn't do it. He couldn't trap her.

She rushed to his side. "Are you okay?"

He shook his head. No, he had never been less okay in his entire miserable existence.

"Come here." She helped him over to a log, urged him to

sit. "What is it? Did you get bit by something? Or is it your appendix? Should I jump you to the hospital?"

She was so concerned about him. Worry played across her beautiful features. He had almost destroyed her soul. She would have been lost, gone forever.

With shaking hands, he reached for her face. "I need only you."

"Sebastian?" Her brow furrowed. "You're acting weird."

"I know." He reached for her face, his gaze falling to her perfect pink lips. "Kiss me, Siobhan."

She did. With no argument, her lips feathered over his.

This was the reward for his restraint. The silver lining. Having her so close he could breathe in the hot sweet scent of her. She smelled like vanilla. Like a home Sebastian had never known.

He kissed her and fell a little harder.

"You thought that you could control me…." A voice hissed from the shadows behind him.

Sebastian drew back and shoved Siobhan behind him. He scanned the darkness between the trees looking for the telltale red eyes.

"I will devour her magic." Louse emerged, darkness coating his fully formed body. He had fed recently otherwise he wouldn't appear so intact.

Sibby went pale. "What is that thing?"

Sebastian shoved her back toward a patch of sunlight. "Siobhan, get out of here."

Her nails dug into his forearms. "I'm not leaving you behind to face whatever that is."

"It is a wraith, little witch." Louse gathered the shadows closer. "An eater of magic. And now I can control the elements, the way your recently departed sister could."

Siobhan shook her head. "I don't believe you."

Overhead a cloud covered the sun, plunging them into a half-light.

"It's after you, not me," Sebastian barked. He was desperate to get her out of the clearing, away from Louse. "Just go. *Now*."

"Come with me," she begged.

Louse lunged, and Sebastian threw himself between the wraith and Siobhan.

"Go," he said as the malevolent spirit settled inside him. "Before he gets control."

A tear slid down her face but Siobhan disappeared.

Sebastian growled as he fought off the possession. Louse had grown stronger. It was more than just Kyle. The wraith must have fed from one of the wolves. Only a supernatural being would have made him so strong. Black talons of soul sank inside Sebastian.

"Traitor," Louse hissed using Sebastian's own lips. "You call yourself dark fae? Pathetic. Laid low by a witch. You and your petty threats mean nothing to me now. I will take your power as well as theirs."

Sebastian fell to his knees in the dirt. "Like hell."

Gritting his teeth, he grabbed hold of the wraith and yanked it from him. It was like ripping a particularly sticky Band-aid off of one's soul.

Louse struggled and fought, but Sebastian was stronger, more determined. He pulled the creature loose and flung it into the sunlight.

It hissed and popped under the late afternoon sun. And then vanished.

Sebastian collapsed back in the dirt. Exhausted in both body and soul.

He had won. For now. But if Louse fed on Alys, nothing could stop the wraith.

# SIOBHAN

I appeared in Brock's kitchen the same way I had hours before. Unlike before, it was full of naked werewolves.

I shoved them out of the way. "Where's my sister?"

"Sibby," Maeve called from the other room. "Are you hurt? What happened?"

I fell into her arms, still out of breath. "I left him. Left all of them." That hadn't been my plan. My stomach lurched and I thought I might vomit as I recalled the desperation in Sebastian's eyes as he begged me to go.

"He told me to go. But I shouldn't have left him behind." The weight of guilt threatened to flatten me.

I should have grabbed him and gone. But my magic was unreliable. And something about that creature made it slip through my fingers like fine-grained sand.

"Where's Alys?" Maeve asked.

"It said it killed Alys," I sobbed. "Oh, God, Maeve. What if that thing got her?"

Brock appeared. His eyes shone werewolf gold. "Where is she?"

"I don't know."

"Try calling her," Brock barked to someone. "And Nate too."

"Nate left his phone in Sebastian's car." Sebastian...What would that creature do to him?

"Alys's phone is going straight to voicemail." Simone moved up beside us and put a hand on my back. "Do you know where she was headed?"

I shook my head. "We took different paths."

Brock's shoulders were squared off in determination. "Can you take me to the spot you last saw her? If I get close enough, I can scent her."

I looked up into his desperate brown eyes. I had enough juice left for one trip. "What about Sebastian?"

"It's too risky." Maeve came forward. "That thing took control of Debbie. Fed off her and made her leave Lia somewhere. She's a werewolf. If she couldn't fight it off, what chance does a human have?"

I shook my head but Brock grabbed my shoulders. "Siobhan, listen to me. We can't help him by ourselves. But if we get Alys back, she's strong enough to do something."

"It said she was dead," I whispered.

"It was trying to trick you."

I looked up into his face. "How do you know?"

"Because I just got her," he said. "And there is no way in hell I'm going to let her go now."

His determination was contagious. I looked to Maeve who nodded.

"I'll wait here."

I took Brock's hand. Took a deep breath and traveled to the last place I'd seen my sister.

*Hold on, Alys. Help is on the way.*

ALYS

Absolute darkness. No stars, no light of any kind. Cold seeped into my skin where it was pressed into the bare ground. No scent, no sound of any kind to give away my location.

I knew this dream, recalled it vividly. But some parts were missing. No scent of earth or coldness seeping through my clothes. My senses denied any insight into my location. Fear coursed through me and I forced myself upright. How had I gotten to this place? I tried to recall but my thoughts were sluggish, as though I had woken after an unplanned nap. I would wake up any second now. Any second....

I tried to listen to my heartbeat, heard nothing. Felt nothing.

Nothing but me in the darkness.

"Where am I?"

A hand landed on my shoulder. I looked at it and it seemed to glow with a golden light.

The light didn't reach much beyond the pale hand that was touching me. I followed the glowing limb up to the shoulder, taking in the leggings and oversized red sweater that covered a plush female figure.

I wanted to swallow but my mouth was dry, just as numb as the rest of me. I looked up into a face that was so familiar and so far gone. Maeve's face, but older.

A sprinkling of light freckles across the bridge of her nose. Gray and brown curls braided into a long rope down her back. Laugh lines around her mouth and eyes. No make-up, but she didn't need any, she had always been so beautiful, just the way she was.

"Mom?" I whispered.

She nodded.

I shook my head. "What are you doing here?"

"I've come for you, Alys. It's your time. Just like you knew it would be."

Something coiled in my stomach. "My time for what?"

"To go on."

"On?"

Her glowing hand reached up and stroked my cheek the same way she had every night before bed.

"Alys, sweetheart. You're dead."

# CHAPTER TWENTY-SIX

**D**ead. The word echoed inside my mind.

I'd known it was coming. Knew I wouldn't make fifty. I just hadn't expected the end to be so sudden. So final.

"Weren't you ready?" my mother asked. "I gave you all the warning I could."

"Warning? You mean those dreams?"

She nodded. "I thought it might help make it easier for you to transition."

Panic was starting to take over as well as a healthy dose of anger. "So that's it then. My life is just over in the blink of an eye and I don't get a say in it?"

"Alys, none of us get a say. Our time to die is as unique as the life we leave behind. Did you think I wanted to abandon you girls without your mother? Even with Ethan—"

"Who's Ethan?" I interrupted.

"My phantom lover."

"Say what now?"

She waved it away. "He's the spirit attached to Jess's house."

I held up a hand. "Wait, you're telling me that Aunt Jess's house is haunted? And you were sleeping with the ghost?"

"Of course not. He's his own person. The house acts as his anchor to the mortal plane. It's built on a convergence you know."

At my blank look, she frowned. "A spiritual place of power, where ley lines intersect? Didn't Jess tell you about all this?"

"Aunt Jess told us nothing. We hadn't even been inside the greenhouse before a few days ago!"

Her genial expression turned into a frown. "This isn't right. You and your sisters have a destiny to fulfill. Jess was supposed to teach you, to guide you into your craft. You can't just go off and die and leave it undone."

"Isn't that what you did?" My words were coated in bitterness.

She looked at me sharply. "I told you. I didn't have a choice in the matter."

I knew that. She'd been found at the bottom of a ravine. She had fallen, busted her leg, and been unable to get out. Had died of exposure. The police had ruled it an accident but in my secret heart, I blamed her.

"What were you doing there?" I asked her. "Why were you out there by yourself? Did something attack you?"

She shook her head. "I don't remember."

"Not good enough." My hands clenched into fists. "Why didn't you fight harder! I needed you to fight harder. Do you know what it was like? I was barely an adult when you left us. When you left me behind!"

She didn't speak, her expression remained impassive. She just let me shout at her.

"Say something," My voice broke.

"What do you want me to say?" she asked.

I didn't know. All I knew was that I needed to hear something out of her. Something more than that she hadn't been given a choice and that it didn't matter in the grand scheme of things that I had needed her. That my life had gone off the rails and never really recovered because I had never gotten over losing her.

To my horror, tears came to my eyes and I turned my back on her.

"Alys."

I held up a hand, indicating that I needed a minute. "Damn it, I hate it when she's right."

"Who?"

I blew out a long breath. "Sibby. She said I had unresolved issues with you."

"Sibby is smarter than anyone gives her credit for. Do you remember how she always managed to wriggle out of her car seat?"

A wet laugh bubbled up out of me. "You used to have to stop and pull over and strap her back in."

"And five miles later it was the same deal. Sibby never liked to be contained in any way." My mother looked at me and I saw something in her that I'd never seen before.

Contentment.

"What's it like?" I whispered.

"What?"

"Being dead."

She shrugged. "Your mileage may vary."

I rolled my eyes. "Really? That's all you've got for me? Your mileage may vary?"

"What can I say? I spent a lot of time behind the wheel. I like him by the way."

"Him who?"

"Your werewolf. He's coming for you even now." Her expression turned sad. "He'll be devastated when he finds your body. So will Sibby. And Maeve."

I reached out and gripped her by her glowing shoulders. "Mom, please. Tell me how to go back."

She shook her head. "I told you—"

I didn't want to hear it. "There must be a way."

She studied my face. "If anyone can find it, Alys, it would be you."

Behind her, a pinprick of light formed. It glowed with white-hot intensity. She moved toward it. Not walking, just drifting farther away from me.

"Mom, wait!" I had so many questions, so many things I wanted to say to her. But she was growing smaller and I was stuck in place as though my feet were rooted to the spot.

"I love you, Lys. You and your sisters were my whole life." She said and then was gone. Leaving me alone in the darkness once more.

The pinprick of light remained though. And some instinct warned me that if I managed to free myself and followed her if I crossed into the light, there was no going back.

I screamed. Agony tore through me. The scab covering the loss I'd never gotten over ripped free and bled and bled and bled. I screamed until I ran out of air. The sound burst out of me and seemed to shake the void I was in.

And in the distance thunder rumbled.

I froze. That was me. That was the weather responding to my magic.

I looked down at my feet and realized what held me in place.

My body.

It was there, just beyond the darkness.

Again, I looked to the light, the direction my mother had gone. She said I had a destiny, had said it mattered.

So was that destiny more important than my time being

up? Was my mother nature magic strong enough to help ground me in my body for a little bit longer?

I looked from the light to my feet and back.

And I made my choice.

PAIN ECHOED THROUGH MY SKULL.

I wanted to laugh, wanted to weep. It had worked. There was no way my body could hurt so badly if I were dead.

Beyond the pain was cold and darkness. Not the darkness of the void, but the darkness of the cave. And then wet, slurping sounds that made every hair on my pain-wracked body stand on end.

A child's cry. A whimper of animalistic pain.

Slowly I forced my lids up. My vision was blurry and there was no light. My skull throbbed where it had hit the stone.

Something was feeding on me. For a moment I worried it was Nate in wolf form. But my fingers were touching something soft and still. Something that felt a lot like a wolf's pelt.

Whatever was eating me wasn't tangible. It wasn't consuming my flesh. No, this went deeper. Whatever it was feasted on my soul. On my magic. I could hear the slurping sounds and feel the pull as if something was being tugged out of me a little bit at a time.

It pissed me right the hell off. This was my body and my magic. And yet here was another damn creature just like my ex who wanted a piece of me. And another and another until I was little more than a carcass picked clean of all that I could have been.

*Fuck. That. Shit.*

Whatever it was, it was about to get more than it bargained for.

269

Beneath me, the ground quaked. The incremental suctioning stopped. I sat up and scooted closer to the werewolf.

"So, you're not dead yet," the thing hissed.

"Who are you?" I asked the creature. "Are you a magic hunter?"

"Yessss."

I blew out a breath. No surprise there. "Okay then. Well, you have two choices. Either You can bugger off or I will end you."

The thing laughed and it was a manic sort of sound. "End me? What makes you think you have that power?"

"Good genes," I respond. The mountain shook again. Stalactites came crashing down. I curled my body over Nate.

Light spilled inside as the rock crumbled. I blinked at the sudden brightness then took in my surroundings.

We were in some sort of mine shaft, clearly abandoned. Nate was by my side and to my relief, he was still breathing. I couldn't see whatever it was that had been feeding on me, but to my left, I spotted a small figure.

"Lia," I gasped and started to crawl to her. Ignoring the pain, the blood, everything.

The child sniffled and then was yanked up into the air.

"Stop or I drop her." The voice came from behind me. "Give yourself to me or the child dies."

Fear filled me at the thought of her small body being splattered on the stone. The quaking stopped. Beside me, Nate moaned.

I could feel the thing gloating in satisfaction. It thought it had won. That I was giving up.

Not hardly. "What do you want?" I asked the creature.

"I want it back."

"Want what back?" I eyed the distance between where I was and where Lia hovered above me.

"The magic Margret Ellen Silver stole from me."

My lips parted. "How do you know her?"

"Because I traded my soul to a dark fae for a chance to regain what I lost. What she took. I could have feasted on the werewolves, but their magic isn't pure. I want what is rightfully mine." The creature snarled.

"And what is that?"

"What you have. And I will suck every last drop out of you and your sisters. One sip at a time."

"You're not our type." My anger unleashed and a swirl of wind knocked the thing away.

"Alys!" Brock's voice echoed through the space. He was close.

"Here!"

Glowing red eyes glowed even brighter as the magic hunter stalked forward. "Give yourself to me or watch them all die."

And then, from out of the darkness a second set of eyes appeared. These the color of polished amethysts. Before I knew what was happening, the second being yanked Lia free and tossed her to me.

"You," the red-eyed beast snarled. "How?"

"You underestimated me, Louse. I told you it would be the last thing you ever did." The voice was smooth as silk and darker than midnight.

A pulse of purple and gold flooded the space. It blinded me and I threw an arm up over my eyes. Lia screamed and behind me, Nate stirred. The beam struck the red-eyed monster and sent him crashing into the opposing wall.

"Go." The purple-eyed thing thundered in a voice to rival my earthquakes. "Before it takes one of you."

I didn't need to be told twice. With Lia safe in my arms, I gripped Nate by the scruff of the neck and limped toward the newly formed crack in the side of the mountain.

There was something really wrong with one knee but I ignored the pain as I limped over the rubble-strewn ground.

"Lys!"

Nate barked and charged ahead just as Brock appeared at the edge of the space. He lowered himself through the gap and took Lia from me.

"Are you all right?"

I nodded though I wasn't sure if that was the full truth. My gaze was drawn back to the fight behind me. "What are those things?" I breathed.

"The one with the red eyes is a wraith. That's what took over Debbie."

And probably Nate as well. Why else would he have attacked me until I fell into that mine shaft? "And the other?"

He shook his head. "No idea. Whatever it is, it's powerful though."

"It saved me." I let out a shaky breath. "The wraith. How do I kill it?"

"You can't," Brock said. "It's not fully alive. The best you can do is disperse it."

"How?"

"It's a creature of shadow. It can't hold itself together in the direct light."

I turned back around and reached inside myself, looking for the deep well of emotion that I had kept so tightly sealed up for so long. It was open now, the seal broken and the cover gone. Drawing on it, pulling strength up from my very soul.

"Cover your eyes," I said to Brock. "And Lia's too."

He did, turning his back and pressing the little girl's eyes against his t-shirt. Even Nate ducked his head.

I let loose.

A blue and white bolt of lightning streaked into the mine-shaft and struck the wraith between the eyes. It screamed and for a moment I saw it as it had once been. A short, paunchy middle-aged man. He wore clothing from another era.

And then he was gone.

Amethyst eyes glowed at me for a long moment. I braced for an attack. If this was another magic hunter, I'd send him to the abyss hot on the heels of the other.

"Alys!" Sibby charged up the hill. The eyes shifted to her and grew brighter, more focused.

I prepared another bolt.

The eyes closed. And a moment later the presence was gone.

SEBASTIAN AWOKE BACK in his body and aware that he had just expended his valuable magic to save Alys Stevens. He told himself it was because he didn't want to deal with Louse all juiced up on her mother nature strength. That Louse had betrayed him and gone against the code of their kind. Louse was supposed to serve him. Had bargained with him for his revenge. But the creature had gotten greedy. Had overstepped. Had gone rogue. That warranted severe punishment.

Sebastian was a dark fae. He could lie to anyone. But this was the first time he'd lied to himself.

His cell phone rang.

"What?" He held the device up to his ear as he stared up at the purpling sky.

"*What the hell is going on?*" Kyle's voice pierced his ears and he held the phone away.

"I don't know what you mean."

"Someone told me that you're with Alys and her sisters."

Enough.

Sebastian got to his feet. In the blink of an eye, he traveled from the woods to Kyle's house.

The place was a wreck. And seemed to be listing to one side.

Kyle was pacing like the worthless junkie he was around what at one time must have been a very tastefully decorated living room. A trail of red seeped down his neck from two small punctures. Louse had fed off Kyle as he'd been ordered, incapacitating the irritating human. But the wraith's destruction had caused Kyle to regain consciousness.

"Well?" Kyle barked into the phone he was holding.

"Well what?" Sebastian said from behind him.

Kyle whirled. "Where did you come from?"

He ignored the question. "I thought I should tell you in person that I quit." He pivoted and headed for the exit.

"What?" Kyle chased after him. "Why?"

Was the man serious? "You're broke, Kyle. And you're a junkie. Besides, I like your wife a hell of a lot more than I like you."

"You're fucking her aren't you?"

Sebastian didn't bother to reply.

"You are. She got to you. Or was it her sister? I always knew the youngest one was a freak in the sack—"

The rest of his sentence got cut off because Sebastian had gripped him by the throat and hefted him off the ground.

"Don't," he said in a calm tone, "Talk about Siobhan. Don't look at her. Don't think about her."

No further threats. No *or else*. None needed. He dropped Kyle to the floor and turned to go.

"I'll go to the police." Kyle rasped.

Sebastian stilled.

"I'll tell them that you approached me." The mortal sounded triumphant.

"Unless…?" Sebastian purred over his shoulder.

Kyle apparently hadn't thought the blackmail threat all the way through. "Unless you give me half a million dollars."

"So that's your offer?" Sebastian glanced over his shoulder. "Your silence for half a million in US dollars?"

"Yy...yes." Kyle didn't sound so sure.

"And here is my counter offer. A year and a day."

Kyle frowned. "What?"

"A year and a day. That's how long you will be a mindless thrall enslaved and forced to do my will. Unless I trade you."

Kyle's eyes went wide. "You're crazy."

"Yes," Sebastian said. "Crazy like a fae."

And he unleashed the damper on his essence. It was a handy little charm he'd lifted off of one of his other victims. It allowed him to blend in with the mortals without worrying about enthralling the people he ran across.

Unless he wanted to. And when he did the effect was instantaneous.

Kyle's eyes glazed over and he slumped where he sat.

Sebastian crouched down beside him, tilted his head. "I'm doing you a favor, you know. You won't even remember the withdrawal. Or what my kind will do to you."

He snapped his fingers and the broken house sat empty once more.

# CHAPTER TWENTY-SEVEN

## MAEVE

"Mommy, mommy!" Bella ran down the hall, hair flying and a big grin on her face. Two bouncing corgis followed her progress down the hall.

I crouched down and opened my arms. She ran to me and I just held her for a moment.

"Bedtime, Bella," Kal said from the top of the stairs.

"But Mommy just got home." The words came out in classic little girl whine.

"Tell you what? How about tomorrow we do a mother-daughter day. Just you and me. We can do whatever you want."

"Can we get pedicures?" she asked.

I nodded "Any color you want."

She squealed and then gave me one more hug. "I love you, Mommy."

"Love you too, baby bell. Take the entourage with you."

"Gimli, Grogu, come." Bella clapped her hands and ran up the stairs followed miraculously by two bouncing corgi butts.

"Hey," Kal descended the stairs and drew me into his embrace. "You okay?"

Was I? I didn't even know how to answer that question.

The silence stretched out for so long that he stepped back. "What is it, Evie?"

I needed to tell him. Everything. But I just didn't have it in me at the moment. "Just exhausted and glad to be home. Is there anything left from dinner?"

I turned my back but not quickly enough to bypass the hurt in his eyes. Too much. This was all too much. I didn't want to talk or eat. I just wanted to cuddle up with my husband and cry.

I didn't even know why. Because I was sick? Because my sister insisted that she'd died and seen our mother? Or because both my sisters had left me behind twice today without a backward glance.

Because I was a liability. Even with magic, I was a damn burden. I hadn't been able to help with the search or bring magic to the foreground. My contribution, the doll that I'd so carefully coated had been abandoned in the woods.

Like it didn't matter at all.

*That's a shitty thing to think, Maeve. Be happy that everyone is safe.*

I was. But at the same time…I hadn't done anything to help.

I headed into the kitchen just as Philip came stomping in through the back door. "Whoa, dude you are filthy. Shower tonight, huh?"

He grunted and then headed for the stairs.

"What was that?" I frowned after him.

Kal scrubbed a hand over his face. "He got into it with some of the other soccer players earlier. He quit the team."

"What?" I rounded on him.

He held up his hands. "He's not good, Evie. He knows it and they know it. They're teasing him now."

"Those little bastards," I growled. "And their asshole parents. I will gut them like trout."

"You're sexy when you're all bloodthirsty." Kal moved forward and took me in his arms. He smelled of oregano and basil, a clear hint he had been out in the garden earlier.

"I'm glad you think so." I rested my chin on the notch of his sternum. It was the perfect height. "Today was really awful, Kal."

His dark gaze roved across my face. "I thought you said they found the girl. That everyone made it out okay."

I turned my face and pressed my cheek into his chest. "They did. But it was still awful. I didn't do anything useful."

"That makes two of us." His voice rumbled low and from my position, I could feel the vibration of it.

"What do you mean?"

"All day I felt like I ought to be doing something else. Something to help ease your burden."

"You did. Knowing you were here with the kids, that they were safe. That's everything to me."

He lifted my chin and brushed a soft kiss over my lips. "You know you can tell me anything, right?"

My heart started to pound. I could just blurt it out. Shove out the stupid words and be done with it. *I'm afraid I'm sick. I enchant people when I'm afraid. Magic hunters are after me and my sisters and they will suck out our souls to get what they want.*

But I held my tongue even as I nodded. "I know."

Tomorrow was another day.

## ALYS

"Happy birthday." Sibby was at the counter carving a pumpkin when I stumbled to the coffee pot the next morning.

I let out a breath. Fifty. I'd made it. Barely. "Thank you. Do you really think we'll get any trick-or-treaters all the way out here?" I asked her as I secured the bedroom door. Brock was still fast asleep.

"Probably not." She shrugged and then pasted on a false grin. "But we can be ready just in case."

I rolled my eyes. "Okay, how many bags of candy did you buy?"

She pretended to think about it. "Three."

"And, how many do you think will be left by Halloween?" It was a whole two days away.

"Less than three."

"I'll buy more," I added cream to my mug and then looked at her. "Have you heard from Sebastian?"

"Not since he called to tell me he's all right." She yanked a fistful of seeds out of the pumpkin with excessive force. "And that he's moving back to the city."

I knew that much. Was relieved about it, actually. Because even though Sebastian hadn't done anything other than represent Kyle, I still didn't trust him.

He knew too much about us. Had seen the wraith. It had probably freaked him out and sent him scurrying back down the mountain.

Leaving Sibby to deal with the fallout.

"It's probably better this way," she muttered as though trying to convince herself.

"Why's that?"

She didn't answer, just kept carving.

"I'm gonna go take a shower. We're heading up to the Mid-Century Modern today. Did you want to come?"

Sibby looked up at me and winked. "Always."

I rolled my eyes. "You know what I mean."

"I would be delighted to accompany you and your were-wolf escort," she said.

Brock was awake and chuckling when I re-entered the bedroom.

I raised a brow at him even as I sauntered over. "What?"

"Nothing," he reached out and I offered him the mug. He took it from my hand and then set it down on the nightstand before scooping me off my feet and tossing me back onto the mattress.

"I'm calling in sick today," he murmured as he kissed his way down my throat. "You should too. Since it's your birthday and all."

"Um, no." I gripped a fistful of his shaggy blond locks. "We are already behind schedule on that house. We can't afford to, *ohhhh...*"

The rest of my thought unraveled as he kissed his way down my body. After what had happened the day before it didn't take much to convince me that maybe life was better lived when I stopped playing by other people's rules.

One sick day was probably in order since I'd died yesterday. Seeing as I was a fifty-year-old witch and my twenty-nine-year-old werewolf lover was currently trying to kill me with pleasure, it was time to toss the rulebook.

Much later, I was sitting out on the porch steps staring at the lake when Maeve arrived. She had on bright blue nail polish and had a pink butterfly clipped in her hair. I hid my grin as she fought with a giant balloon bouquet in the back of her minivan. Two of them were silver one with a 5 and the other a 0.

"Need some help?" I called out.

"I got it." More muttering from the van, followed by a pop.

"She sounds cranky," Sibby muttered as she carried the wine bottle and three plastic glasses out to the porch.

"The more things change, the more they stay the same." I took the bottle, inspecting the cork.

"It's legit," Sibby huffed. "No magical mixtures this time."

"Can you blame me for checking?"

"Happy birthday, smartass," Maeve said and shoved the balloons at me. "Where's your boy toy?"

"She's such a badass. She sent him to work and took the day off." Sibby shook her head. "The whole day. Can you believe it?"

"No." Maeve accepted a glass from Sibby. "What are we toasting to?"

I raised my glass. "To Mom."

They stared at me.

"What?"

"You said she didn't fight hard enough to live," Sibby whispered. "You always said that."

I nodded. "I know and that was shitty of me. I was just so angry for so long. I didn't know how to be any other way."

Maeve had tears in her eyes. "I'm glad you got to see her."

"Me too." I wasn't sure if my sisters believed me when I told them that I died. But it didn't matter. What mattered was that I was with them.

"To Mom," Sibby said.

Plastic clicked together and we all drank.

Maeve rested her chin on her hand and stared out at the lake. "So what now?"

"What do you mean?" I asked her.

"Well, we're magical. Sort of. We're on the outskirts of this whole new world. There are magic hunters out there who want to suck out our souls. I'm afraid to go to Walmart because what if a spider crawls on me and I freak out and the whole store follows me home."

Sibby snorted. "Is this what keeps you up at night? That is when you're not doing unspeakable things to Kal's body?"

"Now," I said to stop Maeve's retort. "We live every day to the best of our ability. We fight as hard as we can and love as much as we can for as long as we can. Because nothing is guaranteed."

"I'll drink to that," Sibby said.

I closed my eyes and the wind gently lifted the hair off the back of my neck.

It was good to be home at last.

*Come back to the Silver Sisterhood in Witch Way Did She Go. Coming in October.*

### Wife. Mother. Enchantress. Can a magical talisman cure what ails her?

Multiple Sclerosis. Ever since Maeve's doctor spoke the words out loud, Maeve has lived in fear of what that means for her life, her family, but most of all her marriage. Terrified that her husband will leave her—or worse, stay with her out of a sense of obligation rather than love—Maeve has put off

telling him about her diagnosis. Desperate for answers, she convinces her sisters to accompany her to an underground magic market in search of a cure for her chronic illness.
When a mystic sends the trio in search of the Mother Superior of Magic and her healing amulet, the three midlife mavens are pitted against a host of new challenges. Followed into a secret realm by the dark fae who has been keeping tabs on their growing powers, can the trio escape supernatural zombies and find what they so desperately seek? Or will the gamble cost them all their magic…and their souls?
*Witch Way Did She Go* is the second book in the charming Silver Sisters paranormal women's fiction series. If you enjoy strong female characters who put it all on the line for love, magic at midlife books, and stories full of heat and heart, you'll adore Jennifer L. Hart's enchanting tale.
Buy *Witch Way Did She Go* and embrace the witch within now!

# IT'S NOT MY WORDS THAT COUNT. IT'S YOURS!

Please consider leaving an honest review for this book. Reviews help readers like you select the kind of books they like and help authors like me sell books to the right readers. I found one of my favorite series from a two star review.

Thank you for reading!

Jennifer L. Hart

# ABOUT THE AUTHOR

*USA Today* bestselling author Jennifer L. Hart writes about characters that cuss, get naked, and often make poor but hilarious life choices. A native New Yorker, Jenn now lives in the mountains of North Carolina with her imaginary friends. Her works to date include the Damaged Goods mystery series and the Magical Midlife Misadventures.

Want exclusive behind the scenes access to what Jenn is working on next? Become a Patron today!

Made in United States
North Haven, CT
22 January 2022

15136159R00163